Felicia's Favorites

By Danielle Steel

FELICIA'S FAVORITES • THE DEVIL'S DAUGHTER • THE COLOR OF HOPE
THE PORTRAIT • FOR RICHER FOR POORER • A MOTHER'S LOVE
A MIND OF HER OWN • FAR FROM HOME • NEVER SAY NEVER • TRIAL BY FIRE
TRIANGLE • JOY • RESURRECTION • ONLY THE BRAVE • NEVER TOO LATE
UPSIDE DOWN • THE BALL AT VERSAILLES • SECOND ACT • HAPPINESS • PALAZZO
THE WEDDING PLANNER • WORTHY OPPONENTS • WITHOUT A TRACE
THE WHITTIERS • THE HIGH NOTES • THE CHALLENGE • SUSPECTS • BEAUTIFUL
HIGH STAKES • INVISIBLE • FLYING ANGELS • THE BUTLER • COMPLICATIONS
NINE LIVES • FINDING ASHLEY • THE AFFAIR • NEIGHBORS • ALL THAT GLITTERS
ROYAL • DADDY'S GIRLS • THE WEDDING DRESS • THE NUMBERS GAME
MORAL COMPASS • SPY • CHILD'S PLAY • THE DARK SIDE • LOST AND FOUND
BLESSING IN DISGUISE • SILENT NIGHT • TURNING POINT • BEAUCHAMP HALL
IN HIS FATHER'S FOOTSTEPS • THE GOOD FIGHT • THE CAST • ACCIDENTAL HEROES
FALL FROM GRACE • PAST PERFECT • FAIRYTALE • THE RIGHT TIME • THE DUCHESS
AGAINST ALL ODDS • DANGEROUS GAMES • THE MISTRESS • THE AWARD
RUSHING WATERS • MAGIC • THE APARTMENT • PROPERTY OF A NOBLEWOMAN
BLUE • PRECIOUS GIFTS • UNDERCOVER • COUNTRY • PRODIGAL SON • PEGASUS
A PERFECT LIFE • POWER PLAY • WINNERS • FIRST SIGHT • UNTIL THE END OF TIME
THE SINS OF THE MOTHER • FRIENDS FOREVER • BETRAYAL • HOTEL VENDÔME
HAPPY BIRTHDAY • 44 CHARLES STREET • LEGACY • FAMILY TIES • BIG GIRL
SOUTHERN LIGHTS • MATTERS OF THE HEART • ONE DAY AT A TIME
A GOOD WOMAN • ROGUE • HONOR THYSELF • AMAZING GRACE • BUNGALOW 2
SISTERS • H.R.H. • COMING OUT • THE HOUSE • TOXIC BACHELORS • MIRACLE
IMPOSSIBLE • ECHOES • SECOND CHANCE • RANSOM • SAFE HARBOUR
JOHNNY ANGEL • DATING GAME • ANSWERED PRAYERS • SUNSET IN ST. TROPEZ
THE COTTAGE • THE KISS • LEAP OF FAITH • LONE EAGLE • JOURNEY
THE HOUSE ON HOPE STREET • THE WEDDING • IRRESISTIBLE FORCES • GRANNY DAN
BITTERSWEET • MIRROR IMAGE • THE KLONE AND I • THE LONG ROAD HOME
THE GHOST • SPECIAL DELIVERY • THE RANCH • SILENT HONOR • MALICE
FIVE DAYS IN PARIS • LIGHTNING • WINGS • THE GIFT • ACCIDENT • VANISHED
MIXED BLESSINGS • JEWELS • NO GREATER LOVE • HEARTBEAT • MESSAGE FROM NAM
DADDY • STAR • ZOYA • KALEIDOSCOPE • FINE THINGS • WANDERLUST • SECRETS
FAMILY ALBUM • FULL CIRCLE • CHANGES • THURSTON HOUSE • CROSSINGS
ONCE IN A LIFETIME • A PERFECT STRANGER • REMEMBRANCE
PALOMINO • LOVE: *POEMS* • THE RING • LOVING • TO LOVE AGAIN
SUMMER'S END • SEASON OF PASSION • THE PROMISE
NOW AND FOREVER • PASSION'S PROMISE • GOING HOME

Nonfiction

EXPECT A MIRACLE: *Quotations to Live and Love By*
PURE JOY: *The Dogs We Love*
A GIFT OF HOPE: *Helping the Homeless*
HIS BRIGHT LIGHT: *The Story of Nick Traina*

For Children

PRETTY MINNIE IN PARIS • PRETTY MINNIE IN HOLLYWOOD

DANIELLE STEEL

Felicia's Favorites

A Novel

Delacorte Press
New York

Felicia's Favorites is a work of fiction. Names, characters, places, and incidents are the products of the author's imagination or are used fictitiously. Any resemblance to actual events, locales, or persons, living or dead, is entirely coincidental.

Delacorte Press
An imprint of Random House
A division of Penguin Random House LLC
1745 Broadway, New York, NY 10019
randomhousebooks.com
penguinrandomhouse.com

Copyright © 2026 by Danielle Steel

Penguin Random House values and supports copyright. Copyright fuels creativity, encourages diverse voices, promotes free speech, and creates a vibrant culture. Thank you for buying an authorized edition of this book and for complying with copyright laws by not reproducing, scanning, or distributing any part of it in any form without permission. You are supporting writers and allowing Penguin Random House to continue to publish books for every reader. Please note that no part of this book may be used or reproduced in any manner for the purpose of training artificial intelligence technologies or systems.

DELACORTE PRESS is a registered trademark and the DP colophon is a trademark of Penguin Random House LLC.

Hardback ISBN 978-0-593-97305-9
Ebook ISBN 978-0-593-97306-6

Printed in the United States of America on acid-free paper

1st Printing

First Edition

The authorized representative in the EU for product safety and compliance is
Penguin Random House Ireland, Morrison Chambers,
32 Nassau Street, Dublin D02 YH68, Ireland.
https://eu-contact.penguin.ie

To my so greatly loved children,
Beatrix, Trevor, Todd, Nick, Samantha,
Victoria, Vanessa, Max, and Zara,

May you be forever blessed,
together and stronger for the love you share
and the love I have for each of you.

You are my favorites, always were,
and always will be, forever.

With all my heart and soul, I love you,
                    Mom / d.s.

Felicia's Favorites

Chapter 1

The identical letter reached each of the five recipients on the same day, according to Felicia Morgan Weston's precise instructions. The day the letters were sent was the second of December, a month after her death. It was sent to her five daughters by her attorney, Scott Freeman, and said only that he had a letter written to them by their mother, she had written it six years before, at the same time she wrote her will, when she turned sixty. Scott wanted them to come to his office, so he could give them each their copy. He knew it contained some long-overdue explanations, which their mother was aware would shock them, or surprise them at best.

Felicia had been strong, busy, still beautiful, and in good health when she wrote the letter and her will, and nothing had changed when she died in a freak accident at sixty-six, a month before.

She had run in the New York marathon for twenty years. She did it every year to prove to herself that she could, and she prepared for it all year. It cleared her head, and gave her a feeling of accomplishment.

She was one of the victims of a deranged sniper who had opened fire on the runners with an assault rifle shortly after they crossed the starting line. She was the first of the nine people he killed. He injured eight more before the police shot and killed him.

Her daughters were devastated. They were all close to her, and their mother was the only family they had. Their father had died in a commercial airline crash when they were between two and ten years old. The three oldest girls, Charlotte, Quinne, and Olivia, still had a few vague memories of their father, but the two youngest, Veronica and Isabelle, had been too young to remember him. Felicia was thirty-four when she was widowed, her husband Bill Weston forty-four when he died. The plane crash was officially determined to be due to pilot error. As a result, the insurance payments to the families the passengers had left behind were enormous. They paid Felicia enough to assure her and her five daughters a reasonably comfortable life for twenty years, until her youngest daughter finished college. Felicia had never remarried and had been widowed for thirty-two years when she died.

Bill had worked as a literary agent at a major literary agency, and had a solid career. Felicia had worked as a junior editor in a publishing house before they married and had children. They had met at a party at the Frankfurt book fair, when a more senior editor got sick and dropped out. Felicia and Bill were both from New York and books were their passion. They dated for a year. She got pregnant almost immediately after their wedding and quit working when her first child Charlotte was born, and she stayed home after that. Bill was able to support them without her working.

His parents had been college professors and died before he did. He had inherited a small amount from them and sold their house on Long Island. The money they left was Bill and Felicia's buffer for emergencies, and helped make it possible for Felicia to stay home with their children. The insurance money from the airline made it possible for her not to change their lifestyle after Bill's death, but she was an intelligent woman, and looking into the future, insisted she knew that the insurance wouldn't last forever. She began thinking about getting a job a few years after Bill died. She went back to editing at a publishing house, which was the only profession she knew. Bill had often consulted her about his new literary clients, and he often shared manuscripts with her. He respected her opinions. She was a voracious reader, and had a good sense for finding people with undeveloped talent. He had often encouraged her to write herself but she brushed off the suggestion as absurd. She didn't have the desire or the talent. Bill didn't press her but he was certain she had a book in her. Felicia's father was a literature professor, like Bill's father, and her mother was a Latin teacher at an elite girls' school. They prized education, and had left Felicia their savings, to help send her daughters to college. They died a year apart, not long after Bill. Felicia raised the girls alone, and tried to share her love of books with them, which appealed to some of them more than others. Her daughters had diverse talents and interests and were entirely different from each other.

She went back to work when she was thirty-seven, three years after Bill died, when her youngest, Isabelle, entered kindergarten. She worked part-time for the first year, and moved to full-time when Isabelle started first grade. She enrolled all of them in after-school daycare, where the older ones could do homework before she picked them all up on the way home. She had a housekeeper who babysat for the girls when Felicia needed her to.

When she went back to work, she was disappointed by the caliber of the books she was editing. Many of them were intellectually ambitious and boring to read. The more commercial books always seemed to have a flaw in them, or something lacking, an absence of passion or credible characters. They weren't exciting and didn't strike her as great reads. In frustration one night, she began working on an outline for a book of her own. She didn't know if she'd finish it, or even start it, she wrote the outline as an experiment, to see if she could write a book, more for fun than with any serious intent. She was stunned to find that the story raced along once she started to write, and it fairly flew beneath her fingers. She loved writing the book and finished in three months. It was a complicated thriller that challenged the reader, took constant unexpected turns, and kept the reader guessing until the end. She fell in love with the characters as she wrote, edited it carefully afterward, and wasn't sure what to do next. Not knowing where else to go, she submitted it under a pseudonym to the publishing house where she worked. They normally didn't accept manuscripts that weren't sent by a literary agent, but she argued persistently for the book, and when she convinced her boss to read it, her senior editor agreed, liked it, and was eager to publish it. It was published on

Felicia's Favorites

Felicia's thirty-ninth birthday, under the name Morgan Reed, and it quickly became that rarest of birds in the publishing business, an overnight success. Readers and critics alike were fascinated by the plot, were enchanted by the endless twists, fell in love with the characters, and loved the ending, which surprised them completely. She had invented a complicated but convincing identity for the mysterious author, supposedly a recluse in the wilds of Montana. She took her late husband's boss, famous agent Robert Farr, into her confidence. He agreed to be her agent, and promised to shield her identity. Readers weren't even sure of the sex of the author with the name she had chosen, Morgan Reed, her own maiden name and an entirely fictional last name. Robert Farr never gave away her secret and her true identity remained unknown. He was vastly impressed by her talent, and he was one of the most respected agents in New York. She was a number one best-selling author at forty.

In time, she discovered that she could write three or four novels a year, and her fans devoured them. She grazed the top of the bestseller lists with every book. Felicia was highly praised at the publishing house for having spotted the manuscript and the unknown author's talent, and after her third big success with a bestseller, she left the publishing house, saying that she had been hired by the now very successful author, to be her private editor and work directly for her, editing manuscripts sent from Montana. Every editor in the house envied her, and she stuck to the same story with her children. They never knew that she was Morgan Reed. She wrote the books by day when they were in school and at night while they slept, and the sight of manuscripts on her desk seemed familiar and normal to them since she was a private editor for the woman she had created and called Morgan Reed.

Felicia knew from Bill's career as an agent, and after working in publishing herself, she saw what happened to people's lives when fame intervened. She wanted none of that to interfere with raising her children, their values, or the way they lived. They lived in a respectable but not luxurious building in the East Nineties, near her children's schools. She was able to keep them all in private schools, thanks to the airline insurance, the small inheritance from her parents, and eventually the impressive contracts her agent got her. Her book contracts provided a comfortable lifestyle and a firm foundation for their future. It was always a condition that the reclusive author would do no publicity for the books, would never appear in person or do book tours or appearances, but the books kept coming steadily and continued to improve. By the time Felicia died, she had been a dazzling success for twenty-seven years and no one had ever seen or spoken to Morgan Reed. And she had written a hundred and eight books.

Her agent, Robert Farr, shielded her from all direct contact. Several times over the years, he had tried to encourage Felicia to step into the limelight, but she saw no reason to. She was comfortable as she was. When the children grew up and moved out after college, she took a smaller apartment in a slightly better neighborhood in the East Eighties, looking out at the East River, and said she was happy there.

Robert also knew that she had bought a large property in Connecticut in the name of a corporation her attorney set up for her, and she spent time there anonymously. As Morgan Reed's "editor," she was frequently asked to give interviews about her, which she always turned down. Morgan Reed's name was prominent on Robert Farr's client roster. Felicia's appeared nowhere except on private documents that only Robert handled himself, and kept locked in his safe. At the time of Felicia's death, her secret had never been revealed. It had been her intention to continue working into her old age, and to divide her very considerable fortune and all of her possessions between her children. The house in Connecticut was a beautiful two-hundred-year-old farmhouse, which she maintained impeccably. It had forest land around it, rolling hills, and a small lake. It was a peaceful place, and eventually she wrote her books there and rarely came into the city. When she did, she saw her children at the modest apartment, where they believed she lived, and she kept it for that reason, and eventually only went there when she saw them or spent the night in town to go to the theater, and didn't want to drive back to Connecticut. The rest of the time she was writing and lived in seclusion in Connecticut. She led a very quiet, solitary life, and worked all the time.

Her attorney, Scott Freeman, tried to get her to at least tell her children about her remarkable career and share it with them, but she didn't want the money to corrupt them, or to diminish their motivation to make something of themselves. When she came up with money to help them, if they were in distress, as she had to for her middle daughter, Olivia, she assured them that Morgan Reed paid her handsomely for her editing, and she had enough put aside to be able to help them. None of them even remotely suspected the fortune she had amassed in twenty-seven years, with careful investments to enhance the proceeds from her advances and royalties. And she didn't want her attorney to tell them until a month after she died, whenever that happened, so the initial dust would have settled by then, and they would have recovered somewhat from her passing, at whatever age it happened. Bill's untimely death had taught Felicia that it could happen unexpectedly at any time, and her own parents had died young, her father of a stroke and her mother of pancreatic cancer, which had been shocking and fast. Felicia kept her affairs in order, and was wise and responsible with her money for her entire life.

Felicia had been a modest woman, who had no desire for fame or public attention. The success of the books spoke for itself, and was enough satisfaction for her. More than anything, she didn't want her daughters drastically changing their lives because she had made money, or living on borrowed grandeur, based on someone else's accomplishments. She wanted them to achieve their own success, whatever they considered that to be. She didn't want to rob them of the satisfaction of their own victories. But they were going to have to face their lives now without her, and both Robert and Scott knew that the whole story of the second half of her life was going to shock them profoundly, and that her daughters might even resent her for her silence and the secrets she kept. But they had lacked for nothing and she had been an attentive mother, without the frills of luxury. They had comfort and stability and love. She respected hard work more than anything.

Felicia was an only child, and had always been shy. She'd been busy with her family and writing while her children were growing up, with full responsibility for them, and she had become truly reclusive once they left home and she moved into the smaller apartment. As far as her agent and attorney knew, she occupied her enormous Connecticut estate alone, without a partner, but when the two men had lunch together one day to go over her investments and contracts, they both realized that they knew nothing about her personal life. She could have had a man in her life, but she never said so, and there was no sign of it when they visited her. They were the only guests in Connecticut. She employed only live-out day help there, and spent her nights alone, and they both knew that she worked primarily at night. She had successfully hidden both her private and her professional life from all who knew her, even her children. She had no desire for fame in any form, and didn't want people chasing or befriending her because she was famous. Scott often realized how lonely she must be, but she seemed like a lively engaged person, wasn't maudlin or strange, was still close to her children, and had written well over a hundred books in her lifetime. It was a remarkable achievement, which she had shared with no one except her agent and attorney, as far as they knew. And certainly not with her children, with intentional determination. She guarded all her secrets closely.

"It's going to be a hell of a shock to them," Robert Farr commented to Scott Freeman, when Scott called him before he sent the letter to her children about coming into his office, just to confirm the timing.

"I know." Scott was serious. "I'll do whatever I can to help them."

"If they let you," Robert added, knowing her children, which Scott didn't. He had never met them. Robert had been a slightly remote, serious grandfather figure to them for their entire lives, and occasionally offered them advice, as he did to Felicia, when asked. After estate taxes, her daughters were going to inherit eighteen million dollars each and the property in Connecticut jointly, which was valued at about fifty million. Both men wondered how it would change all of their lives. They were sensible, intelligent, discreet young women, and they were about to inherit a great deal of money. Robert knew them and had known Bill when he worked for him. And he had been Felicia's agent for all twenty-seven years of her literary career. Robert was eighty-two, but still active and in good health. Scott had only represented Felicia for ten years, and was forty-eight. He didn't know her as well but admired her immensely. She was honorable, intelligent, direct, and kind. She had been an unusual woman, and they both liked her, and were going to miss her as a client and a friend. She said she had had a lonely childhood with cold, critical parents, which had made her drive herself harder to win their approval. She had grown up in New York, had a relatively normal childhood as an only child of dull, socially responsible, stern, intellectual parents with high standards for academics. And she had been happily married to Bill. She was close to her daughters, but she admitted that she saw little of them now, since they were busy and had their own lives, and she was determined not to be a burden on them, or interfere in their lives. Robert could see in her writing that she had been a lonely woman, and had filled the void in her life with her work. He marveled at how she came up with one fascinating plot after another, which were never repetitive. She had honed her skills sharply over the years, edited her books herself, and held herself to a high standard of excellence. She wrote constantly. Robert had moved her to another publisher eight years earlier, who paid her higher advances.

Felicia's Favorites

It had been a good career move for her. The new publisher gave her books more publicity, were masters of social media, and played up the mystery of her identity, which only made her an object of greater fascination to her readers. She always spoke respectfully of the fictional Morgan Reed she worked for, and made her seem real when she spoke of her as her "boss" to her children.

It seemed tragic to both Scott and Robert that a woman who was creative, vital, and talented, and still so productive, should be killed by a random sniper. The man who had killed her was twenty-two years old, had grown up in foster homes, had managed to escape psychiatric treatment, and had a long history of mental problems that had gone untreated. He had no motive for his rampage. Her name was mentioned in the news stories about the shooting only as Felicia Weston, an unknown book editor, and her story faded quickly from the news. Robert had enough of her recent unpublished books for another contract when her current one ended, but after that Morgan Reed would fade away onto the shelves of publishing history as a phenomenon and only he as her agent, her lawyer, Scott Freeman, and her children would ever know the truth of who Felicia Weston had been and what she had done.

She had admitted to him once over a long dinner with a bottle of wine that she had never won her parents' approval despite good grades. They had set the bar so high for her that she had never achieved their goals. They had been cold intellectuals and she had grown up starved for affection, which explained her deep love for her daughters. Her cold parents' merciless criticism had made her shy and reclusive all her life. It was a life well lived that ended too soon, with no fanfare, or the lavish praise that would have been heaped on her as Morgan Reed. Felicia had remained true to herself and her values for her entire life. She had led an exemplary life as a good mother, good wife, good person, hard worker. She had lived for her work and her children, with little frivolity, and not enough fun, in Robert's opinion. But she always seemed content with her life.

After the two men spoke, Scott sent his letter to each of Felicia's daughters that afternoon. He could well imagine that it was going to be a hard Christmas for them, seven weeks after their mother's death. But she had left them an enormous gift, and a legacy her millions of fans would cherish. He could only hope that her daughters would too. Scott's letter had requested that they contact him as soon as possible, so he could arrange a meeting with all five of them, to explain their mother's bequests to them. It was going to be a very interesting meeting, the first time Scott had seen or spoken to her daughters, when he met with them at the farm in Connecticut, as Felicia had requested, the farm that none of them even knew existed. He had been there several times. It was a beautiful place and he loved going there, and she always received him warmly and was kind to him.

Felicia's daughters had a whole world and a whole persona to discover. Scott couldn't wait to meet them, and he wondered how well they would match Felicia's descriptions of them. As she was in all things, she was honest and direct, although never cruel or unkind, but very straightforward and keenly perceptive about people and astute about their strengths and flaws, their weaknesses. She even understood their fears and dreams and was deeply empathetic. She was fascinated by people and the human condition. Her daughters seemed almost like characters in a book to Scott from the way Felicia had described them. She knew each of them completely, their needs, their fears, and their strengths. Each of the five women he was about to meet already seemed real to him, as though he already knew them. She knew each of them intimately, to their very soul, and they knew her not at all. She had admitted to Scott that she had never allowed them to know her fully, and had remained hidden in the shadows for her entire life, with everyone she knew, even her children. It was comfortable for her. She kept everyone she knew at a safe distance, so no one could hurt her, or reject her as her parents had. She always spoke kindly of her husband, and as far as Scott knew, there had been no men after him. She never spoke of her personal life. She was as much a mystery as was the author of the hundred and eight bestsellers she had written. And the surprise ending this time was not a good one, written by a lone deranged gunman with an assault rifle, who had ended the life of a wonderful woman Scott admired deeply, and whose daughters were about to learn their mother's secrets. Scott wondered how they would all react and if their mother's description of them had been accurate. At the meeting at her farm, he was about to find out more about them.

Charlotte Weston's life had been a struggle for almost twenty years. She had felt the burden of being the firstborn heavy on her shoulders almost from the beginning, and took her mother's advice as criticism. Felicia was careful not to criticize her children.

But Charlotte hated her mother's counsel and opinions, and hated even more that Felicia was so often right, which was easy to do with Charlotte, because Charlotte was a risk-taker and the risks she took were so often ill advised. She had grudgingly come to admit that her mother was usually right, as her sisters always pointed out to her, which set Charlotte at odds with them too. Charlotte was always doing battle with someone. Her mother, her own teenage children now, Adam, her ex-husband, her business partners when she had them. Her ex-husband had given up custody of their children and moved to Spain, and was killed there in a motorcycle accident. Her mother had warned her about him, and Charlotte had brushed off her wise advice. At twenty-two, Charlotte had married a devastatingly handsome, charming, fast-talking "snake oil salesman" as she called him later. She had started a business with him, an online magazine destined to fail, and had two babies, and the business had crashed quickly when he kept taking money out of it for himself, and stealing money from her. The marriage had failed a few years later. He cheated on her with her friends, emptied her bank accounts, abused her credit cards and her soul, and by twenty-nine, she was out of money, severely disillusioned, and fighting Adam's demands for support. He was a small-time crook, as her mother had feared. Adam was unemployed, and Charlotte had a job. She wound up paying him spousal support for three years, and was bitter beyond repair after the divorce.

He left for Spain with his alimony and the settlement he got. He gave up custody of their two children by his own choice. And three years after the divorce he was killed in a motorcycle accident in

Spain, and Charlotte had been angry ever since. Her mother and sisters had tried to warn her about Adam before she married him. She refused to listen, and paid a high price for it. Her son Sean was now nineteen, her daughter Julia sixteen, and were both good kids.

Felicia had helped her daughter and bailed her out financially when she needed it most, which Charlotte found humiliating, even though Felicia was nice about it. In the past ten years, her mother's faith in her had been justified, and she had had a very considerable success in business with an online delivery service that wasn't unique but was extremely efficient. She was a hard worker and hoped to take the company public in the next few years. It supported her and her children handsomely and Felicia was proud of her. But despite her success in business, and two nice children, Charlotte was never happy. Anger and disappointment emanated from her pores. Charlotte had remained sour about men ever since Adam.

Her taste in men hadn't improved, and she had sworn off marriage forever. She'd had several predictably disastrous relationships with irresponsible, usually opportunistic men. None of them had had solid careers, and were using her as a stepping-stone to wherever they wanted to go. She was still naïve about men, and believed their lies.

She no longer needed her mother's help financially. Her business was called To Go, and was a huge success. And to her credit, she had worked hard for ten years to achieve her success in business, and there had been some very lean years when she no longer accepted her mother's help. She wanted to make it on her own and had eventually paid her mother back every penny she'd given her. Felicia respected her for it. There was often tension between them, especially when she warned Charlotte about men she was currently dating, who seemed dangerous or "off" to her. Charlotte was always blind to their faults until too late. Felicia was usually right about them, which infuriated Charlotte. It was a lesson she hadn't learned yet, and Felicia worried that maybe she never would. Charlotte could never resist a handsome face and a man who needed her help to get some project off the ground, which never happened. They either failed abysmally, or never tried and ran off with the money, which added to her bitterness about men and her lack of faith in them. The only one surprised by her poor choices was Charlotte. She was beautiful and bright, but not wise. She was naïve about people's faults until too late.

Charlotte had a good life, and a very reasonable success to her credit, and still wasn't a happy person. The glass was always half empty in her eyes. There was always something to complain about, someone she envied, who she thought had more than she did, or a happier relationship than her current one. All Felicia wanted for her was to be happy with a good guy who made her life better, not worse. She hadn't found that so far, and Felicia wondered if she ever would.

Charlotte was a hard worker, but the grass was always greener somewhere else. She was a fighter for her business, but a loser in relationships. Her ex-husband had been irresponsible and dishonest, and didn't care about their children. He had lived with a series of very young women after the divorce and she was still bitter about him. She had been sure the marriage would work, and been shocked when it didn't. She was the only one surprised when her marriage to Adam crashed and burned.

In typical fashion, she was angry when she read the letter from Scott Freeman. She was annoyed at him, and her mother. Why did her mother always have to make everything so complicated? Why couldn't she just have a will like everyone else and tell them what she was leaving them? Charlotte asked. Why did she have to be mysterious and try to control them with money from the grave? She ranted to her next younger sister, Quinne, who was good-natured, and the most willing to listen to her complain. The others all got along with their mother easily. The five sisters had been close as children and had stayed that way, but the others got impatient with Charlotte's complaints about their mother, who was generous with all of them equally.

"She never tried to control you with money," Quinne reminded her fairly in a gentle voice on the phone when Charlotte called her. "She gave you money when you needed it for your business, with no strings attached. You paid her back when you could. It was a clean deal, Char. What's to control?"

"She hated the men I dated," Charlotte said. She was beautiful and blond like their mother.

"So do you, eventually. So do most people. You've dated some pretty awful guys. Mom didn't want you to get hurt, and she can't control you now," Quinne said sadly, missing their mother. She had a deep love and respect for her and was still traumatized by her death. They all were, and showed it in different ways. Charlotte was angry and Quinne was grieving deeply.

"She probably put all kinds of ridiculous conditions on whatever we inherit. I don't care, I don't need the money," Charlotte said petulantly. Her business was extremely lucrative.

"That's lucky for you. And that wasn't Mom. She loved us unconditionally, no matter what we did. She never made anything difficult for us," Quinne reminded her. "She was proud of you, Charlotte, and of all of us. She helped us whenever we needed it, even when she didn't have much." They all knew that divided by five, what she had left wouldn't be a lot. None of them expected a big inheritance. Their mother had always said that Morgan Reed paid her a fair salary for her editing, and she lived modestly, and saved what she could. Charlotte just liked to object in principle to whatever her mother did, still acting like a teenager with her sometimes, like her own daughter. She was a smart woman. She had a gift for business, more so than her sisters. She and her daughter Julia were engaged in constant battles now too. Charlotte complained about her. Her son Sean had avoided any battles with his mother by going to college on the West Coast and taking summer jobs far from home. He got along better with his more open-minded grandmother and aunts. Sean and Felicia had gotten along particularly well, which made his mother jealous.

"And why do we have to go to Connecticut for the meeting, all five of us?" Charlotte groused. "It's just another flaming hoop for us to jump through. Why can't we just go to Scott Freeman's office in town, instead of Connecticut? I have meetings that day." Quinne listened to Charlotte's complaints until she got bored and ended the call. Charlotte's problem was that she had been burned by her ex-husband and several boyfriends so badly that she no longer trusted men. She had two good kids and a successful business.

And her bitterness kept most men away, so there was no man in her life.

In contrast to Charlotte, at thirty-nine, Quinne had been a hard worker all her life, but wanted none of the responsibility or the glory of owning a business, with its headaches and demands. She had no head for business. She didn't want marriage or kids. She was content with a job, not a career, and had been in television production since college, working on successful projects where someone else got the glory and big bucks, and Quinne got the hard work she never shirked. She just didn't want the headaches or the stress of success. She had risen to the top in her field, was a talented TV producer, and was paid decently. She had more than enough to live on, and to coast comfortably between projects. She had been in love with the same man since college, Cooper O'Neill. He was Irish and they had met at USC, and had lived together since senior year, for eighteen years now. He made a good living with supporting actor roles in TV and movies. He wasn't a star but made a steady, very respectable income. They were in sync on how they lived and what they wanted. Quinne was phobic about marriage, after watching her sister's nightmarish divorce and others like it. Felicia was sorry that Quinne didn't want to marry or have children. Quinne loved her niece and nephew, and Felicia liked Coop a lot and enjoyed him at family gatherings. They were happy. They didn't want a lot materially, and were content as they were. They lived in the Village in New York in a small walk-up apartment that suited them. Neither of them wanted a fancy life.

Charlotte lived in a nicer apartment than Quinne, in Tribeca, and was talking about buying a better one after her company went public. Quinne and Coop lived in a simple apartment that suited them, and when they went on location for several months, they locked the door and left it until they came back. They had no desire to be burdened by possessions or bound by responsibilities or traditions. It wasn't what Felicia would have wanted for her, but she respected Quinne's right to make her own choices and decisions. Quinne and her mother spoke two or three times a week and the conversations were warm and easy. Charlotte loved to argue with her mother. It was like a sport she enjoyed. They were always arguing about small things that didn't matter. Felicia tried not to be upset by them. And she had Quinne and the others to console her when Charlotte hurt her feelings. All of the sisters had their own distinct personalities.

Olivia was the strongest of them all and had had the hardest challenge to face. Her mother had helped her more than the others, which no one resented in her case.

Olivia's passion had been ballet since the age of three, and she had been formally trained, seriously talented, and totally dedicated. A car accident at twenty-five had changed her life forever, while she was dancing with the American Ballet Theatre. Now thirty-seven, she had been a paraplegic in a wheelchair for the twelve years since the accident. Her career had ended brutally. The driver, a close friend she danced with, and another passenger died in the accident. Olivia had survived, but nothing else in her life had. Her life as a dancer vanished instantly, with a severe spinal cord injury. She had to rethink and rebuild everything in her life. She and one of the dancers and choreographers she worked with, François Vernier, had been in a serious relationship for seven years and were engaged at the time. Olivia had ended the relationship immediately afterward, as soon as she understood what her future would look like. She refused to be a burden to François, or an object of pity, or a tragic figure. She ended it with François while still in the hospital. He was devastated, but she was relentless in her decision, and refused to see him afterward. He wanted to stay with her to care for her and still marry her, and she refused. It had been twelve years since she had contact with him, since the accident. He had waited seven years to marry. She was the love of his life. He had finally married when he realized she wouldn't come back. He had been married for the last five years and Olivia hoped he was happy. She was thirty-seven years old, still stunningly beautiful even in a wheelchair. She taught advanced ballet classes from her chair, and worked on both set and costume design for a small but respected dance company. She made enough to live on, in a small ground floor apartment near Lincoln Center on the West Side in Manhattan. She did everything physically for herself. She had a woman come in to help her every morning with the tasks she couldn't do on her own, but in every way she could be, she was independent, and never sorry for herself. Felicia had wanted to hire live-in assistance for her, and Olivia had refused, said it wasn't necessary and she knew their mother couldn't afford it, and she managed fine on her own, after extensive training and rehab. Olivia made the best of everything, and had a strong upbeat personality. It had broken Felicia's heart to see her at first, but it was impossible not to be overwhelmed with admiration for her. She never complained, unlike Charlotte. Olivia's strength and indomitable spirit were a sharp dose of reality for them all. There had been no man in her life since the accident, and she no longer heard from François Vernier at all, nor did she want to. It was past history, like her life onstage. She fended well for herself. It was a source of sorrow to Felicia, and one of life's cruel blows, but Olivia wasn't an object of pity. She had refused to become that after the accident. She was determined and positive about everything she did, she loved her job and her students, and was deeply concerned about others, with a generous nature.

Veronica and Isabelle were the closest to each other, as the two youngest. Veronica had made a difficult life choice that her mother didn't approve of. She had graduated from Columbia Law School, passed the bar the first time, and landed a job with an important law firm, with a brilliant career in corporate law ahead of her, until she met Anson Phillips in her first job. He had been the CEO of two major corporations, had gone into politics, and was an extraordinarily charismatic man. Veronica was twenty-six when they met, and he was forty-seven when he ran for senator. She had campaigned for him. He was a client of the law firm where she worked, and he spotted her quickly, and fell in love with her. Their affair began while he was campaigning, and then he won the election. She traveled with him as an assistant, and he ultimately set her up in an apartment where they could meet discreetly. It was a passionate love affair. He had been in a bad marriage since his twenties, but he and his wife were Catholic and he was afraid a divorce would hurt him politically. His wife was fiercely opposed to the idea of a divorce, and Veronica and Anson were excruciatingly careful and never got caught. He was honest with her that there was no hope of marriage with him, and he wanted her near him and available at all times. She gave up her job and her future law career for him, and he set her up in a beautiful apartment. She had been his mistress for ten years. There was no hope of marriage or a future where she could be visible, but she loved him and had given up her life for him and had no regrets. She spent her time waiting for him, and preparing for their time together.

Felicia objected vocally and strenuously to Veronica's decision, but Veronica was unwavering in her love for Anson. She was thirty-six now, and Anson fifty-seven, and she never swayed from the path she had chosen, much to her mother's dismay. Her sisters didn't support her decision either. Anson was a charming, handsome, powerful man, and he made it up to Veronica in countless ways with a luxurious apartment, employees who had signed iron-clad confidentiality agreements, wonderful trips where they met most often abroad, and visits to her at the apartment in New York when he could get away. She had everything she could have wanted materially, a beautiful home, an elegant wardrobe, jewelry he bought her from discreet jewelers. She could share no social life with him, and stayed mostly out of sight except when he could easily explain her presence publicly with some excuse or lie. She couldn't have a job, in order to be available to him whenever he wanted. Her sisters were shocked by how completely she had given up her life for him, but she never doubted for a moment that it was the life she wanted and was right for her. She knew she could never marry him. Veronica loved him deeply, and was happy when she was with him.

Charlotte predicted it would end in disaster for her sister. Felicia was desperately upset about it, Quinne felt sorry for her, and Olivia tried to be supportive, although she too was sorry for her. Veronica lived in golden isolation, waiting to be at the beck and call of the man she loved, and who she knew loved her. It was a high price to pay for the time they spent together, which was never enough, but she was a consenting and willing partner in the life she had fashioned to accommodate him for the past ten years. She had even given up the hope of having children, but she was willing to give it all up for him. And she had no financial needs since he paid for everything in her luxurious lifestyle, which was all he could give her. He was a very wealthy man and could afford it, as long as he didn't get caught. He was willing to risk that for her, although he was extremely careful, and everything he paid for was through convoluted channels via his lawyer. He had a whole secret financial structure for Veronica's support.

Isabelle was the youngest of Felicia's children. Her dreams were more human scale than her sisters'. She was a beautiful woman, and having grown up without a father—she was two when her father died—all she wanted was to be married and have children and a "normal" family life. She was married to the son of a wealthy New York very social banking family, and like Veronica, she had a luxurious lifestyle, provided by her husband. She was thirty-four years old, and had three children, Tyler, Charlie, and Penny, and had been married for twelve years. Her lifestyle was more respectable than Veronica's, but materially their lives were similar, with beautiful homes, numerous employees, and an extremely pleasant way of life, and they didn't have to work for what they had. And both of them were dependent on their men. The two sisters had that in common.

Charlotte was critical of them both at times. She thought they were wasting their lives. Veronica had achieved her life by being a mistress, and Isabelle by being a wife. But Charlotte had an independence that neither of them had, because she had earned every penny she had herself. She depended on no man, unlike Veronica and Isabelle.

Isabelle never had any career aspirations, and never wanted a career, just a husband and children. She had a happy, sunny nature and appreciated the life she had. Olivia and Quinne didn't care about money, and didn't envy the others. The only jealous one in the group was Charlotte occasionally.

Of all of them, Isabelle appeared to have the most perfect life, a handsome, respectable, wealthy husband, three beautiful children, armies of help, a beautiful home in the city. She hadn't done anything remarkable in her life, but it was the life she had dreamed of since she was a child. Veronica and Isabelle lived much more luxuriously than their mother in her small apartment. And even Charlotte's apartment was larger than her mother's. Felicia was happy for them, although she'd been unhappy about Veronica's circumstances, her relationship with Anson Phillips, and her life as his mistress. She was ever watchful of Olivia's health since the accident. She shared in Olivia's heartbreak and disappointment, but Olivia handled it well, and had since her accident. She was a strong woman with a positive outlook on life.

All five sisters were severely shaken by their mother's tragic, senseless death, whatever their relationship with her, even Veronica, whose lifestyle as Anson Phillips's mistress Felicia least approved of. She thought Veronica's life in the shadows was demeaning and she hated that for her.

All were startled by the letter they received posthumously from their mother's attorney. None of them understood the mystery surrounding the meeting to share her will with them, or why the month's delay at their mother's request. They understood even less the reason for the meeting being held at a house in Connecticut, which Scott Freeman said was at their mother's request, with no further explanation. It made no sense to them. Why Connecticut and not her attorney's office in the city? Scott also mentioned that their mother had stipulated that if they wished to spend the weekend or the night together in Connecticut after the meeting, Scott could arrange it. His letter offered no explanation of the location, and they all assumed that she must have added an amendment if she had rented the property somehow before her untimely death. It couldn't have been part of her original will written six years before or they'd have known about it. As far as they knew, she had no secrets from them.

The five sisters called each other as soon as they received the letter from Scott Freeman, and couldn't figure it out.

Charlotte grumbled about going, predictably. Veronica hesitated. She didn't want to go to the meeting, and was afraid that whatever Felicia had left them would be subject to conditions Veronica wouldn't agree to, like giving up her married lover. Isabelle had suffered a terrible shock at her mother's death, and now there was a second one. Her marriage had been perfect for twelve years, but the night before the letter arrived, she discovered that her husband, Ian MacPherson, was having an affair with a twenty-three-year-old intern who worked for him. Isabelle was still staggering from the blow the next morning, unsure how to react, feeling her whole life in jeopardy. Her rock-solid foundation with a loving husband was suddenly shaken to its core, a month after she lost the mother she adored. She told Veronica, whom she was closest to, about Ian's affair. Veronica was deeply sympathetic. Isabelle didn't feel in any condition to go to the meeting, but finally agreed to go with Veronica to support her. Quinne and Olivia were eager to go, and curious about it. And Charlotte was the last to grudgingly accept. In the end, all five sisters agreed to go to the mystery house in Connecticut on Friday morning to hear Scott Freeman reveal to them their mother's final will and testament, at a location that made no sense to any of them, and was inconvenient, out of the city.

Veronica and Isabelle rode in a car together, with Veronica driving. Isabelle felt too shaky to drive after the shocking news about Ian's affair. A close friend of Isabelle's who was related to one of Ian's associates had heard the rumor from a reliable source and thought she should know. Isabelle and Veronica rode in a car alone so they could discuss it. Isabelle wasn't ready to share the bad news with the others, and they had other things on their minds: their mother's will and the mysterious meeting. Drama and secrets weren't their mother's style.

Isabelle felt as though she had already lost Ian, if the rumor was true, which made it a double loss for her, if she lost her mother and husband within a month of each other. Both were huge losses for her.

Charlotte, Quinne, and Olivia rode in a car together. Quinne drove. They were quiet as they left the city, still unable to guess the reason for the secrecy and the mysterious unfamiliar location. It was unlike their mother to complicate things. She had always been honest, transparent, and straightforward with them. They were certain she'd had no secrets from them, nor anything of great value to leave them. The greatest gift she'd had to give them was the love she shared with them, unconditionally, for their entire lifetimes. It had been so much for each of them to lose her so suddenly and in such a shocking way. They each drifted with their own private thoughts of her as they drove to Connecticut. It was a cold gray winter day, and none of them suspected even for an instant how radically their lives were about to change. Losing her enormous presence in their lives had been hard enough.

Chapter 2

Charlotte and Olivia rode in the car with Quinne, who drove them in the battered station wagon she and Cooper had purchased jointly. They shared it, and he had auditions that day and didn't need it. Charlotte complained that they should have taken her car. With the profits from her business going through the roof, she had just bought a new Mercedes, but she didn't feel like driving, and Quinne didn't mind. She was always willing to accommodate the others. It was a freezing cold December day and was liable to snow before they got back to the city, and Charlotte didn't like driving in bad weather, so she was happy Quinne was driving. Olivia was comfortable riding in the back seat. She was in great shape and agile with the exercise routine she followed every day to keep her upper body strong. She was glancing at a magazine, and joined their conversation from time to time. She liked being with her sisters, and all three of them were busy, so they didn't get together as often as they used to. Olivia had her ballet classes to teach, and numerous charitable activities. Charlotte had her business to run, and her daughter Julia, at sixteen, still kept her occupied, driving her places and keeping an eye on her. She was a good girl, more so than her mother had been at her age, but the two of them had been engaged in constant battle for the last year over the rules that Charlotte imposed on her. She was an attentive mother, as their own had been when they were teenagers. Felicia always knew what was going on and stayed a step ahead of them. She was less strict with the others than she had been with Charlotte and they had been better behaved. Charlotte still groused about how strict Felicia had been, but the others never agreed with her.

Quinne was always busy with the TV productions she worked on, and she and Coop spent all their free time together. Spending a morning or a day with her sisters in Connecticut gave them a chance to catch up and talk. Charlotte and Olivia were both blondes and looked like Felicia. Quinne had dark hair, but they all had a family look with blue eyes, and they were tall and slim as their mother had been. Veronica had dark hair like Quinne, and Isabelle was a strawberry blonde, smaller than her sisters and very romantic looking with long wavy hair. They were all strikingly attractive women, and were in good shape, as their mother had been with her marathons. Charlotte went to a gym at six o'clock every morning before work. Quinne had to be on set too early to go to a gym when she was working, but she and Coop played tennis on the weekends, and swam frequently. And Olivia still went to a rehab center several times a week to maintain her upper body strength, which she needed in order to take care of herself efficiently, and be able to live alone.

Felicia's Favorites

The Connecticut countryside looked bleak and wintry, the trees were bare, and there was still snow on the ground from a recent snowfall.

"Why do you suppose Mom wanted us to meet at some godforsaken place in Connecticut about her will? Just to make things difficult?" Charlotte asked, as the countryside looked more rural an hour out of the city. They had left the city at eight-thirty in order to get there by ten.

"No," Olivia said, "probably to make us spend some time together, so we're not all running off in ten directions. I had to get someone to take one of my classes for me. Char is always in a meeting, Quinne is always on set. Veronica cancels at the drop of a hat if Anson has an hour to see her, and Isabelle gets stuck at home with a sick kid, or the nanny is sick," she said, and Quinne laughed. It was true. They were close to each other, and called often and sent texts, but they hadn't seen each other since their mother's funeral four weeks ago. "We're not easy to pin down." But they had all freed their schedules for the meeting in Connecticut. They wanted to know what their mother's wishes were. She had left separate instructions about the funeral, but they didn't know if she had left specific bequests for the things in her apartment, which they still had to pack up and vacate, and they didn't know where she wanted to be buried. Her ashes were still at the funeral home, waiting to be picked up. There was an unsettled feeling for all of them, not knowing what was in her will. They needed closure, and Isabelle's husband, Ian, had reminded them that they would have to pay estate taxes, which Scott had confirmed, and they didn't know the value of her estate. They knew it wouldn't be much, but whatever it was, they needed to settle the final painful details. They all hated the finality of it.

It was still shocking to think that Felicia was gone. She had been so youthful and so alive, so strong and full of energy, and so loving. The sisters had grown closer to each other just in the last month without her. Charlotte had been grumpier than usual, Quinne admitted that she cried every time she thought about her, Olivia had had trouble sleeping, Veronica felt suddenly anxious, and Isabelle looked dazed when Veronica picked her up for the drive, since they lived near each other uptown. They all agreed that they felt suddenly lost without Felicia, even though they didn't see her all the time, but they knew she was there if they needed her, that strong, comforting voice that always knew what to do, would listen at any hour, and remained calm in a crisis. She was the one person in their lives they knew they could always count on. What would they do now without her?

"I feel like an orphan," Quinne said softly as she drove. Charlotte stared out the window and nodded silently, and Olivia was glad they were together, and grateful for the time with them, even if it made no sense to drive all the way out to Connecticut to finally learn what was in their mother's will. It wasn't about what they were going to get, for any of them, it was just about knowing what she wanted. They were quiet for a while, thinking about her. They were all well aware of how hard Christmas was going to be without Felicia. Isabelle had been with her in-laws for Thanksgiving, while Charlotte had gone away with Julia to spend it with Sean at Stanford since he said traveling home would be a nightmare. Veronica had been on call for Anson, who couldn't come at the last

Felicia's Favorites

minute so she'd been alone. Olivia had volunteered to serve at a homeless shelter, and Quinne had stayed in bed and hadn't acknowledged Thanksgiving at all.

They were all nervous about what Christmas would be like without her. Felicia loved Christmas, she always made a big fuss, and they crammed into her small apartment on Christmas Eve, with a tree that was always too big, eggnog and hot toddies, a turkey she cooked herself, and a mountain of gifts for her children and grandchildren. It was her favorite day of the year and she made it special for all of them. None of them had had the heart to make their Christmas plans yet, as though a miracle might occur and she might come back, if they didn't.

The three women in Quinne's car were silent, thinking about Felicia, and Veronica came through the gates right behind them at the correct address, and followed them up a long tree-lined driveway. The gates had been left open for them at the location they'd been given. They were on time. The property had a rustic look to it but was neat and well cared for, and they wondered who it belonged to, and why their mother had requested they meet there. It was a long way to the main house, and when they reached it there was a circular driveway, and a large stone house, with tall old trees all around it. There were neat flowerbeds and a lawn, a number of cottages and outbuildings, and a pool. It was a handsome estate and had a historical feel to it. The farm, dating back to the days of the American Revolution, was more than two hundred years old, and was beautifully maintained.

"Maybe they rent out for meetings and conventions," Charlotte suggested, as Quinne parked and turned off the engine, but it didn't look like that kind of place. It looked like a beautifully cared for private estate. They had driven past a similar property when they got to the address. It was obviously a wealthy area with large private properties. Scott Freeman was standing in front of the house, waiting for them, in a business suit, white shirt, and tie, although Felicia had told him to come in jeans the few times he had met her there. He was handsome and looked younger than his forty-eight years, with dark hair and brown eyes, and he'd wanted to look respectable and serious for them, and respectful of Felicia. He looked slightly overwhelmed for an instant as all five women got out of the two cars, and he was struck by how beautiful they were, even more than he had expected. Quinne got Olivia's chair out of the trunk and opened it, and Olivia maneuvered herself expertly into it and followed her sisters to meet him and introduce themselves. They were smiling but looked serious. They had dressed informally for the country and the weather, but even in jeans, down jackets, and casual clothes, they were a striking group, and like their mother, none of them looked their age. They were a group of beautiful women, and took turns shaking hands with Scott. There was a brisk wind and the air was cold as they followed him into the warm house. There were no steps for Olivia to negotiate.

The entrance hall was spacious and airy, with handsome American antiques, a large vase filled with fresh flowers, and a very pretty painting. All five of her daughters were looking around filled with curiosity. They took off their down jackets and coats and he led them into a large sunny living room, with tall windows leading out to a garden, a stone patio, and an open pavilion where one could dine in summer. There was a view of a lake in the distance that Scott told them was part of the estate, as was the forest land behind it.

They were admiring the view when a tidy-looking elderly woman in a crisp white apron brought in a silver tray with a coffee service and cups for six and set it down on a long antique table. There was a large fireplace in the room, a fire had been lit, and there were comfortable-looking couches and chairs where they could sit for their meeting. Veronica loved antiques and noticed the silver coffee service as the housekeeper set it down. She said her name was Ellen and looked at them with interest and then left.

"That's funny, Mom had a silver service just like that, and Anson and I bought an almost identical one at the silver vaults in London, because it reminded me of hers." Scott didn't comment. The women were looking around the room, admiring the shelves of antique books, and Charlotte was staring at the painting over the fireplace. It was a picnic scene, and she couldn't take her eyes off it. The artist was French and she turned to the attorney with a puzzled look.

"Our mother had one just like that, the same one. What's it doing here?" she asked him, and he looked serious.

"Let's sit down and get started," he said. Charlotte suddenly felt a chill of anticipation, as they took their places on the couches, glancing at each other, a thousand questions in their eyes. They waited politely for Scott to begin, the mystery of the painting over the fireplace foremost in their minds. Had he brought it to make them feel at home? Had their mother instructed him to do so with her penchant for minute detailed instructions? What was it doing there? And more importantly what were they doing there, and why?

He took a breath and began, sitting in a large comfortable chair, with a stack of papers on a table next to him, and all five women were staring at him expectantly.

"I know you have pertinent questions, which will all get answered by the end of our meeting. Your mother left very specific instructions. I'm sure you all know how precise she was. But it's hard to know where to start. There are two important things for you to know. After that the rest will all make sense and fall into place." He tried to sound reassuring, but he could see that the two youngest sisters, Veronica and Isabelle, looked scared, and he wanted to put them out of their misery as soon as he could.

"First of all, I assume you all know the name Morgan Reed."

"My mother was her private editor for years, separate from the publishing house where she used to be employed. My mother worked for her directly," Veronica explained, which they all knew, and he did too. For the moment, she was the star student with the correct answer, or so she thought.

"That's not exactly true, although it's what she said," Scott said cautiously, knowing he was about to shock them profoundly.

"Did Morgan Reed die and leave my mother some money?" Charlotte interrupted bluntly. She was getting an odd feeling about the house, and wondered if it belonged to Morgan Reed, who allowed Felicia to use it.

"That's not quite the case," Scott said, and leapt in. "In fact, there is no Morgan Reed. Or there was. Morgan Reed is the pseudonym your mother used to write the books. In truth, your mother was Morgan Reed. She never revealed that to anyone, except Robert Farr and myself, that she wrote the books. Morgan Reed was your mother." They were all stunned into silence for a moment and stared at him in amazement.

"Mom was Morgan Reed?" Isabelle said in a squeaky voice and felt as though she had missed something. "Why didn't she tell us?"

"She never wanted anyone to know. She guarded the secret carefully for her entire career, for a hundred and eight books."

The sisters looked around at each other, trying to absorb it.

"Holy shit," Charlotte was the first to comment.

"I think she was surprised by their initial success. I didn't know her then. Her books were an overnight hit, and they just got bigger and bigger with time. She didn't want fame to intervene in your lives or hers, so she never told anyone. They're the biggest bestsellers that anyone publishes."

"They must have paid her a lot for them," Charlotte said practically. "What happened to the money? Our mother lived a very small life, she was never extravagant." Charlotte appeared to doubt what Scott was saying.

"She invested most of it for all of you, which is part of what we have to discuss today." He moved on to the next surprise then. "This property belonged to your mother. She left it jointly to all five of you. She spent most of her time here in the last ten years. She kept the apartment in the city as a pied-à-terre, and for her visits with all of you. Her success came so quickly, and the money that came with it, that she didn't want to change your lifestyles or your careers. She preferred to save and invest her money so you would have it later, and not when you were too young to handle it responsibly. And this property was a refuge for her. She did all her writing here. She bought the property about twelve years ago for a reasonable amount. She had it reappraised two years ago. At current market value then, it was estimated at fifty million dollars. There's quite a bit of forest land, and a lot of acreage, and it's a historical property. You each own a fifth of that, she left it to you jointly. That's why you recognized the painting, Charlotte. This is your property now, all of yours. She was hoping you might all like to use it together, or separately with your families. With the outbuildings she did over as guesthouses, there's room for all of you. Of course you can decide to sell it, if that's what you all wish to do, or buy each other out, if some of you want it and others don't. In addition, her investment portfolio was very well handled, and her contracts increased exponentially each time. After the estate taxes are paid, you will each receive in the vicinity of eighteen million dollars. She saved most of what she earned, in order to leave it to the five of you one day. And her body of work is an important legacy. We'll need to work with Robert to handle it and make sound decisions about reprints, television series, feature films, syndications, and her royalties from all her international publishers." He let it sink in, and all five of the sisters were stunned into silence for a moment, trying to absorb what he had said.

"Eighteen million dollars each? And this property? What are we going to do with that?" Quinne asked. She couldn't imagine it. She was perfectly satisfied with what she had, her walk-up apartment in the Village and her on-and-off production jobs that gave her all the income she needed to pay her half of the rent with Cooper. And now suddenly, she was worth nearly thirty million dollars, including her share of the property in Connecticut. Tears sprang to her eyes, and she was shocked by what their mother had done for them. They were suddenly very rich women, but she would have given anything to have their mother back instead of the money.

"Why didn't she tell us any of this?" she said, and wiped her eyes.

"She thought you were all pretty much on track on the paths you wanted to be on, and she didn't want to upset the balance of your lives. She didn't really lead a life of luxury herself, except for this property. But she turned it into a home, a haven where she could write, not a showplace. You know yourselves, she wasn't a showy woman. She was always very down-to-earth, and all she wanted was to write the books, and see all of you when you had time." She had built an empire for them, and he was intrigued to know what they were going to do with it. Quinne seemed very much like her mother, and Scott could see that material success had not been one of Quinne's goals, and that the windfall she was about to receive came as a total shock.

"I could do another startup," Charlotte said with stars in her eyes, "without investors to drive me nuts this time." Veronica and Isabelle were noticeably silent and looked stunned.

"We could set up a foundation, and bring inner-city kids here for two-week camp sessions all summer, or even all year," Olivia said, visibly excited. The suggestion was so typical of her that the others smiled. She was deeply philanthropic, and was already thinking of who they could help.

"Do we want to keep the property?" Veronica asked them, catching her breath. "It looks gorgeous. Maybe we should keep it for us," she said cautiously, not wanting to offend her charitable sister Olivia.

"Let's look around before we make any decisions," Charlotte said sensibly. "It's too soon to decide anything. We've owned it for ten minutes, although Sean and Julia would love it."

"I could spend summers here with the kids, and I wouldn't have to go to my in-laws in Maine anymore," Isabelle said, smiling, but who knew how all of that would shake out if the rumors about Ian having an affair were true. Maybe he was going to leave her. She didn't know what to believe. Within twenty-four hours she had learned that she might be losing her husband, and that her mother had left each of them a bequest worth nearly thirty million dollars each. She couldn't wrap her mind around it yet, and she didn't want to tell Ian about it now. She didn't want him to stay with her for that. She felt as though she no longer knew him. His family had always treated her like a lesser person because she didn't have money, and now suddenly she had more than they did, and a much nicer country home. While Ian was about to ruin everything with another woman in his life.

Veronica was wondering how Anson was going to react to her windfall and unexpected inheritance. She had been completely dependent on him ever since they'd been together and she'd given up her law career for him, and she had no income. She depended on him for everything and he always said he didn't mind. She didn't like to be beholden to him, but there was no other choice if he wanted her to be constantly available at a moment's notice, with no other life, no friends to take up her time, no projects or engagements to occupy her. No children. No job. Her whole life was a waiting game, expected to be there to offer him comfort, support, love, and nurturing, and sex any time. She was in effect a paid courtesan, which was what her mother had objected to so strenuously about her situation. Now Felicia had changed all that in an instant, and materially Veronica would no longer be dependent on Anson. She wondered how he would like that, or if he wouldn't. She didn't want to upset him, and had already decided to wait until the right time to tell him, and not right away. She and Isabelle had good reasons to hide their news

Quinne wasn't sure either how Cooper would react. They didn't live in abject poverty, but they led a very simple life, and contributed equally to everything they did. They had an entirely equitable relationship which was about to change dramatically, and Coop was sensitive about things like that. Maybe he'd trade her in for a poor girl. They'd both been living on what they earned, and their combined incomes were very modest. Felicia had changed all that, for all of them.

The only two who had no partner to consider were Charlotte and Olivia, who were very much alone in their lives, and only had themselves to think about, except for Charlotte's children, Sean and Julia. She had no intention of telling them that they had become rich overnight, thanks to their grandmother. She would tell them one day, but not for a long time. They were too young for her to explain wealth of such magnitude to, and they were liable to tell their friends about it.

Charlotte thought of something else then, and turned to Scott. "Are you going to tell our mother's publisher that Morgan Reed is dead?" she asked him. He had thought about that as well.

"You'll have to discuss that with Robert, and see what he advises. As I understand it, he has six or seven of her latest unpublished manuscripts that aren't part of the current contract, so you don't need to rush telling them, which gives you time to make a wise decision. That's really his province, not mine, and you'll have a lot to discuss with him, now that you know the truth about the books and who wrote them."

They all had a great deal to think about after the meeting. Scott discussed their mother's investment portfolio with them, which was in very good shape. She had been a consummately responsible person, a practical woman, and since she was doing it all for her children, she was particularly careful, and never invested in anything high-risk. He assured them that they had all the money needed to pay the estate taxes. Felicia had an insurance policy for that, and additional money set aside in case of surprises. She was leaving them a whistle-clean estate and an astounding inheritance, and a beautiful property they could use and enjoy.

It took two hours to go over all the details and bring the sisters up to date, and he handed them each the letter from their mother. It was brief and handwritten to each of them, apologizing for never telling them the truth about the Morgan Reed books, but saying that she thought it was best handled the way she had chosen. None of their lives had ever been disrupted by the impact fame would have had on all of them, which had been her goal in using a pseudonym for her entire writing career. It protected all of them from the price to pay for fame, which she had ardently avoided for her entire literary career.

She apologized to all of them for not telling them about the farm in Connecticut. It had been her hideaway, her safe haven, and now they could enjoy it among themselves, and she hoped that they would be as happy there as she had been.

"She was such a solitary person," Quinne said sadly, "and none of us spent enough time with her in the last ten years. We've all been busy with our own lives, and we thought she was busy editing and didn't need us. She was so self-sufficient, but she must have been lonely here. It's such a beautiful place, it makes me sad to think of her here alone."

"Mom preferred it that way," Charlotte said, and Quinne suddenly wondered if they had known their mother at all. She had kept some very deep secrets from them for more than two decades, such as an important writing career, one of the most major literary careers in the States. She was the queen of thrillers, and she kept the secret of her home from them, and the money she was saving for them. Quinne wondered if there were other things they didn't know about her. Anything was possible. Veronica wondered the same thing. Charlotte had always misjudged her mother. She had assumed that the façade Felicia showed to the world, and even to them, was the real one. And Veronica and Quinne were no longer so sure. Who was Felicia really? They didn't know her at all. The beautiful country estate was proof of that.

Olivia's mind was racing wildly, thinking about the foundation they could establish in their mother's name, to honor her memory and do philanthropic deeds. Ever since her accident, her focus was always on what she could do for others less fortunate than she was. Isabelle's mind was clouded now with worries about her marriage. Losing her marriage, if she did, meant even more to her than the fortune she had just gained. It was hard to focus on both at the same time. Life was so strange. It gave with one hand, and took away with the other. Her head was spinning by the end of the meeting.

When Scott was finished speaking to them, he suggested they look around the property they had just inherited and explore the main house and the cottages and outbuildings, which they all wanted to do. The housekeeper appeared with a platter of sandwiches for all of them. They helped themselves before they began looking around, and they thanked Scott for all his explanations. Everything they had heard that day was good news, but their mother was still dead and was never coming back. Quinne wiped away tears and blew her nose and commented to Charlotte before they ate their sandwiches.

"You were so wrong about her," she said. "You always were. She wasn't trying to complicate anything for us. She's given us incredible gifts."

"I'm beginning to think that I never really knew her," Charlotte said, mollified after the revelations of the morning.

"I don't think any of us did," Veronica said sadly. "She kept all of this secret from us. She didn't even live in that tiny, overcrowded little apartment where we used to see her. She was here, writing, in a beautiful place, all by herself, for the past dozen years. We should have spent more time with her, all of us. I've been busy with Anson for most of it, and you've been busy with your business and your kids," she said to Charlotte.

Felicia's Favorites

"And I've been living day-to-day working freelance and living with Coop," Quinne volunteered. "I could even set up my own production house now, if I wanted to." She had never wanted to own anything until then, but the discoveries of that morning might change that. She glanced at Isabelle then. "And you've been all wrapped up in your perfect marriage with your handsome prince and your adorable babies, living happily ever after," she said, and tears filled Isabelle's eyes when Quinne said it. Her happily ever after had just crashed in flames, and she didn't feel ready to tell her sisters, although she knew she would eventually. They never kept secrets from each other. But their mother had. She had kept the biggest secrets of all, and she wasn't there now so they could thank her. She had let them lead their lives the way they chose, with the people they had chosen, in exactly the way they wanted to, and now she had given each of them security for the future, the freedom to do what they wanted. She had freed them from their burdens, and given them a beautiful home to share. She had let them be exactly who they were and wanted to be, without ever sharing with them who she was, or what her fears and burdens were. She had never wanted to be a burden to them, and she hadn't been. She had been there to love and protect and support them, to pick them up when they fell, to stand by them when they needed her to. Olivia knew that even better than the others. Felicia had done everything she could to restore her daughter to a normal life after the accident, in whatever way Olivia wanted to do it, so she could be independent despite her injuries.

"I just want you to know that I think your mother was an amazing woman," Scott said to them before he left to drive back to the city. "She wanted the best for all of you, and she loved you more than anything in life. I think you know that now. And the house is yours, free and clear. You can stay here now, if you want to. I think she would have liked that. She couldn't wait for you to see it one day and enjoy it too. And now it's yours." He gazed at all of them with a gentle smile.

"I wish we could have shared it with her when she was alive," Isabelle said softly.

"She thought that this way would be better," Scott said quietly. He could see that they loved their mother and had a lot to digest now. "Maybe she needed to be alone here to write," he said. "There are some things we'll never know about how or why she did things. The way she did them. She was a very private person, with enormous talent, and she loved you. That's the thing you can be sure of now. There is no question about that. Call me if I can do anything to help," he said, and left a few minutes later, after giving each of them a full set of keys to the house and the other buildings on the property. They sat quietly for a few minutes and then put on their coats and went to explore the house and the estate that were theirs now. They all had a lot to think about, who their mother was, and what she had done for them, while she was alive, and now after she was gone. She had done even more for them in death than she had when she was alive, and Veronica smiled when she thought of something, as they finished the sandwiches, before they began their tour of the house.

"Do you remember how Mom always told each of us we were her favorite, when she tucked us into bed at night? She told each of us not to tell the others. I believed her. For years, I thought I was her favorite, and then I found out she told you the same thing." They all smiled at the memory. They had each found out in the end, one day when they had an enormous fight and one of them announced she was her favorite. At first, they were crushed, and then they all thought it was funny. And they'd always remembered it. "She was telling the truth, as it turns out. We were all her favorites and we still are. She divided everything perfectly between us. It's up to us what we do with that now. We're still her favorites, all five of us. So she wasn't lying after all. She just proved it to us. I love you guys," Veronica said emotionally.

They went upstairs to check out the house a few minutes later, and it was more beautiful than they could have imagined. There was an elevator so Olivia was able to join them easily. They found photographs of themselves in her bedroom and library, and favorite objects Felicia had moved from the city that they'd never noticed were missing. She even had some of their artwork from when they were kids, and things they had made her for Christmas and Mother's Day. And there was no doubt about it when they finished the tour. They had each been her favorites, all five of them, and she was much more amazing than they had ever imagined. She had rejected fame, for them, and her own peace of mind, and saved everything she could so they would have a better life in the future.

It shocked them to realize how secretive Felicia had been and how little they had known her. They had a lot to think about now, about how what she had left them would impact their lives and their future.

Chapter 3

The tour of the house was amazing. The main house where their mother had lived was wonderful, and felt like home to them, with all the familiar objects they discovered. The two guest cottages on the grounds were big and comfortable. The grounds were beautiful to walk, and there was one neighbor's house they could see through the bare trees at the front of the property that they had noticed on the way in. But other than that, there were no other houses around. They each had their own ideas about what to do with the property, but by the time they finished the tour, they agreed that for now they wanted to share it, and remain in their mother's aura, and they had no reason to sell it and no financial need to, thanks to her.

When they got back to the house, they asked the housekeeper who owned the house on the property next to their mother's. She wasn't warm, but she answered their question. So far, she had viewed them as intruders. She was protective of her turf and their mother's memory. She had been fiercely dedicated to Felicia.

"Spencer York," she answered, and all five women looked surprised.

"The famous writer?" Charlotte asked, and Ellen, the housekeeper, nodded, and went back to the kitchen. She was worried that they would sell the house and she'd be out of a job, or worse, that they would use it, and invade her territory.

"I wonder if Mom knew him," Quinne said. "She must have. He's her closest neighbor, and the only one." Veronica looked thoughtful.

"Maybe our mother wasn't as solitary as we thought she was," she said pensively. "I'm beginning to think we didn't know her at all."

"Let's not get carried away," Charlotte said. "Knowing Mom, she wrote her books here and kept to herself." She hadn't had many friends, and had spent all the years they knew her writing, editing, and with her children. Nothing they had learned about her was really out of character except that she had been more successful than they'd ever guessed, under a pseudonym, made a lot of money, and had bought a beautiful house where she wrote her books. Charlotte doubted that there was more to the story, and Felicia had always been shy and retiring ever since their father died. Charlotte had been ten when he died and still remembered him. And Quinne had been seven and had dim memories of him too. Olivia was five and only recalled a tall handsome man who spun her around in the air, and she had a vague recollection of how sad her mother had been when he died, and nothing else about him. And to Veronica and Isabelle, he was just a face in a photograph. None of them could recall men of any significance in their mother's life after that. She was busy with her daughters and editing books, which they now knew were her own books.

"You all talk about being her favorites," Veronica reminded them, "but I became the black sheep in the family when I got involved with Anson. I wasn't her favorite then. She was furious with me."

"She didn't want you to be unhappy because he was married, and you cut yourself off from everyone else," Quinne corrected her. "You gave up a lot for him," she said gently. "You gave up your law career, and your future, after graduating magna cum laude, to be Anson's slave."

"I thought he was worth it, and I still do," Veronica said staunchly. He had protected his marriage and his political career, which was easy to understand, and he had been honest with her. He told her right from the beginning that he would never leave his wife and couldn't marry her. He had been truthful, and she had accepted it. And she owed him a lot now. For the past ten years, he had set her up in an apartment and a lifestyle that she could never have afforded without him. He paid for everything so that she was constantly available to him, when he had time. She had given up her law career, and the idea of marriage and children. He had four children of his own and didn't want a child out of wedlock with her, and the risk of a scandal. He had been running for senator when they met, and won. He would face another campaign soon, and he had a good chance of running for vice president in the next presidential election and didn't want anything to jeopardize that. They were unfailingly discreet. He slipped in to see her whenever he could, and she met him in other cities when he traveled, and they took brief vacations in Europe. The sacrifices she had made still seemed worth it to her. They had been careful and the secret had never leaked. Only his banker knew about the transfers he made, and all the papers pertaining to her, and the apartment he rented for her, were in a safe in his office. He was fifty-seven years old and one day he might even have a shot at the presidency. And every aspect of her life was dedicated to him.

She felt as though she owed him a great deal. She had a golden life she would never have had otherwise. At thirty-six she had given up the idea of marriage and children, and her career as a lawyer, but he was an exciting, fascinating man and they loved each other. She had lived up to her end of the deal. She was constantly available to him, as his mistress. It was a life that her mother had never approved of, no matter how charming and charismatic he was. Her mother had been certain that Veronica would be the loser in the end. She had sacrificed her youth, her education, and her future to him, and was alone most of the time, waiting for him. He spent holidays with his family, never with her. She accepted that too. He made the rules, according to his needs, not hers. Felicia had hated that for her, and saw it clearly.

"Do you want to spend the night here?" Quinne asked, after they toured the property. Their letter from their mother had suggested it. They had much to think about now, and needed time together to discuss it.

Charlotte called her housekeeper and asked her to spend the night with Julia. Olivia had no classes to teach the next day on Saturday. Veronica knew that Anson had a political dinner that night, and texted him on the phone he kept just for her. And Isabelle called the nanny and explained that she would be home the next day. And she didn't send a text to Ian.

They let their mother's housekeeper know that they were spending the night. She showed them where everything was, and there were enough bedrooms for all of them. They didn't sleep in their mother's bedroom. And there was a ground-floor guest bedroom perfect for Olivia. She wondered if her mother had thought of all of it when she bought the house. She always thought of everything, down to the last detail.

Quinne called Robert Farr at home that night and told him that they had met with Scott, and were at the house in Connecticut, and they knew all about her pseudonym now, and everything she'd left them.

"I tried to get her to tell all of you years ago, once you were old enough, and she wanted to wait to tell you. No one expected her to go this soon, and she shouldn't have. I need to meet with all of you next week. You've got some decisions to make about the books. She's got a new publishing contract coming up, and there's a serious offer for a series from a streaming platform. We've got seven unpublished books for the next contract, and there are papers I need you all to sign if you want me to continue to represent her estate."

"Of course we do," Quinne said firmly. He gave her a date for the coming week and she told the others.

They made pasta and a salad and ate it in the kitchen, and Ellen, the housekeeper, discreetly disappeared. She was overwhelmed by five grown women suddenly invading the house, but at least she still had a job, and it sounded like they were planning to keep the house. She had been worried ever since Felicia's death that her daughters would sell it, but they seemed to like what they'd seen so far, and they'd been warm and polite to her, just as their mother had been.

They brought up two very good bottles of French wine from their mother's wine cellar and toasted her over dinner.

Charlotte looked at her sisters after her second glass, and said in a stunned voice, "Do you realize that suddenly we're all very wealthy women? What do you suppose that's going to do to our lives?" she asked, and no one answered for a minute. None of them had figured that out yet.

"I can't imagine it," Quinne said honestly. "And I have no idea how Coop will react. He doesn't believe in personal wealth."

"I want to start a foundation," Olivia said again with a determined look, and the others were sure she would. She had been living on her income from teaching and the insurance settlement from her accident for twelve years, and she didn't live an extravagant life, nor want to. She had everything she needed.

Charlotte looked at Veronica. "And you don't need to be a sex slave to Senator Phillips anymore. You can support yourself now," she said somewhat harshly.

"I'm not with him for the support. I'm with him because I love him," Veronica said quietly.

"You've paid a hell of a price for it," Charlotte said. It was one of the few things that she and their mother had agreed on. She hated to see her sister waste her life in the shadows, waiting for a man who would never give her more than she had now, which she insisted was enough for her, and Charlotte didn't believe her.

Isabelle looked at them mournfully then, loosened up by the wine and the overwhelming emotions of the day. "I just found out that Ian is having an affair with a girl in his office. She's twenty-three." And Ian was forty-four. Isabelle was thirty-four, and they had had a perfect life until then, and now everything was teetering on the edge of a cliff.

"Have you talked to him about it?" Quinne asked her, as Isabelle's eyes filled with tears and she shook her head.

"I just found out two days ago, and I didn't know what to expect here today. I'm going to talk to him about it this weekend. The person who told me said it's been going on for six months."

"Don't tell him about today," Charlotte said firmly. "It'll just muddy the waters and you don't want to wonder for the rest of your life why he stayed, if he does. He needs to stay because he loves you. Let it give you confidence when you confront him, but don't tell him what Mom left us," she said wisely. Isabelle realized she was right. It was something they all had to deal with now. They were going to become targets for fortune hunters and greedy men. It was what their mother had wanted to spare them when she steered well away from fame, but it couldn't be helped now. Sooner or later it would leak out that they had inherited money, especially with their partners. It wasn't a happy thought to contemplate. "Put your foot down," Charlotte said harshly. "Don't let him jerk you around or ask you to be patient. You're a good wife to him, and a wonderful person, and you don't have to put up with him being a jerk, if he wants to have his cake and eat it. I learned that lesson with Adam. I should have thrown his ass out long before I did. I think Mom would say the same thing to you now. It's good motherly advice."

"I want to save my marriage," Isabelle said sadly.

"That's up to him now," Charlotte said, and Quinne agreed.

"I want to be his wife, I don't want to be a rich divorcée."

"Hopefully you won't be," Quinne said more gently. "But don't settle for less than you deserve."

"I never thought he'd cheat on me."

"Char and Quinne are right," Veronica said softly. "I settled for something I never thought I'd do. I love Anson, but you lose a piece of yourself when you settle for less than you deserve. I have no choice with Anson, because of his life in politics. But you do with Ian, the others are right, don't let him jerk you around, and tell you he can't decide. He has to. You're his wife. She's just a girl at the office, she doesn't deserve to ruin your life."

They talked late into the night, about their mother, and everything that had happened that day. All that they had learned about her had brought them closer. Their bond was stronger than any of them had realized. Their mother had counted on it. She knew them well. She wanted them to be there for each other when she was gone, and she hadn't expected it to come so soon.

They had breakfast together in the morning, and went back to the city. Isabelle was quiet on the ride with Veronica. They both were for a while. They were all proud to know that their mother had been a famous and very successful writer, but there was so much more to the story and to figure out now.

"Do you think the inheritance will change things between you and Anson?" Isabelle asked.

"I don't know," Veronica said honestly. "I thought about it all night. I'm not sure how he'd feel about it. I'm not going to tell him for a while. I need to get used to it myself."

"I'm not going to tell Ian either. I have to confront him about the girl in the office and I'm scared. What if he really loves her?"

"If he does, he's an idiot," Veronica said. "You're a great wife, and you two have a wonderful life. He's crazy to put that in jeopardy."

"Maybe I bore him. I don't have a career or do anything interesting. I don't have Mom's talent, or your law degree, or Char's talent in business, or Quinne's. And Olivia was a fantastic dancer before the accident, and she's still involved in it now, even in the chair. All I ever wanted to be was a wife and mother."

"And you do it better than I ever could have. You run a beautiful home for him, and you're a great wife and mom. Hold your ground, Isabelle, don't let him make you feel that you have no value." Isabelle wanted to feel stronger than she did, but she didn't. And the girl in the office had youth on her side, and was probably sexy and exciting. Ian was handsome and successful. She felt as though she had already lost the battle before she started, and she was afraid to lose him. She had been dependent on him financially for their entire marriage, but at least now that wasn't the case. If he left her for the girl in the office, she wouldn't have to beg for support. She could support herself now, better than he ever had. At least it was something. She wasn't a beggar. All she wanted was for him to love her.

In the other car, her sisters were discussing her situation and felt sorry for her.

"You and Isabelle are the nicest of all of us," Charlotte said to Olivia. "She doesn't deserve this. I hope she has the guts to be tough with him. He's a fool to risk their marriage. He probably figures she won't do anything if she finds out, and can't afford to. But now that's changed."

Quinne dropped Olivia off at her apartment on the West Side, and Charlotte in Tribeca, and reminded them of their meeting that week with Robert Farr, their mother's agent. He was almost like an uncle to them, had been the closest person to their mother, knew the sisters well, and had worked with their father. They shared history, and they needed his advice about how to handle their mother's enormous body of work. It wasn't someone else's problem now, it was theirs. Scott could help them with taxes and legalities, but Robert was vital for advice on their mother's backlist of more than a hundred books and the opportunities that would stem from them. Their mother had always said that there were sharks in the waters of publishing, and Robert would be able to steer a safe course for them. And Felicia had also said that he was a fierce negotiator. They needed all the help he had to give as the agent for their mother's work. They were innocents, and had been thrown into the deep end of the pool with the discovery that their mother was Morgan Reed.

* * *

Felicia's Favorites

All five women showed up at Robert's office on Wednesday afternoon for the appointment he'd given them, and he looked solemn when they filed into his office and he invited them to sit down. He hadn't seen them since their mother's funeral. He had looked ashen, and sat in the pew behind them at the service. He was still vital and active at eighty-two, but Felicia's death had hit him hard, and it had been so senseless, at the hands of a mentally deranged sniper, running a marathon. There had been no apparent motive. The police sharpshooters had taken him out, killing him before he could tell them. No one had been able to shed light on a motive in the five weeks since. It was all still so fresh for all of them.

"Your mother was a woman of mystery," Robert said, smiling at them. "I tried for years to get her to tell you about Morgan Reed. She insisted it wasn't important. She was a very modest woman. She thought celebrity would be harmful for all of you, and for her. Fame meant nothing to her. She liked the money because she could leave it to you one day, and make a difference for each of you. The rest didn't matter to her. She was a wonderful writer. Your father always thought she would be, and he was right.

"When he worked for me, he was a terrific agent. He could spot a bestseller a mile away, and a writer who would grow into one. I liked him a lot, but he gave your mother a raw deal. She never wanted to tell you, and taint his memory, but I always thought she should have. He fell in love with an agent I hired. She was a hotshot from a big agency, young and good-looking, from L.A. He told your mother he was leaving her, shortly before the crash. The girl wasn't as beautiful as your mother, but she was bold and brash. She went after him and she got him. They were on the way to L.A.

for a premiere she was invited to. He was all excited about going. They died together in the crash, but he had already told your mother he was divorcing her. And then he was killed." Isabelle felt a shudder run down her spine as she listened to the story, thinking of Ian. And all five women were staring at him, shocked by the story.

"Mom never told us any of that," Quinne said in a hoarse voice.

"I know she didn't. She should have. She made him out to be a hero to you. She was the hero in the story. It was fortunate that the airline was responsible—she supported you all on the insurance money until she got her writing career going as Morgan Reed. She had an incredible talent. I think she was so wounded by what he did that there wasn't another man in her life for nearly twenty years. She dedicated herself entirely to you. It was all she cared about, that and writing the books, and building her career. For the last fifteen years of her life, she was happy. No one deserved it more. I wanted her to share it with you, but she wouldn't. She thought you'd be upset, so she kept it to herself, like everything else she did. She met Spencer York here in my office, by accident. He's one of my clients. He was a widower with a son around the same age as you, Quinne. Sparks flew immediately. They fell in love, and I've never seen two people happier or more devoted to each other. They were crazy about each other, and good for each other. He lived in Connecticut, and they went back and forth, both of them with heavy writing schedules. They were a perfect fit. Three years later, the farm next to his became available. I think the couple who owned it were very old and they died. Your mother bought the farm in Connecticut then, and she and Spencer restored it together. They were so happy, and for the last twelve years, they've lived there side by side. When one of them was writing, the other could retreat to their own house if they needed to, but they were almost never apart. They were wonderful together, and so good to each other. It was a fairy tale with a nightmare ending.

"She insisted on running the marathon. Spencer didn't want her to. He was afraid she would get injured. It never occurred to anyone that she might get killed. I drove out to Connecticut that night to tell him and I was afraid he wouldn't survive it. He was a few years older than your mother. He was devastated. I stayed with him for three days. I doubt he'll ever get over it. He wanted to marry her, and she never wanted to. They felt married anyway, and she was afraid you would be upset if she remarried. They lived together on their farms and she came into the city to see you. I'm sure she wouldn't want me to tell you, but I wanted you to know that your mother had been loved by a good man who cared deeply for her. And I always said she should have told you about Spencer York. He's heartbroken without her. He truly loved her."

Charlotte looked shaken when she found her voice. It had been another shocking meeting with revelations about their mother, of a deeply personal nature. More than ever, they felt as though they hadn't known their mother at all. She had been passionately in love with a man for fifteen years and they had known nothing about it, hadn't suspected, and had never even met him. And now she was gone.

"Where is he now?" Charlotte asked Robert.

"He couldn't stand being in the place where they'd been so

happy, once she was gone. Friends lent him a flat in London for six months. They're shooting a movie in Africa. He left two weeks ago. His son is house-sitting for him. He's a writer too. He lives in Aspen, and flew in when he heard the news. I think Spencer's son comes and goes. It's a little quiet for him out there and he comes into the city. But he's keeping track of the house for Spence. His father is in seclusion in the flat in London. He's not seeing anyone. He's in deep mourning." All five sisters were shocked into silence by the story of their mother's love affair with the famous writer.

"Could we write to Spencer?" Veronica asked. They had all been deeply touched by what Robert had told them, and this new revelation about their mother, as a woman deeply in love with a man for many years, without ever telling them. "I'd like to thank him for making her happy, and tell him how sorry I am for his loss. Maybe we could meet him when he comes back from England." The others all nodded, agreeing with her. It had been a week of startling discoveries. Their mother hadn't been as solitary as they believed her to be, and their father hadn't been the saint she claimed. Charlotte felt as though an entirely different woman had replaced their mother. The new one was stunningly famous, immensely rich, lived on a farm, and had found her soulmate fifteen years before and was part of a loving couple. It reminded Charlotte again of how little time they had spent with Felicia, and how little effort they had made to get to know her once they were adults. They took everything about her at face value, and she had continued to play the role of the single parent, with a menial job as a minor book editor for a famous author, instead of the star she had been, and the woman of many facets, none of which they knew, never looking beyond the exterior, which was only a cardboard façade. All the while, she was preparing for their future, so they would be safe and comfortable forever. Charlotte wished they could start all over again and truly get to know Felicia and show her how much they loved her, in all her guises and disguises, and as the real woman she had been behind the façade. She had even protected their father so as not to hurt them. Charlotte could only imagine how lonely she had been for the seventeen years after their father's death until she met Spencer York.

"I think Spencer would like to hear from you," Robert said to Veronica, and smiled at all of them. "Your mother will probably haunt me forever for revealing her secrets to you, but I thought for a long time that you had a right to know, especially now after losing her. These are happy secrets, that she was loved and happy in her final years. And I think it would give Spencer considerable comfort to meet you. Some of you are very much like her, and there will be solace for him in meeting you. She lives on in all of you. I'll have my assistant send you his address, and email contact."

After that, they talked about the offers he currently had pending for their mother's work, from publishers around the world and from streaming platforms. Scott had been right. There would be many decisions they'd have to make in the coming years about Felicia's work. It was a living body of work that would stretch far into the future, which was a way for them to keep their mother alive too.

It was five o'clock when they left Robert's office on Madison Avenue, and Charlotte looked at her sisters. "I need a drink. If I find out one more thing about Mom, that she had six more children we don't know about, was a belly dancer in Paris, had three more houses, and was married to an Italian prince, I think I'm going to have a heart attack. I'm maxed out. I need a martini," she said, and the others laughed.

"I think I need one too," Olivia said, and she rarely drank. "One of you can push my chair afterward so I don't end up on my ass on the sidewalk."

"I'm in," Quinne said with a grin. Isabelle and Veronica agreed, and they headed to PJ Clarke's a few blocks away, got a table, ordered drinks, and smiled at each other after the first sip.

"Mom sure had a lot of major activities we never knew about." Charlotte summed it up. "A huge best-selling career, over a hundred books under a pseudonym, a fifty-million-dollar farm we just inherited, and a boyfriend she was crazy about for fifteen years. Why the hell didn't she tell us anything? We're not kids anymore, and we loved her, and cared about her."

"Maybe she was too busy listening to us, and worried about us," Quinne suggested, "but it would have been nice to have some warning that we'd be responsible for the afterlife of her entire body of work now. I don't know a damn thing about it."

"At least you know about TV," Charlotte reminded her. "You can help the rest of us with that. And Veronica, you're an attorney, you can look over the contracts."

"I haven't practiced in ten years and I was in my first job as a lawyer then. I don't know anything about book contracts, or TV. I will start reading up on literary law," she said seriously.

"Well, you'd better read fast," Charlotte said in a stern voice.

Felicia's Favorites

"Don't you trust Robert?" Veronica asked her, surprised.

"Yes, but he's eighty-two years old, what happens if he gets sick or retires?"

"He's the best in the business, the best literary agent, and Scott can help us with the contracts," Veronica said. "Until I get up to speed." There was so much to think about.

"I think we all better start learning about Mom's business so we can make good decisions about the deals we get offered. Have any of you read the Morgan Reed books?" Quinne asked. "I read two, years ago. They were terrific, but they made me too anxious before I went to sleep at night."

"I read one when I was in rehab," Olivia said. "Mom gave it to me. It was great, but I don't usually read thrillers or mystery books. I prefer Eastern philosophy."

"My book club read one a few months ago. I never get time to read anymore. I dropped out," Isabelle said, looking embarrassed. The fact that they believed Felicia only edited the Morgan Reed books wasn't enough to make them read them.

"Great." Charlotte ordered her second martini and turned to Olivia. "You'd better get another designated driver for your chair. I'm planning to get seriously drunk."

"It's obvious that we need to do some major catching up. We at least need to know what we're selling," Quinne said seriously. "Mom wrote a hundred and eight books. We each need to read twenty-one of her books, and then we'll all know what we're doing and we can talk about it."

"It'll take me twenty years," Isabelle said, looking glum.

"I'll read thirty," Veronica volunteered. "That way you only have to read ten," she said to Isabelle. "I read fast and I have nothing else to do, sitting around, waiting for Anson to show up." They agreed to do it, and Charlotte had an idea halfway through her second martini.

"I'm going to take my kids to Paris for Christmas. Paris is gorgeous at Christmas. And Christmas is going to suck this year without Mom."

"I'll bet the farm is beautiful at Christmas," Isabelle said wistfully, wondering if she'd still have a husband by then.

"Why don't you and I spend Christmas there?" Veronica said to Olivia. "I can't see Anson on the holidays and it will be like being with Mom. We can bring some of her decorations from her apartment." Olivia's face lit up when she said it.

"I've been dreading Christmas without her," she confessed.

"We all have," Charlotte said, delighted with her Paris plan.

"Coop and I could come out for New Year's," Quinne said, smiling.

"We're spending Christmas with my in-laws," Isabelle said, "if Ian hasn't left me by then." Christmas was two weeks away, and it was beginning to sound better than it had since their mother's death.

"What about Dad?" Charlotte said, glancing from one to the other. "That was quite a revelation about him. He was going to divorce her, and she never told us in all these years. She protected him and made him sound like a hero."

"At least she was happy for fifteen years with Spencer York," Quinne reminded them. "I have no idea who our mother was by now. But whoever she was, I think she was an incredible woman and I think I love her even more than before. I wish I could tell her."

"Yeah, me too," Charlotte said. "I'm sorry for all the mean things I said about her, and the arguments I had with her about crap that didn't matter. And she was right about Adam. He's even worse than she said."

"I'm not giving up Anson," Veronica said staunchly, "I love him, even if he's married and I'll be in the shadows for the rest of my life." It was a heavy admission from her. She hadn't given up on him.

"Maybe you could do some legal work," Olivia suggested, "and learn about copyright law and intellectual properties. We have a goldmine on our hands, and you could explain some things to us."

"I'll get some books," Veronica promised, and looked excited about it.

"Or you can handle my divorce," Isabelle said, beginning to feel drunk.

"You don't need to divorce him," Quinne said sensibly, "just lay down the law and scare the hell out of him."

"Maybe he'll leave me," Isabelle said sadly.

"He won't," Charlotte said. "He's not that dumb. You two have too much going. You just have to get through this."

"I want to write to Spencer York," Veronica said, "and meet him when he gets back."

"We can invite his son over when we go to the farm for Christmas," Olivia suggested, and Veronica liked the idea. She wanted to know more about the man their mother had loved and who had loved her so passionately.

Charlotte picked up the check, and took charge of Olivia's chair on the way out. She bumped into two tables, and Quinne took over. She seemed more sober than the others.

They hugged each other then and hailed two cabs, and got Olivia's chair into the trunk of one of them, after Olivia slid onto the back seat. They all had a plan for Christmas, which was a first step. And as Quinne had said, with all that they knew about their mother now, they loved her more than they ever had before. It made the loss both better and worse. They were only just beginning to know the person they had lost. She had been a stranger to them before, and had hidden from them all her life. And now they wanted to get to know her, with all the secrets she had kept.

Chapter 4

By the time Sean came home from Stanford for the holidays, Charlotte had bought the air tickets to Paris and reserved two rooms at the Ritz. She and Julia could share. She wasn't used to spending extravagantly and lived within her means, but with her new inheritance, she had decided to splurge, which surprised her children. She could indulge any whim she wanted now, without thinking about her business first, and what she was spending on private school tuition for Julia and college for Sean. Her business did well, but she was still careful.

She told them about the trip to Paris at breakfast on Sunday morning. Sean had been out late the night before with friends.

"I have a surprise for you both," she said, and her children looked at each other with dread. A surprise usually meant a new tutor she'd hired, or a class she wanted them to take to improve their grades. She expected excellence from both of them and set the bar as high for them as she did for herself. Sean was an excellent student and had been accepted at three Ivy League colleges. He had turned down Princeton and Yale to go to Stanford, and was excited to be on the West Coast. He was in his sophomore year, and wanted to find a job in venture capital in San Francisco when he graduated, so he didn't have to come back to New York. He loved the casual outdoor life in California, wearing gym clothes to work, and the weather. It was a plan he hadn't told his mother yet, and he knew she wouldn't like it. He wanted to go to business school after he'd worked for a year or two in Silicon Valley.

Julia was struggling through her junior year in high school at sixteen, and her grades had slipped, which had won her two SAT tutors, since her college acceptances would depend on her junior grades and SAT scores. But there were so many more interesting things to do after school in New York. She and her brother had both been shocked and saddened by their grandmother's death. Charlotte thought her mother was a better grandmother than mother. Felicia wasn't as demanding, nor did she expect as much of her grandchildren as she had of her own children, and she always reminded them to be sure to have fun. Felicia told Charlotte she was too hard on them and overscheduled them with extra classes. She had been the champion of their causes and now she was gone.

"We're going to Paris for Christmas!" Charlotte announced, and they both stared at her.

"Can we afford it?" Sean asked her. She usually complained about every penny he spent, and wouldn't let him have a car, which was very limiting. He always had to hitch a ride with friends, and take the train or a bus when he went into the city, even on a date, so he stayed on campus most weekends, and went to restaurants in Palo Alto on his dates.

"Yes, we can," Charlotte answered simply without further explanation.

"What changed?" He scrutinized her carefully. They loved each other, but argued a lot.

"I think it would be a hard Christmas here this year without your grandmother, and we could all use some cheering up. Paris is beautifully decorated at Christmas, and we haven't been to Europe in a long time, so why not?"

"I want to see my friends, Mom," Julia said plaintively, and Sean nodded agreement.

"Me too," Sean seconded his sister's statement.

"We've already got the tickets. We leave next week. You'll see, it will be fun," their mother said firmly.

"Can we be home before New Year's Eve? I have plans. I'm going to Sugarbush with friends," Sean said, and she nodded agreement.

Julia added her voice to his. "And Kelly Martin is having a sleepover on New Year's Eve and she invited me to stay for the whole weekend. I told her I could go. I didn't think you'd mind."

"Okay," Charlotte agreed. For once she didn't argue with them. She wanted all three of them to enjoy the trip, not fight over details. She had taken the reservations until the second of January, but they could be changed. "We'll come home on the thirtieth so it doesn't screw up your New Year plans." She didn't have plans of her own, but she didn't care about New Year's Eve. It was Christmas at home she was trying to avoid. It made her want to cry just thinking about Christmas Eve without her mother for the family dinner she hosted every year, with all of them crowded around her dining room table and the Christmas tree brightly lit in the living room beyond, their gifts piled high, each person's gifts in a different paper so they knew at a glance what was for them. She never disappointed them. She had a knack for picking the right gifts for each person. It was going to be a sparse year without her for Julia and Sean, since Charlotte hated to shop. She did as much as she could online, and hadn't even started yet. But now they could shop in Paris and pick what they wanted.

Sean and Julia were talking excitedly between themselves. The idea of the trip had caught hold and had been an easy victory for Charlotte. "We're staying at the Ritz," she added. "It's a fabulous hotel." She hadn't been to Paris in years either, and had taken the children when they were much younger. Julia hardly remembered it. Charlotte had taken them to Disneyland Paris. This was going to be a far more grown-up trip, and she could share some of her favorite haunts with them. She loved the bistros in Paris, the art galleries and antique shops, the wonders of the Louvre, Notre-Dame, the Musée d'Orsay, the Tuileries Gardens, and the little shops in the arcades of the Palais Royal, with its distinguished history, and the flea market on the weekend. And the Christmas lights on the Champs-Élysées and the Eiffel Tower were sure not to disappoint them. Paris was a feast to the eye during the holidays. She had been there with her mother several times as a child, with her sisters. They had stayed at the Plaza Athénée, but Charlotte thought the Ritz would be more fun. She was going all out. After everything that had happened in the past week, she could go with a clear conscience, without worrying what they spent.

Felicia's Favorites

Sean and Julia rushed off after breakfast to text their friends and tell them about the trip.

As she went to her own room to look over her wardrobe for what seemed suitable for a trip to Paris, Charlotte wondered how her children would like the farm in Connecticut, but she wasn't ready to tell them about it yet. She didn't want them to think they had suddenly become rich overnight, and have them behave like spoiled brats, and she had no idea how to explain that their grandmother had owned an enormous estate that she had never told them about. It was going to take some finesse to introduce the subject, and she wasn't ready to deal with it yet. She hadn't adjusted to the idea herself.

Veronica didn't mention the farm to Anson either when he came to visit her later that week. As usual, he came on short notice, and sent her a text less than an hour before he arrived. His cheeks were red from the cold, and he beamed the moment he saw her, as she hurried toward him in black velvet pajamas, with the diamond studs in her ears that he had given her several years before. He had always been generous with her. He gave her beautiful gifts for her birthday and Christmas, and the apartment was in a small elegant building in the East Seventies between Fifth and Madison, a block away from Central Park. From her high floor, she had a view of the park from her living room windows. It was snowing the night he came to see her, and Central Park looked like a Christmas card.

She poured him a glass of his favorite red wine, Chateaux Margaux, and he put his arms around her and kissed her. The world around them and all its problems always faded away as soon as he was there. She forgot everything except Anson, and everything related to him. And he loved having her full attention. She dropped everything the moment he arrived. Their relationship was all about him, and always had been. He had set her up in an extremely comfortable life so she could focus on him and be available whenever he wanted.

She never told him that she was busy or that it was an inconvenient time. If she had other plans, she changed them or canceled them immediately. She had never said no to a visit, and was ready at all times to receive him in the haven he had helped her create for him. He said it was the only place on earth where he felt relaxed, safe, and unconditionally loved. She never complained about his marriage, or even mentioned it, and he never talked about his wife. When they were together, it was as though she didn't exist. Only they did, in their safe little bubble in a magical world.

She had a small sitting room off her bedroom, where she read or watched TV at night. She was comfortable in the apartment alone, although happier when he was there. They sat in her little study sometimes in their bathrobes after they'd made love or before they went to bed, on the nights when he could stay with her. They were at the mercy of his wife's schedule, when she was in Greenwich, or in the city. His family home was farther up Fifth Avenue, a dozen blocks away, an easy walk for him, if he even had half an hour to spend with her. Sometimes he showed up just to kiss her good night, or make love to her if he had time. They usually went to bed shortly after he arrived, which was a sign that he

Felicia's Favorites

couldn't stay for long. She liked their quiet nights together, when they had time to talk, or sit by the fire, drinking wine. She created an atmosphere for him that was like a warm embrace in his busy world. She always had time for him, to make him feel special and important, which he was to her. She was the perfect mistress. Never tired, or sick, or too busy for him, or in a bad mood, or with problems of her own, or worried or sad. She kept anything unpleasant to herself and didn't trouble him with it. She was beautiful for him at all times, exquisitely dressed, her hair and nails perfect, her smile flawless, her arms outstretched, and her body hungry for his. She thrilled at his touch and drank in his every word. He was already an important man in the world, but he felt more so with her.

They had just made love and taken a warm bath afterward, and were sitting in her study in their robes, when he noticed the books she had ordered about intellectual property law after their meeting with Robert Farr. She had started reading them, and they were fascinating. She loved reading them now, with her mother in mind. Anson looked surprised when he saw them.

"What are those? Remnants of your law school days? You can throw them away."

"I've been reading them. They're very interesting," she said evenly, not wanting to contradict or upset him. "Just keeping up my legal skills."

"Why? You won't ever need them again. That's ancient history now." He dismissed them, picked them up, and dropped both books in the wastebasket near her desk. She was startled and didn't know what to say. He had made himself clear.

"It's good to keep my mind alive. I was an attorney, after all."

"For about five minutes. You've probably forgotten it all by now." He looked less relaxed than he had before he saw her books, but happier again once he'd thrown them away.

"Actually, I was surprised that I remembered some of it, and I was never well versed in intellectual properties. The firm I was working for was all about estates, taxes, and business. Intellectual property seems like more fun."

"None of that is fun," he said with a determined look. "I'm your fun now, Veronica. And your joy, I hope. What are you doing for Christmas?" He changed the subject, knowing that she usually spent Christmas Eve at her mother's and wouldn't this year. He had never been able to spend holidays with her, and she didn't expect him to.

"I'm going to spend it with my sister Olivia. Charlotte is taking her kids to Paris, Quinne's with her boyfriend, and Isabelle will be at her in-laws, so Olivia and I are at loose ends. There's a farm in Connecticut we thought we'd stay at. It's very peaceful." He frowned as soon as she said it.

"I don't like that idea," he said firmly. He was a very handsome man, exuded power and strength, and was used to the people around him doing what they were told. He was almost fatherly with her at times. At fifty-seven, he was twenty-one years older than she was. She was thirty-six, and had been his mistress and willing slave for a decade. "I'll be in Vermont with Anne and the kids. If I get some free hours, I could come down to see you. That won't work if you're not here. I'll be on a tight turnaround." He often was, but they both knew that it was a four- or five-hour drive from his house in Vermont, in good weather, and the round-trip drive alone would take him nine or ten hours. There was no way he could see her in "a few hours," but he wanted her there anyway. And his plans changed constantly, between the time he spent in Washington, D.C., engaged in politics, planning his campaign, meetings, conference calls, and events he had to drop in on. He had very little free time, was most often rushed, and almost never left his family on vacation, although he had once or twice if Veronica was nearby. Sometimes he had her stay at a hotel in the area or even the same hotel when he was traveling. He liked the security of knowing that she was close at hand, and waiting for him at all times. It was the arrangement she had agreed to ten years before and had lived up to, to the letter. This was the first time she had mentioned going out of town herself and it upset him.

"You'd need a helicopter to come down from Vermont fast enough and get back in time," she said calmly.

"I could say I have an important meeting," he insisted, determined to cancel her plans, and he could sense her resistance.

"This Christmas is going to be hard for us," she said gently, "and Olivia and I are both going to be alone. We need a change of scenery, or we'll sit around crying about my mother, especially with the others away. They have children, and Quinne has her boyfriend. Olivia and I are both alone."

"Stay in the city and go to a movie, or midnight mass. The country would be depressing, and you could get snowed in for days." She didn't answer him, but what he said weighed heavily on her. She didn't want to refuse him, but she and Olivia had their hearts set on Christmas at their mother's farm, with their mother's decorations all around them. It was the next best thing to spending it with her. And they were planning to stay for a week or ten days, through New Year's, which Veronica didn't say to Anson. She didn't dare.

"I'll talk to her about it," she said quietly. She didn't want to argue with him in the little time he had. "Will I see you again before Christmas?" she asked in a soft voice, not wanting to pressure him, which he always reacted badly to. She got more from him if she didn't ask, but she liked to know, so she didn't have false hopes of seeing him, and get disappointed.

"I'll come by to give you a kiss before we drive to Vermont," he said vaguely, and didn't say which day. He never did, until an hour or less before. But she never lost sight of the fact that she owed him her lifestyle and everything she had. She had a financially stress-free life because of him. She never had to worry about money. And didn't need to now, thanks to her mother, but Anson didn't know that. He thought he was still her only benefactor, but the landscape had changed, which he was unaware of. She was grateful to him anyway.

He didn't spend the night with her that night. He dressed slowly and reluctantly and hated to leave her, but he needed to get home. He had early meetings the next morning and was appearing on a morning news show to talk about a bill he had proposed. He kissed her tenderly when he left, and she fished her law books out of the wastebasket after he was gone. She put them in a drawer so he wouldn't see them the next time he came. She didn't change her plans to go to the farm with Olivia. She didn't want to disappoint her sister, or herself. She had never defied Anson before. She always did what he wanted, but there had been the slightest shift, and after the revelations about her mother, something deep inside her had changed. She still loved him, but she had more confidence in herself, and she liked the legal aspect of having a hand in defending her mother's work. She couldn't give that up for him, or the chance to visit the farm again. She was certain he would never know. He wanted her to be in the city, waiting for him, but he never spent holidays with her, and she knew he never would. He would never know she was gone, and when he snuck off for a minute on Christmas Eve or Day to call her, he could reach her on her cellphone. That was all he wanted from her or had to give on holidays. He belonged to his family then, and never to her. She was excited about going to her mother's farm. It subtly changed the balance with him, as did her unexpected inheritance. She was no longer dependent on him. He didn't know it, but she did.

Veronica went to her mother's apartment and picked up her Christmas decorations, which were neatly put away in boxes in a storage closet. It was emotional seeing them and made her cry for a minute, and then she carried them to her car. She loaded up her car with them, had taken a single suitcase with her, and picked up Olivia, who was waiting in front of her building in her wheelchair, with the doorman carrying her valise. He put it and the wheelchair in the car and they took off, like two giddy girls. Olivia had called Ellen, the housekeeper, to tell her they were arriving. She didn't sound too pleased, but they had a gift for her, a warm scarf and matching gloves and a wool hat.

They chatted on the way to Connecticut and played Christmas carols on the radio.

"Have you heard from Char in Paris?" Olivia asked her.

"She sent me a photo of the kids in the front of the Eiffel Tower all lit up red, and she said they're having a ball. I'm glad they went," Veronica said, smiling. "And I'm glad we're going to the farm." She didn't tell Olivia that Anson had told her to cancel. She didn't want Olivia to worry about her.

"I'm glad too," Olivia said. "I brought my homework with me. Three of Mom's books. I should be able to get through them over Christmas." Veronica had sent each of them a reading list, so they wouldn't read the same ones.

"I brought two, and two textbooks on intellectual property laws. It's a little dry, but applying it would be fun. I haven't read a law book since I passed the bar. I'm a little rusty, but it comes back to me as I read."

When they got to the farm, Ellen had mushroom soup and sandwiches waiting for them, and they showed her the decorations they'd brought with them.

"They were our mother's," Olivia explained reverently, and Ellen smiled and disappeared. She came back a few minutes later with stacks of boxes piled up in her arms.

"And we have lots more," she told them. "Your mother loved Christmas. We have some beautiful antique decorations she bought. She used to string little lights in the trees outside too. She did it herself with a ladder. Mr. York loved it. They did it every year." She brought them the cartons of lights a few minutes later. And after lunch, they got to work decorating. They used up all the decorations from the city apartment quickly, and Ellen showed them where Felicia had placed the others every year. There was a beautiful crèche, Ellen said, that Spencer York had bought her in Italy. "The gardener will chop down a tree for you, if you want, we have a stand for it." By the end of the afternoon, Ellen was their best friend, with stories about their mother, and she showed them Felicia's favorite decorations and where everything went. The gardener promised them a tree by the next day, and once it was dark, before dinnertime, Veronica and Olivia went outside to put the lights in the trees surrounding the house. Ellen had already put wreaths on the front and back doors. Olivia was the lighting director, observing from her chair at a little distance, telling Veronica where there were holes and when to move a string to the right or the left. It took them two hours and the trees looked magical when they were finished.

They were just walking back into the house and taking their coats off when Veronica's cellphone rang. She saw the call was from a blocked number, and wondered if it was Anson. She felt guilty when she answered, and was surprised that it was Scott Freeman.

"Hi, Scott, how are you?" she said easily.

"Fine. I have some papers for you to sign, nothing serious, just tax stuff. I can run them uptown for you if you like," he suggested.

"Are they urgent?" she asked him.

"No, but they need to be signed by the end of the year. I'll just bring them up, have you sign, and take them back with me."

"That's nice of you, but I'm in Connecticut, at the farm with Olivia. And we're here till after New Year's."

He hesitated for a moment and sounded cheerful when he answered. "No problem. I'll drive them out to Connecticut for you tomorrow, if that's okay with you."

"I feel terrible having you do that. That's a long drive for a signature," but she didn't want to go back to town just for that.

"They need original signatures. Charlotte and Isabelle sent me theirs before they left town, and Quinne promised to drop hers off tomorrow. That leaves you and Olivia. I honestly don't mind coming. It would be nice to see you both again. I'll bet it's beautiful out there."

"We just finished decorating. Olivia is the artistic director. My mom loved Christmas, and we used all her decorations."

"I'd love to see it," Scott said warmly, sounding casual. "I seriously don't mind coming out to you."

"All right. If you're sure." She wondered why he hadn't sent her the papers before. It was getting close to Christmas, and she told Olivia about it over dinner. Ellen had roasted a chicken for them, and they were both starving after two hours outdoors, working steadily. "It's nice of him to do it," Veronica commented.

"He's a nice guy," Olivia said, delighted with their day's work, and they still had the tree to decorate the next day when the head gardener brought it. Whoever they talked to, they had the impression that their mother had been greatly loved by the people who worked for her, and by Spencer York too.

They went to bed early that night, and woke up early the next day. The gardener showed up right after breakfast with a ten-foot tree that he stood up in the living room, and it looked beautiful.

Ellen got the stand, and they filled it with water to keep the tree alive. They couldn't wait for Charlotte to see it too. It was worthy of their mother.

They were still decorating when Scott arrived an hour later. He had left the city early and said there was no traffic. Veronica was teetering on the top step of the ladder, perilously perched, and Olivia was warning her to be careful. Veronica looked down at Scott with a smile as he held the ladder steady for her.

"Why don't you come down," he suggested. "I'll get the angel on top." She came down the ladder then and handed it to him, and a minute later the beautiful angel was elegantly seated on top of the tree, and Scott was back down, and they both thanked him. "I'm a full-service attorney," he said. He was wearing a heavy cable-knit sweater, and looked very handsome. They invited him to sit down. He had a cup of coffee, and he took out the papers for them to sign. And after that, Veronica invited him to stay for lunch.

It was three in the afternoon when he finally left them, and they'd had a good time talking and laughing. It had been nice to have a visit.

"I think he likes you," Olivia said with a grin after he left.

"I think he likes all five of us. He was very nice to everyone the day of the big revelations. That must have been stressful for him too. And I think he's a good lawyer."

"I mean he *likes* you. You know, like a guy." Veronica stared at her with a frown.

"Don't be silly. He likes you just as much as he likes me," Veronica insisted.

"When was the last time a lawyer drove two hours to get a signature, and made a point of telling us he wasn't charging for the time?"

"I told you, he's a nice guy."

"You are blind," Olivia told her with a grin. "He lit up like a Christmas tree every time he talked to you."

"No, he didn't, and Anson would have a fit if that's true. He doesn't like it when men flirt with me or come on to me."

"Then maybe he should consider leaving his wife," Olivia said gently, "and not going on vacations with her."

"That's part of the deal," Veronica said matter-of-factly. "He never hid the fact that he's married, and he never promised to leave her. In fact, he told me he never would. He thinks a divorce would hurt him politically. He has a heavily Catholic constituency. It's just the way it is," she said coolly.

"Is that enough for you?" Olivia asked her. "A guy who only sees you on the fly, and will never spend holidays with you?"

"I love him, and that's the only deal he has to offer."

"Don't you want marriage and kids? We're not getting any younger," Olivia pointed out, and Veronica smiled.

"I'd want those things with Anson, but not someone else, and even if we could get married, which we can't, he doesn't want more kids. He told me that in the beginning too. He has four and he thinks he's too old. When we started and I was twenty-six, I didn't think it would ever matter to me. Now I realize it does matter. But I've spent ten years with him and I love him. A little of Anson is still better than a lot of someone else."

"He's a lucky man. I hope he knows it."

"I'm lucky too," Veronica said seriously. "He's given me a wonderful stress-free life and everything I could possibly want."

"Except Christmas," Olivia said soberly. "For me, it wouldn't be enough." There hadn't been a man in her life since the accident that severed her spinal cord and left her paralyzed from the waist down. She had been madly in love with the French choreographer and planning to marry him when it happened, and she had broken it off with him and sent him away.

"Do you ever hear from François?" Veronica asked gently about the choreographer Olivia had been engaged to, and her face hardened when she answered.

"Never. And I don't want to. He's married now anyway." He had waited seven years for her and tried to convince her to come back to him, and he had finally married another dancer five years before. She was well known in France. Olivia never let herself think about it. There was no point. It was the past. She only lived in the present, and the future. And she knew the future would be no different than it was now.

Chapter 5

The days at the farm before Christmas were peaceful and relaxing for Veronica and Olivia. Anson hadn't called Veronica. He had texted her whenever he had the chance but he hadn't called, which was a relief. She didn't want to lie to him about where she was. And she would never have canceled their plans and left Olivia on her own, this year especially. They needed each other, and being at the farm, with Felicia's decorations and favorite belongings everywhere, made them feel close to their mother.

Veronica wondered if Anson would feel differently if he knew she had inherited the farm with her sisters, but she didn't feel ready to tell him any of that yet, so she said nothing, and let him believe she was in the city. It was a sin more of omission than of commission, and she wasn't hurting anyone. But she felt guilty about it anyway. And he was with his family. She had spent ten lonely Christmases without him so far, and this was the hardest one of all, seven weeks after her mother's death. None of them had adjusted to it yet. It was going to take time, especially after all the surprises Felicia had revealed after her death, and even some she hadn't, like her relationship with Spencer York, which sounded like a real love story. Veronica was glad she had had that, and had known some happiness in her life. Her mother had worked hard.

She and Olivia were going down the long tree-lined drive one day toward the road to get some air and exercise, when they saw the York house come into view through the naked trees. In the summer it would be obscured, but in winter, without leaves on the trees, they could see it clearly, and they saw a man come out of the house. He watched them for a few minutes and then made his way through the branches and walked toward them.

"Who's that?" Olivia asked, as he walked in their direction. Olivia was rolling slowly in her chair while Veronica walked beside her. They'd been talking about their mother's books that they'd been reading, and they loved them. They had new meaning for them now. They felt as though there was a message to them on every page. There were little bits of her philosophy and values woven into the stories, her innermost thoughts, her history, and even her humor. It was like visiting with her each time they picked one up, and they were both sorry they hadn't read more of them when she was alive. Veronica had lots of questions about them that would never be answered now, about what was true and what wasn't. And they had realized by then that almost all of the books had been dedicated to them, except for a few that were dedicated to "S.Y. with all my heart," which they knew now was Spencer York, and they had never noticed the dedications before. They had missed them entirely. But they had read very few of her books. Felicia's whole life history was in them, woven in with the products of her imagination, and Veronica was never sure which was which, since she had shared almost no details of her own history and early life. From her books they had begun to understand that she'd had a lonely childhood, with cold demanding parents who had expected a great deal from her, and gave little in return. She was never enough to win their approval or their love.

The man who had come out of the York house and headed toward them caught up with them a few minutes later on the drive. He was tall, with a mane of blond hair, and hadn't shaved in a few days. He was wearing work boots and a heavy jacket in the cold, and smiled cautiously at them.

"Hello, we're more or less neighbors, I think," he said, glancing from one sister to the other, "if you're Felicia Weston's daughters." He wasn't sure if they were just houseguests or renters. Olivia looked a little like her mother, with fair coloring, but Veronica didn't. "I'm Andrew York. Andy. I'm house-sitting for my father," he said. Veronica and Olivia both smiled and introduced themselves. He had a boyish quality and look to him, although the little smile lines near his eyes said that he was older than they were.

"We've been wanting to reach out to you," Veronica said, "but we didn't want to intrude. I've been meaning to write to your father."

Andrew nodded. "He's in London. He was heartbroken when your mother passed away. It's a terrible thing," he said sympathetically.

"We never knew about your father until after she was gone.

Their agent told us. It sounds like such a beautiful story. I wish we'd known before. We didn't even know about this farm, and now we own it," Veronica said, as he walked along with them.

"It's a beautiful place," Andrew agreed, "and they were so happy here. They had the perfect arrangement, together most of the time, when they wanted to be, and then they'd retreat to their own houses when they wanted to write. They never got on each other's nerves that way. I always wanted to meet you, she talked about you all the time. She was very proud of you. I lost my own mother when I was very young, so I feel for you."

"She was too young to die," Olivia said sadly.

"And so senselessly, in such a horrible way," he added.

"Would you like to come up to the house for some coffee or wine?" Veronica offered, and he ambled slowly up the drive with them.

"I've been wanting to meet you, but I was afraid it was too soon. My father was in terrible shape when he left. He says he can't be here without her. I don't know what he's going to do. I hope he doesn't sell the house, and can make his peace with it. It might help him to meet you. You're like a part of her. And it makes it seem like she's still alive. I think it's going to take my father a long time to get over the shock," Andrew said, obviously worried. "Do you have children?" he asked them. "I know she had grandchildren, although she didn't look it." He smiled as they reached the house. Veronica invited him in and he followed them inside.

"We don't," Veronica said, "but two of our sisters do, and another one doesn't. There are a lot of us." Veronica smiled and led the way into the front hall, which was familiar to him. Andy had been there many times, although it was still new to them. He caught sight of the Christmas tree immediately, with the beautiful decorations, and stared at it.

"They were like children. They both loved Christmas. They collected those ornaments together. Fifteen years is a long time." It made it seem even more incredible that Felicia's daughters had never known. "Are you staying for Christmas?" he asked them, and they said they were.

"Are you?" they asked him.

"I am. I'm a bit stuck here. I promised my father I'd watch the house, he's afraid a pipe will burst or the house will burn down. I go to the city occasionally, but I feel so guilty, I come rushing back. I was going to go to England to spend Christmas with him, but he's with friends. I've been living in Aspen before this. I used to write screenplays in L.A., for TV and the movies, and I've just written my second book. Robert is my agent too, he's a wonderful man and a great agent. He introduced them to each other."

"Do you have children?" Olivia asked him as she rolled into the living room and they followed. She was intrigued by him, and wondered if his father was as nice as he was. Andy seemed desperate for company and someone to talk to. He had said he was living at his father's farm alone, which had to be lonely.

"No, never married, no kids. I think writers are hard to live with. My father was, until he met your mother. She tamed him, and he was gentle as a lamb after that. My mother died when I was a child, and he never remarried. He locked himself away, and I think he will again. I don't think he'll ever get over your mother. The fairy tale didn't have a happy ending."

"I have to write to him," Veronica said. "I hope he comes back to visit. We all want to meet him."

"He said he would." Andy accepted a glass of wine, and the two sisters had one too, and they talked until it was dark, and the lights in the trees went on and he stared at them through the tall windows. "They used to light the trees just like that," he said, moved by the sight of it.

"The housekeeper told us. Veronica did it all when we got here."

"It's beautiful." He smiled at them both and stood up when he finished his wine. "I don't want to keep you. You'll have to come down the road to have dinner."

"Would you like to come for Christmas Eve?" Veronica asked. "It's just the two of us. Our older sister is coming for New Year's Eve, and maybe another of our sisters. The oldest one is in Paris for Christmas with her kids."

"You're lucky you have each other, and if it wouldn't be an intrusion, I'd love it. I feel a bit shipwrecked being at Dad's house alone. It's pretty solitary. He likes that. I'm delighted you're here," he said, smiling warmly at them both.

"We wanted to meet you too," Olivia said to him, and Veronica offered him a ride back to his place.

"No, I'll walk. I love walking around here. I have to confess, I've walked around your property too. The lake and the forest are wonderful." Both women felt a strange kinship with him. They talked about it after he left.

"If they had gotten married, he'd be our stepbrother," Olivia said, and Veronica nodded.

"It kind of feels like he is. It's so weird that he knew Mom, and we didn't know anything about them. But it feels really comfortable talking to him. I hope we get to meet his father."

"So do I," Olivia agreed.

Andy came to dinner on Christmas Eve, wearing a blazer and slacks and a tie. He had shaved, his hair was combed, and he looked very respectable. They talked for hours about their lives and their parents' books. He had led an interesting life with his father growing up, and it sounded as though his father had been as reclusive as Felicia. They had been perfectly suited to each other.

"Writers are people who like to observe life more than they like to be engaged in it. My father hated fame as much as your mother did. They were perfectly matched, like two puzzle pieces that fit together seamlessly. I've never met a woman I felt that way about," he admitted. "That's why I never married. I couldn't see the point of marrying someone that I knew going in didn't really suit me."

They talked late into the night and drank a lot of wine, and the two sisters could feel their mother near them.

On Christmas Day, Veronica sent an email to Spencer, telling him they had met Andrew and loved him, and she extended her heartfelt sympathy to him and told him that they all hoped to meet him soon. Now that they knew about their relationship, and how important he had been to their mother, he felt like family, and they were all eager to get to know him. She sent him their love and prayers, and hoped that he would find peace soon, after the shock they had all experienced.

Spencer answered that night, with a beautiful, touching, eloquent letter that felt like a warm embrace when Veronica read it and brought tears to her eyes. He tried to express to her how much he had loved her mother and what she meant to him, and as an extension of her, he welcomed them into his family, and said that he was readily available if he could do anything for them. She forwarded the email to her sisters and thanked him. He was obviously a very special person and his love for their mother was plainly evident.

Their trip to Paris was the best time Charlotte had ever spent with her children. They were open to everything, fun to be with, good company. They acted like adults instead of bratty kids. They went to fun restaurants, walked all over Paris, loved the Louvre, the flea market, and the Quai d'Orsay, and went to the top of the Eiffel Tower. They did touristy things, and things that the Parisians did, and they wandered through art galleries and antique shops with their mother. They went to midnight mass on Christmas Eve at Sacré-Coeur, with a choir of nuns who sounded like angels, and they stood looking over the city afterward, while street musicians played Christmas carols and Charlotte and her children sang with them. They went back to the Ritz afterward and had hot chocolate with mountains of whipped cream in their room.

It was the closest Charlotte had ever felt to her children at a grown-up level, and the best idea she'd had in years. It was a trip she knew that none of them would ever forget, and a final gift from her mother.

In quiet moments, alone in bed at night, she made notes for ideas for a new company she wanted to start, but she knew she hadn't had the right idea yet. She wanted to do something different and exciting and build it from the ground up the way she had her first one. They were almost ready to go public with To Go, and were planning the road show to launch it. She was waiting for the right new idea to grab her. She knew she'd hit on the right one eventually.

Sean left for Vermont with his friends the morning after they got home, and Julia went to stay with her friend giving the sleepover for six girls. They were going to have a dance party and watch movies all night on New Year's Eve. None of them had dates for the evening—it was an all-girls' night and the host parents were allowing them to share one bottle of champagne for all six of them since they weren't going anywhere, and they were all sixteen. And Charlotte was comfortable with it. She had let both Sean and Julia drink a little wine on their trip, and they had handled it well.

After the kids left, she drove to Connecticut, and got to the farm at five o'clock. She had brought a long skirt and top to wear in case her sisters wanted to dress up. It felt like home as she walked through the front door and saw her mother's decorations. It suddenly all looked so familiar. Veronica and Olivia were in the kitchen making hors d'oeuvres. They had a pasta recipe which included caviar and lemon, and they were chilling vodka and champagne.

They gave a squeal of delight when they saw Charlotte, and she hugged them and told them all about Paris over a glass of wine. They had set the dining room table with their mother's best linens, and Quinne and Coop arrived half an hour later and joined the merriment. The house felt happy and cozy and like the right place to be. They had given Ellen the night off, and Olivia put Christmas carols on. It felt like the perfect ending to an extraordinary year, full of surprise twists in the plot, just like their mother's books. And after tragedy they were finding joy again, and blessings to share.

"Has anyone heard from Isabelle?" Charlotte asked, as they devoured the hors d'oeuvres and sampled some local cheeses before they went to their rooms to change. "All I got was a text on Christmas Eve wishing us a Merry Christmas and telling me she loved me. Has she confronted Ian yet?"

"She decided to wait until after the holidays. She didn't want to ruin Christmas for the kids," Quinne answered her. "I haven't heard anything much from her either. I think she had a miserable Christmas. They'll be home in a couple of days. I figured she couldn't talk freely at her in-laws' so I haven't called her. I had an idea, by the way. Why don't the five of us spend Mom's birthday here? We could make a weekend of it." Felicia's birthday was in four weeks, at the end of January. The others smiled at her and loved the idea.

"She would have loved that," Charlotte said with a smile. Olivia was pleased too. And Veronica endorsed the idea. She and Olivia were feeling at home there after spending Christmas at the farm, and they helped Quinne and Charlotte pick comfortable rooms.

They all disappeared upstairs to dress and were back an hour later. Cooper whistled as Quinne came down the stairs in a short silver minidress that molded her figure and showed off her legs, with high-heeled silver sandals.

"I feel like the Tin Man in *The Wizard of Oz*," she said, looking embarrassed, but Cooper put his arms around her and kissed her and poured the champagne he'd just opened. They had brought a bottle of Dom Perignon. Charlotte came down a few minutes later in a long black skirt she'd bought in Paris and a silky gold top. Veronica had helped Olivia get into a soft pink cashmere dress with a long skirt, and Veronica was wearing a long red knit dress that was casual and chic, which Anson had bought her for her birthday at Dior. They all looked very festive, as Coop poured them each a glass of champagne. The doorbell rang as he did, and Charlotte went to open it. "Are we expecting anyone?" she asked Veronica over her shoulder, opening the door before Veronica heard her, and found herself looking at a tall handsome man with slightly wild blond hair wearing a dinner jacket, an immaculate white shirt, and a black tie, with jeans and black velvet shoes. Veronica smiled when she saw him and went to greet him, as he stared down at Charlotte with an emotional look.

"You look so much like your mother," he said softly, and it took a minute before Charlotte realized who he was. "Sorry, I'm Andy York. You took me by surprise." He smiled broadly when he greeted the others, and took a glass of champagne from the silver tray Coop was passing around. The two men seemed to have an instant rapport, and within a short time were talking about films they'd worked on in L.A., Cooper as an actor, and Andy as a screenwriter. They discovered that they knew several people in common, and Charlotte was watching them closely as they talked.

"He's definitely a hunk," Veronica commented, as the group moved into the living room, and the two men were engrossed in conversation in front of the fire.

"I'm allergic to men who look like that," Charlotte whispered. "I learned my lesson years ago. I fall madly in love with them, and they turn out to be assholes. Movie-star-handsome men are a death wish for anyone who gets involved with them. I swore them off after Adam."

"Andy is actually a nice guy," Olivia joined the whispered conversation between sisters.

"I'll take your word for it," Charlotte said, looking unnerved. "I'm not going to go near him," she said, as Olivia remembered that she had seated them next to each other at the dinner table.

"Do you want me to move him?" Olivia asked her, and Charlotte shook her head.

"It's a test of ten years of therapy to see if I can remain sane and have an intelligent conversation with him," she said, helping herself to the champagne, and Quinne saw Andy lose interest in Cooper, as Charlotte crossed the room and they exchanged a smile. There was definitely some kind of chemistry between them, whether Charlotte admitted it or not, and Andy wasn't just a handsome hunk, he was a genuinely nice man, and fun to talk to, as Coop had discovered.

Inevitably, during dinner the conversation turned to his father and their mother, and they toasted Felicia and Spencer, and the love they had shared for so many years.

"You look so much like her that it shocked me when I first saw you." But Andy had already noticed that Charlotte was livelier and bolder than Felicia, and she wasn't shy. She had a dry sense of humor and told funny stories about herself that made him laugh. They talked about his books and the films he had written, including a hit series, and he asked her all about the company she had started, which he said he had used himself and thought was fantastic.

Felicia's Favorites

"I'm trying to come up with a new idea, and I haven't thought of anything yet. A lot has been happening. It's been kind of mind-boggling for the last month, the farm, my mom's books, finding out about your father. She had a whole other persona, and a whole different life than the woman we knew."

"That must have been a hell of a shock," he agreed.

"It was, but it was all good. Her dark secrets were all good ones—wonderful books, a beautiful home, and a good man she loved and who loved her. It doesn't get better than that."

"No, it doesn't, and now I have five women who could have been my sisters, and I like everyone I've met. I wish Felicia and my father had gotten married."

"So do I," Charlotte said simply. "She deserved so much happiness. Her parents weren't particularly nice to her when she was young. I think they were cold and nothing she did was ever good enough for them, and it turns out that our father wasn't the prince she made him out to be. We only just found that out too. She never got the recognition she deserved for the books, not even from us, since she never told us, and we didn't read them."

"But my father adored her. They were madly in love, and maybe that was enough for both of them. Some people never find what they had. I never have," Andy admitted. He seemed like an honest guy to Charlotte and she could see why her sisters liked him. He seemed outspoken and honest. And in spite of his good looks, he didn't seem like a narcissist. He was very modest about his books. "What are your kids like?" he asked her, and seemed genuinely interested.

"Monsters some of the time, angels at others. My son's at Stanford, my daughter is a junior in high school. She's more interested in makeup and hair and boys than homework. We just spent Christmas in Paris together, and we had a fantastic time. I couldn't face Christmas at home, without my mother, so we went to Paris. It was an amazing trip," she said, still glowing. "We got back yesterday. They're with friends tonight, and for the weekend, so I got to be with my sisters."

"You're lucky to have each other. I grew up alone with my dad. My mother died when I was nine. And I was a huge pain in the ass in my teens. But somehow we stuck it out, and now we're best friends. I wish I could do something for him now. He's in acute pain over your mother."

"It'll take time, for all of us. She was a lot to lose," Charlotte said softly.

"I didn't know her that well, but I agree. And she was always nice to me. For my father to love her as he did for fifteen years, she was probably even more remarkable than we all think. They had something very special between them," Andy said, almost wistfully.

"Do you believe in that kind of love?" Charlotte asked him candidly, and the question surprised him. "I mean that kind of tidal wave that almost drowns you, it's so powerful. The kind of love that lights up your world." He smiled at what she said.

"Honestly? No, I don't. I think it happens, but very rarely, and when it does, it's kind of a freak event, like a meteor or an eclipse or a rainbow, or a whole mountain range shifting, or a volcano. It's never happened to me," he said.

"Me neither. I think it would scare the hell out of me if it did. I'm used to things going along great for a while, and then falling apart

Felicia's Favorites

and going to shit in some nice, ordinary, predictable way, like the guy sleeps with your best friend, or runs over your dog, or hates your kids. I can handle that. But true love like our parents had? Who does that happen to? And what do you do when it does, other than run like hell?" He was laughing when she said it sincerely and she looked so serious, as though she meant it, and she did.

"I take it you're divorced?" he said. He and Charlotte were speaking in low voices, and the others weren't listening at the end of dinner. They were having some very existential conversation that neither of them cared about, and he liked talking to her.

"Actually, I did time in prison. I killed him."

"Seriously?" His eyes grew wide and she laughed. "No, but I probably should have. It was all very mundane. He slept with almost everyone we knew, so we got divorced. He didn't want to deal with the kids, so he moved to Spain and was killed in a motorcycle accident five years later, with his eighteen-year-old girlfriend on the back of the bike. She survived. He didn't. The kids hadn't seen him since the divorce. It's okay, they're fine. They won't grow up to be axe murderers. It just worked out that way. My mother warned me that he was a disaster, and she had a really annoying habit of being right about the men in my life."

"What are you two talking about?" Quinne leaned over and asked them. They hadn't stopped talking all night. Charlotte's vow to stay away from Andy didn't seem to be holding. And Andy was clearly mesmerized by her.

"I just told him about Adam," Charlotte said blithely.

"Already? You just met him. The poor guy is going to think we're all crazy."

"He's practically my brother. I can tell him anything, can't I?"

"No!" Quinne objected. She'd already had a fair amount of champagne by then, but Charlotte was relatively sober, and so was Andy.

"It's fine, really," Andy said to Quinne. "At last count, I had twenty-one girlfriends who went to rehab, and I paid for it every time. In one case, I paid for her mother to go too, and a set of twin brothers, but they didn't make it through rehab and went to jail for grand larceny. She was a little off too. It's hard to meet serious women in L.A. I finally gave up on actresses."

"You're divorced?" Quinne asked him, feeling totally at ease with him.

"I'm a virgin, and a coward. And probably a cynic. I'm actually happy the way things are, especially now that I have five nearly sisters. I wish your mother had introduced us all sooner."

"So do I. I've always wanted a brother. There were way too many women at our house growing up. A massive overdose of estrogen, but I love them all now. They're very cool, and so was our mom," Charlotte said, looking sad for a minute, and he gently touched her hand, like a whisper. He was painfully handsome in his jacket, and sexy in the jeans and black velvet loafers. He looked very stylish.

They joined the others to play games after dinner, charades and liar's dice and fast card games, until midnight, and then they all went around the room kissing each other and wishing each other a happy New Year.

Quinne heard Veronica's phone ring, and she could guess it was Anson. Veronica swept it off the table where she had left it and slipped into the next room to talk to him, so he couldn't hear the noise around her. They sounded like way more than six people, more like a party, laughing and talking, with music in the background.

It was five minutes after midnight and Anson sounded rushed. "I just wanted to wish you a happy New Year and tell you I love you." But she could tell he was in a hurry to get off the phone before he got caught.

"I love you too," she said. She had been thinking of him all night, with his family. She was with hers. She'd been having a nice time. They were a congenial group.

"Are you alone?" he asked, and she hesitated. She didn't want to lie to him and never had before. She didn't want to start now, after ten years.

"I'm with three of my sisters," she said.

"At the apartment?" He sounded confused, and put her to the test again.

"No, at a farm we just inherited from our mother that we didn't know she had. I didn't want to be alone, especially not this Christmas."

"Where is the farm?"

"In Connecticut," she said quietly.

"I told you that I wanted you at the apartment in the city in case I got free." He sounded livid, but he was controlling his voice so no one would hear him talking to her. She knew the drill.

"Anson, you were never going to leave your family at midnight and drive to New York to see me. And I can be home any time you want me tomorrow. I didn't want to spend New Year's Eve alone.

You're with your family. So am I. That's fair." But he had never promised her fair.

"We'll discuss it when I see you," he said, and hung up without saying goodbye. Usually when he lost his temper, it frightened her. He liked to have his way in all things. He called the shots and made the rules, reasonable or not. But this time, she wasn't afraid. She felt tired, like a wave washing over her. Years before, she would have rushed back to the city, to be there for him even though she knew he wouldn't come. But not this time. She went back to the others sitting by the fire and talking, and tried to look calmer than she felt. Andy caught her eye, as she sat down.

"Everything okay?" he asked her. Veronica looked sad to him.

"Pretty much," she answered, but she seemed tired, and deflated suddenly. And she was. She was tired of Anson telling her what to do, and not do, what to think, what to wear, who to be, who to see. She lived in a cage that anyone would have envied, but it came at a high price. She was the creature he had fashioned out of who she used to be, and could have been. He had thrown away the parts he didn't like and weren't of use to him, and reshaped the parts he liked, and everything he had made of her was for him. She felt as though there were no original parts of her left. She would have to answer to him now for not being at home on New Year's Eve as she'd been told. Andy didn't know what was happening to her or who had called, but he felt sorry for her. She was like a beautiful bird, and he couldn't tell where or why, but he could sense that there were chains holding her tight. She was a prisoner and had lost the key to her life.

Chapter 6

The holidays had been miserable for Isabelle, staying at her in-laws', who had never thought she was good enough for Ian. They had wanted him to marry a rich girl, and she wasn't. It had been painful staying with them at their winter home in Vermont, and Ian had been distant and distracted, and spent most of his time making calls, supposedly to his office, but she could guess who they were to. Tyler, who was nine, developed an earache. Six-year-old Charlie had a stomachache, and Penny, their five-year-old, wouldn't go to ski school, so Isabelle never got to ski. She had raced in the ski club at Boston University, won most of her races, and loved skiing with Ian, but he never skied with her once all week. She spent New Year's Eve with Charlie throwing up, while Ian went out with friends. She wound up crying in their room after the children fell asleep, babysitting instead of out celebrating with her husband. He came home drunk at two A.M., mumbled "Happy New Year," fell into bed, and passed out.

She called Veronica the next day. All Isabelle wanted to do was go home and confront him about the affair. It had weighed on her all week. It was obvious even to her that the rumor was true and he was involved with another woman. He treated her like a stranger now, and he was constantly texting. She couldn't confront him while they were staying with his parents, with all three of their kids sleeping in the next room. She and Ian had been so happy, and she'd thought they had a solid marriage, and now the roof was caving in.

"You've got to talk to him," Veronica said, as Isabelle cried, after Ian had gone skiing with friends on New Year's Day. Charlie was still throwing up so she stayed home with him again. Her mother-in-law had asked if they got proper meals at home. She couldn't understand why Charlie was throwing up, and she thought the children were all too thin. Isabelle had assured her that they had regular checkups, were healthy, and ate well. It was obvious that Ian's mother didn't believe her.

They were going home the next day and Isabelle couldn't wait to leave. "How was your New Year's Eve?" she asked Veronica.

"Really nice. I wish you'd been here. The house is so cozy and there's plenty of room for all of us. The star of the evening was Andy York, Spencer York's son. Olivia and I met him out walking and invited him to dinner on Christmas Eve, and last night. He and Charlotte seemed to hit it off. And Coop loved him. He's a nice man, and a writer like his father."

"What did Charlotte think of him? Did she scare him to death with her usual man-hating routine?" Isabelle asked, laughing.

"He didn't look scared. She was actually nice to him. It's hard not to be. He's a kind person, and she and the kids had a great time in Paris so she was in a good mood. When are you going to talk to Ian?" Veronica was seriously worried about her. Isabelle sounded terrible.

"We're going home tomorrow, so probably tomorrow night. I have to say something. I can't play the game anymore, of pretending I don't know. I want to know the truth, if he loves her and is leaving me."

"He'd be a fool if he did," Veronica said. "Let's have lunch this week," Veronica suggested. She was worried about Anson too. He had been furious the night before that she wasn't in the city, waiting for him, even though he had no intention of seeing her. He wanted an explanation about the farm she and her sisters had inherited, and why she hadn't told him. She had a lot of explaining to do. She had made a decision over the holidays that he wasn't going to like either. She wanted to take some refresher classes to brush up on her legal skills, now that she and her sisters were responsible for her mother's books. It was an awesome responsibility and she didn't want to make any mistakes. She had been reading the books Scott had given her at night.

Isabelle was quiet on the drive back to New York the next day. The antibiotics had cured Tyler's earache, and Charlie had stopped throwing up from whatever bug he had. Penny slept most of the way home, and neither Isabelle nor Ian said a word. She couldn't wait to get back to their apartment so she could breathe again in her own home, where no one disapproved of her. Ian went out for an hour while she was feeding the kids, and he looked happy when he got back. She had just put the children to bed, and she could guess where he'd been, to see the girl that he'd been texting all week. He couldn't stop smiling.

Ian saw her in the kitchen after she put Penny to bed. She was sitting lost in thought, with her head in her hands, when she heard him come in. They were finally alone, and the kids were asleep. She looked at him with despair in her eyes. She felt as though she had already lost the war before she began.

"We need to talk," she said sadly.

"I know." He had been avoiding her for weeks. "I don't know where to start."

"Me neither. Who is she? Are you in love with her? Is our marriage over?" she asked him for openers.

"I don't know." He didn't deny that there was someone else. She knew him too well, and he couldn't lie to her anymore. "It was a stupid thing to do. It was just a mistake at first. Maybe I was bored or I was looking for excitement. She's young, but we get along and she's interesting, and a good person. She's in love with me. It's flattering." He was trying to be honest with her, but it didn't help. Isabelle felt like she had a knife in her chest and a broken heart.

"Are you in love with her?" she asked in a choked voice.

"I'm not sure. Sometimes I think so, and then I realize that she's just a kid. And what you and I have is solid, and I don't want to lose you. We have children, a life, responsibilities. I don't want to give that up. I don't want to leave you," he said softly. "But I can't seem to leave her either. Every time I try, I go back to her. She's like a drug I'm addicted to. I don't know how this happened." He sounded lost and looked confused. "Maybe you and I should take a break."

"Or maybe we should stick with it and try to work this out. But you can't have both of us," Isabelle said, and was surprised at her own words. "You have to stop seeing her, if you want our marriage."

"I can't," Ian said, feeling desperate. This was exactly what he hadn't wanted, to talk to her about it. If he had to choose, he knew he would pick Leila at the moment, but not forever. Isabelle was the kind of woman you married, had children with, and stayed with for a lifetime. Leila was everything he didn't have with Isabelle and wanted desperately, she was a flash of lightning in the sky, but he didn't want to risk everything for her, or lose his family. Isabelle stood up and looked down at him.

"You have to figure it out. Soon. You need to decide who you love and who you want to be with. It boils down to that."

"I love both of you," he said in a raw voice. "How did you find out?" He wasn't surprised, and knew he hadn't hid it well.

"Someone I know heard it from someone in your office." It was bound to happen. "I don't want to live like this. We have a great life, or we did. I don't want to watch it crumbling day by day, until we have nothing left." They were getting there fast.

"Give me a few weeks," Ian said unhappily.

"I've already known about it for a few weeks. I didn't want to ruin Christmas for the kids. You were on the phone to her the whole time we were at your parents'. Do they know?"

"I think they suspect we're having problems. My mother asked me about it, and I said we were working it out."

"They've never liked me. They'd be thrilled if we got divorced," she said sadly.

"No, they wouldn't. They worry about the children."

"So do I," Isabelle said seriously. She had known about it for so long that she was starting to feel numb. She wasn't angry at him, she was sad, although sometimes she was furious, and then she went back to being numb again. She felt totally unbalanced, disoriented, confused, and shocked. It made no sense when her mother was shot and killed. And now Ian was having an affair, which made no sense either. Isabelle had never suspected that either of those things could happen to her.

"Maybe I should move out," he suggested. "It's better for you and the kids."

"What's better for *us*? Maybe it doesn't even matter what's better. It's about what you want. Her or me? You get to pick." For now, and if he didn't pick one of them, she would leave him. She loved him, but she didn't want to be a fool.

"Right now, I want to be with her, and in the long run, I want to be with you," he said, and she shook her head.

"That's not an option. What does she want? To marry you?"

"She wants the whole deal. Marriage, babies, me." Everything he and Isabelle had and she was losing now. She couldn't see Ian giving the girl up. He had said he couldn't. So what did that leave her? A divorce at thirty-four? Twelve years down the tubes, and a broken home for their kids? She didn't have a lot of options. And it wasn't in her hands. It was in his. And Leila's. She knew her name now. She wondered what she looked like, and if she was beautiful. Isabelle was sure she was.

"If you're going to keep seeing her, you have to move out," she said bravely. "I can't do this, Ian. It's only been weeks and it's driven me crazy ever since I found out. I assume you're with her whenever you're not with me. And she works in your office, so you see her all the time."

"That's how it started," he said unhappily. He felt guilty but that didn't make him want Leila less.

"I would never trust you at work again," which was no way to live, she knew.

"I'll look for a place tomorrow," he said, sounding decisive.

"So that means you're going to keep seeing her?"

"For now, until I figure it out." He looked almost as bad as she felt. "This isn't easy for me either," he said, feeling sorry for himself, but she didn't.

"Let me know what you decide," she said in a broken voice. She walked upstairs to their bedroom, went in, and locked the door. And then she lay on the bed and sobbed.

Ian slept in the guest room, and when she got up in the morning to wake the kids for school, he was gone. She wondered if he was going to move in with Leila or get his own place. He was too lazy to find an apartment, and she was sure he'd be staying with her. It was like moving in with his drug dealer, from everything he had said. For the rest of the day, she went through the motions of living and breathing, but every part of her felt dead.

Veronica didn't fare much better with Anson. It took him two days to come and see her after she got back after the New Year. He was punishing her, and he finally showed up at six o'clock at night, with no warning. He looked at her long and hard when he walked in and didn't kiss her. It was the first time she had seen him since before Christmas, but he didn't look happy to see her, and kept his distance. She was sitting on the couch, and he sat down across from her, with a glass of Scotch in his hand.

"Why didn't you tell me about the farm?" he asked her in an ice-cold voice after his first sip of Scotch. He made no move to come near her. He was facing her and staring at her intently.

"Because it was a shock for all of us, in addition to losing her, and I needed time to digest it myself."

"She left you a farm?" He sounded incredulous. "She didn't sound like the type to have large investments no one knew about."

"She's been living there for twelve years. We had no idea. It's a beautiful place. My sisters and I own it jointly," she said simply.

"Are you going to sell it?"

"We don't know yet. I think we want to keep it for a while, while we figure it out."

"Is it worth anything?" he said skeptically. Her mother was just a little editor, and Veronica didn't tell him otherwise. One thing at a time. This was a start.

"I think it's probably worth a lot. I only own a fifth. It would be nice to spend time with my sisters there, when you're busy or not around."

"You're not understanding, Veronica," he said coldly. "I give you all this, this lifestyle, all this luxury and comfort, so that you are here for me whenever I want, when I have time to come and see you. We're not dating. You're my mistress." He made her sound like an object he owned, which she realized was how he viewed her. He had never been as blunt about it before, or seemed as cold. His eyes were like ice.

"I am here for you. I gave up my legal career for you, so that I would be available, in exchange for what you do for me. But I can't sit here doing nothing forever except waiting for you."

"That's the deal. It's not new."

"I'm going to have some things to do for my mother's estate. I want to take some law classes to brush up on my legal skills, so I can help my sisters."

"Hire a lawyer to do it. And your mother's estate can't be that complicated. What did she have? A few stocks? Some savings? By the time you pay the taxes, and divide it by five, it won't be worth your time. Forget the classes."

"No," she said, and felt as though she had just jumped out of an airplane and wasn't sure if her parachute would open. Anson had been her parachute, her safety net for ten years, but he expected her to pay the price now. And the price was her freedom. He could do anything he wanted, but he wanted her in a locked box on a shelf, and he had the only key. Just thinking about it was oppressive. She knew she couldn't give into it. He had never been as blunt about it before. She felt like she couldn't breathe. "I'd like to sign up for the classes. I'm going to need them," she said gently.

"I'm telling you not to." It was a warning.

"They're just refresher courses at Columbia, where I went to law school."

"I don't need a lawyer, Veronica. I need exactly what you've been for the past ten years."

"I'm not twenty-six years old anymore. I don't have children. At least I can put my education to good use for my family." She was on the verge of tears when she said it, tears of anger, disappointment, and fear.

"You have some serious thinking to do," he said, glancing at his watch. "I have to go. I'll call you. I hope you get your head on straight again. We have a good thing, Veronica, for both of us. You have security, and I have you. Don't screw it up." He had been with his family for the past two weeks, and she would have spent Christmas alone if it weren't for her sisters. Her mother had been right yet again. It was a lonely life he was condemning her to, an eternal waiting game, hoping to see him for an hour or a night, whatever he wanted and had time for. Veronica wondered how he'd react if he knew about the money her mother had left her. She felt sure now that he wouldn't like that either. Anson didn't want her to have any independence. "Don't make a big mistake, Veronica," he said. "You'll regret it." She didn't say a word, as he set down his glass, looked at her, got up, and walked out the door, without speaking or kissing her goodbye. Two months ago, Veronica would have run after him and told him she loved him, and not to go away angry at her. But all of a sudden, she couldn't do that anymore. She picked up his glass, walked to the kitchen with it, and put it in the sink for the maid to wash the next day. She lay on her bed for a long time after Anson left, thinking about what he had said and what she was going to do next. The first thing she was going to do was sign up for the classes she wanted to take at Columbia. He couldn't stop her. Her mother had given her the power to resist him and to push back. She didn't even have to push. She just had to be herself and stand up for herself, for what she knew was right. Veronica wondered if Anson was afraid she would cheat on him, but she wouldn't think of doing that to him. This wasn't about other men, and she loved Anson. This was about not being treated like an object by the man she loved, and about respecting herself. He had made her feel cheap when he reminded her that she was his mistress in exchange for the apartment she lived in and the clothes he bought her. He had never made the trade-off as obvious before. Veronica wondered why he felt so threatened by her spending time at the farm with her sisters. But it was all about control. Anson couldn't tolerate her having free will or the right to make decisions for herself. She could already guess that her having money of her own now would be the biggest threat of all and she could never tell him. Just knowing that she owned a fifth of what he assumed was a rickety old farm had threatened him. It would be even worse if he found out that her mother had left a large fortune to each of her daughters and that Veronica didn't have to be his slave anymore.

Veronica had just finished signing up online for the intellectual property classes she wanted to take at Columbia when Robert Farr called her to tell her that the deal had closed for one of her mother's books to be made into a series, on the terms the five sisters had agreed to, and Robert assured her it was a terrific deal and her mother would have been pleased. "I'll send all of you the contracts to sign. They have to line up the cast now. They already have the producer and director. They should be ready to start shooting principal photography in May." The contract was for a very respectable amount of money, even divided by five.

Quinne was particularly excited when he called her, and he told her he'd had an idea and wanted to check it out with her.

"Since you're an experienced producer, would you be interested in being an executive producer?" She was stunned and pleased by the question.

"I'd love it." And it meant additional money for her. "Do you suppose there would be a part in it for Cooper? He's my partner, in life, I mean. I can send you his résumé with all his acting credits."

"I don't know who they're using for casting, or what they have in mind, but send it to me, I'll pass it on. We can turn this into a family production," Robert said, laughing. He had enjoyed talking to all of Felicia's daughters that morning, and he was relieved to hear that they were doing well and getting along. They'd had a lot of surprises since their mother's death, and sometimes good changes were even harder to adjust to than bad ones. "Have you thought about starting a production house of your own?" he asked her. "You could now."

"I gave up on that idea a long time ago," she said. "If I do, I want Cooper to help me with it. We work well together. He's just wrapping a show now. As soon as he finishes, I'll talk to him about it. Maybe the people we just signed with would want to hire us for production." She was an experienced producer. She had just never wanted the responsibility of a production house of her own.

"I can mention it to them, if you're interested," Robert said, thinking about how pleased Felicia would have been to know that her kids were excited about her work, and starting to get involved.

He had tried to push her toward that for years, and for a long time she'd thought they were too young, but they weren't now. They were just the right age to start their own ventures, some of them more than others. And Quinne was a very competent woman.

Veronica was carefully studying the contract Robert sent them that afternoon when Scott Freeman called her.

"I hear congratulations are in order. It sounds like a great deal for a series." He sounded as encouraging and kind as ever. "I spoke to Robert."

"I was just reading the contract. The terms really are complicated in these audiovisual deals. I signed up for a class this morning before Robert called. I need a refresher course to understand it thoroughly."

"I'd be happy to go over it with you, if you want me to have a look," he offered, and the idea was very appealing. "Do you want me to come by after work?"

"How about I meet you at the bar at the Saint Regis?" She knew it was near his office, and she was excited to talk to him and go over the contract with him. She could have done it with Robert, but Scott had offered, and she enjoyed talking to him. He was a lot younger and less serious than Robert, who was more like a grandfather to her. Scott was closer to her own age, only five or six years older. He had gone to Yale Law School and they had exchanged stories about their law school days. But she felt awkward having him come to the apartment, particularly if Anson showed up unannounced. He wouldn't like her meeting Anson there at all.

"Does six work for you?" he asked her. "I'll try to get out of here by then." He was excited to see her, and Veronica took the contract with her when she went to meet him. She put her Columbia application in a desk drawer and locked it before she left the apartment. She hadn't heard from Anson since their unpleasant exchange the day before, and she didn't expect to. It seemed like he was still planning to punish her for a few days, and if he showed up, it would be later, although he wasn't always easy to predict.

Scott was waiting for her at a corner table, when she got to the Saint Regis five minutes late. Traffic had been heavy, and she'd taken a cab. She was wearing black slacks and a striking red coat. He saw her immediately when she walked in, and he stood up to greet her. He was struck again by how beautiful she was. Her cheeks were pink from the cold, and her eyes were bright. Her dark hair was in a sleek bun, her red coat looked chic and expensive, and she had a large striking gold bangle on one arm that he remembered had been her mother's. The sisters had divided the jewelry up among them, without a problem, shortly before Christmas.

Veronica ordered white wine and he had a gin and tonic, and after they chatted for a few minutes, she took the contract out of her Hermès bag. As he looked at it with her, their heads close together, he could smell her perfume. It had a spicy, musky scent that was mysterious and sexy, and he loved being near her. She had an aura of sophistication about her, faintly reminiscent of her mother's, but in a more youthful style. Scott hadn't thought of Felicia as sexy, but he'd thought she was very beautiful, and Veronica was both.

"Does that make sense to you now?" he asked her about one of the deal points in the contract. She said she wasn't sure and he explained it to her again, and then she got it. The contingencies, conditions, and percentages were complicated in audiovisual deals, as she was discovering. "This isn't my usual field of expertise either, but it's more fun than tax structures," he said. They ordered another drink and Veronica was relaxed with him. "Do you miss practicing law?" he asked her.

"I didn't practice for very long. It was a conflict with the man I was involved with, and I quit in less than a year, and I haven't practiced since."

"That's a big sacrifice to make for a man," he commented.

"We're still together, and he still feels the same way about it. He doesn't want me to take the classes I mentioned at Columbia." She said it in a simple, straightforward way without being critical of Anson, which caught Scott's attention. She had a gentle way about her.

"And you signed up anyway?" Veronica nodded. "Is that an act of war?" he asked.

"It's not intended to be. I think it's important that I learn more about intellectual property law so I can help my sisters with our mother's estate. I do have a law degree, after all."

"It makes perfect sense to me," Scott said simply, intrigued by the relationship she was in, if her boyfriend had required that she sacrifice her job. "Was it a conflict for him?"

"It could have been. He's in politics, and his schedule is so crazy and unpredictable and he wants me to be readily available. One overburdened schedule is enough, and that would be his."

"There aren't a lot of women who would make a sacrifice like that today."

"His job was a lot more important than mine, and is liable to become even more so. So I keep myself free, to be available to him." It sounded excessive to Scott, and unfair to Veronica, but he didn't want to pry. He thought she was so fabulous that he couldn't imagine any man asking her to give up so much.

She had a wonderful time talking to him, as she had before, and she was enjoying being at a chic bar with a smart, good-looking man close to her own age. She hadn't done that in a long time, and no one had asked her. Veronica didn't meet many single men. She didn't have a job, and never went out without Anson. He loved her to stay close to him when they went to big charitable or political events, where she always posed as his assistant, not a date.

Veronica and Scott were still talking animatedly when she saw that it was after eight. They'd finished their drinks, she had put the contract back in her purse, and she looked at Scott with regret.

"I hate to say it, but I should get home." The way she said it caught his interest. She sounded sorry to leave.

"Same guy who made you give up your job?" he asked boldly, and she nodded.

"Same guy, ten years later. I try to stay available. He has a demanding schedule."

"And you don't mind being at his beck and call? Why is his schedule more important than yours?" Scott asked her pointedly, wondering what she would answer.

"I wasn't voted into office. He has to keep his constituents happy, and I have to take second place to that." Scott didn't know why but he had a vague suspicion that Veronica's boyfriend was married. And it struck him odd that ten years later they weren't married, when any guy in his right mind would have grabbed her. But he didn't know her well enough to ask her, and he was glad to have seen her for a drink. He had wanted to ask her to dinner spontaneously, but that was obviously not going to happen tonight. He wondered if she dated other men, and if she was single by choice.

"I hope we can do this again," he said hopefully, as he walked her out of the bar, proud to be with her. Heads turned as she walked by. And she turned to look at Scott regretfully then.

"This is kind of unusual for me. As I said, I try to keep my schedule pretty open for my friend, and I have a feeling he wouldn't be comfortable with my having drinks with a single man. He considers me his property." It startled him when she said it. It was a statement most women wouldn't want to make.

"Are you serious?" She nodded. "And you don't mind?"

"Not really. It's not as harsh as it sounds. He's possessive about me, and he has a busy life, and I have to fit in. He's older than I am, so some of his ideas are a little old-school." Listening to her, Scott was even more certain that the man in her life was married, no matter how elegantly she expressed it. To Scott she sounded like a woman under submission to a selfish, domineering man. By what right did he dictate the terms of her existence, who she had drinks with, and cause her to give up a job for which she had spent three years in law school and passed the bar? Scott wondered how her mother had felt about it. Felicia had had very modern ideas about women, that they should have equality and freedom. Veronica didn't sound either equal or free to him, and he was sorry to hear it, for her sake as well as his own.

"Let's see if we can find a time to get together that fits with his schedule," Scott said to her, as the doorman hailed a cab for her. "Maybe I'll get lucky," he said, standing close to her and looking her in the eye, and it made her nervous for a moment, and then she realized she liked it, and smiled at him. "I had a very nice time, and I think Robert got you all a great deal."

"I'm happy to hear it," Veronica said.

"And good luck in school. When do you start classes?"

"In three weeks," she said, her smile growing wider.

"Call me if I can do anything to help. Take care of yourself, Veronica. I'm only a phone call away if there's anything you need." He would have liked to kiss her cheek, but decided it was too forward, and might cause her concern about her boyfriend. Scott felt pulled toward her like a magnet, if only so he could get a closer scent of her perfume. He didn't kiss her, and she slipped into the cab, and waved as they drove away, and he stood looking after her from the sidewalk. She was an enthralling woman, and he envied her strangely controlling boyfriend, and wondered why she put up with it. He felt certain the guy didn't deserve her.

In the cab on the way home, Veronica felt nervous and guilty. There was something so strong, masculine, and appealing about Scott, and he was so intelligent to talk to, that she felt faintly unfaithful to Anson just being there. Even more so because she had enjoyed it. Her motive in seeing Scott had been innocent, but somehow as the evening progressed, it had become personal, and

Felicia's Favorites

it was a heady experience just being with him. She knew she shouldn't do it again. Anson would have a fit if he found out about it. She had committed other crimes recently, inheriting from her mother, spending time with her sisters at the farm they had inherited and the holidays with them, and not being miserable and alone while Anson shared the holidays with his wife and family as he always did. Signing up for a class at Columbia was a major crime she would be severely punished for.

Veronica didn't hear from Anson that night, and she found herself thinking about Scott and remembering things he had said that had interested or amused her.

Anson didn't call or text her, and she knew she was still being punished. Now she had another crime to add to the list, although she wouldn't tell him. Cocktails at a fashionable place with an attractive single man who wanted to see her again. No matter how appealing the idea was, she knew that it wasn't possible, but it had been fun, and she'd had a very good time with him. It was better than sitting at home alone night after night, waiting for Anson to show up and forgive her for the ordinary pleasures he would consider crimes which even she knew weren't.

Chapter 7

After the holidays and being away in Paris, Charlotte was busy in the office when Robert called her to tell her about the TV series they were going to make based on her mother's book. She was still excited about it when her assistant told her there was an Andrew York on the phone for her. She was happy to hear from him and told him about the deal.

"My father will be happy to hear it too," he said warmly, and after a few minutes of easy exchanges, he invited Charlotte to dinner. He had told her he would call, and she was delighted to discover he meant it. He suggested a restaurant they both knew and liked in the city.

"I didn't want to wait to see you until you came back to the farm again. It sounds like you have a busy life in the city."

"I do, and my son hasn't gone back to Stanford yet and I don't want to miss the time with him. I don't think he'll be back here until next summer. He likes his freedom from maternal kibitzing on the West Coast."

"I felt that way about my father too at that age. I took a class on Shakespeare at the University of Edinburgh one summer."

"How was it?" she said, smiling.

"Cold and rainy, but I had a terrific time. I was wondering if I could entice you to a hockey game. I happen to have tickets for a game this weekend." She was happy to hear from him, and she had told him on New Year's Eve that she loved hockey, and so did he.

"That's a fantastic offer," she instantly enthused, and he was pleased.

When the day came, he picked her up at her apartment in Tribeca. They were both dressed for the cold at the game, with down jackets and wool hats, and talked animatedly in the Uber all the way to Madison Square Garden. They were rooting for opposing teams. Charlotte's team won and she lorded it over him all the way to dinner. He said he had some writing to do that week, and told her what the book was about over excellent pasta at Sant Ambroeus, which was her favorite restaurant. Neither of her kids had been home when he picked her up, so Andy hadn't met them yet, but he was looking forward to it. He and Charlotte talked more seriously about the challenge of being both mother and father to them, since they'd been young when their father left, and he was never interested in them before that. It had been hardest on her son, but Charlotte said he was a good kid and good student and had been forgiving of her mistakes.

"My daughter is less generous about it when I screw up, which I try not to do too often. It's a lesson in humility, parenting teenage kids, and it flies by so fast. Julia only has another year of high school after this, and then she'll be gone too," she said wistfully. Andy liked Charlotte's exuberant, realistic, rough-and-tumble view of life. She seemed to roll with the punches, enjoyed her business, and loved her kids. And she was humble about her victories and mistakes. The evening flew by, and he was sorry to drop her off at her apartment. It had ended too quickly. There was always more to say.

"I hope you come back to the farm soon, although it's a little bleak this time of year," he admitted. "But it's nice sitting by the fire on snowy days."

"I'm actually coming out for the weekend with my sisters in a couple of weeks. It's my mother's birthday, and it seemed like a good excuse to come back and spend time together. You haven't met my youngest sister yet. She's having kind of a rough patch at the moment." Andy admired how close the sisters were. They were an impressive group of women, all different, but Charlotte was the woman who had struck him as exceptional, and sexy and fun, the moment he met her. His father had been intrigued but not surprised when Andy mentioned her to him in glowing terms. He had described her as brilliant and cool. Spencer was amused. Felicia had always said that she wanted to introduce them, but that her oldest daughter was famously hard on men ever since her unhappy marriage and bitter divorce. Andy didn't report anything like it, and had enjoyed her a great deal. Charlotte was smart and funny and fun, and Spencer wondered if she had mellowed with age. She clearly hadn't been rough on Andy. He sounded like a teenager when he talked about her.

Charlotte and Andy had lunch when he'd had to come to the city to do an errand for his father, and she showed him her offices at To Go and he was impressed. They were in the heat of preparing their IPO, and she was obviously smart in business too, which was something he wasn't good at. He had spent his entire life in the literary world. Andy had taught literature and creative writing before settling down to write full-time. Charlotte left on the road show for her IPO after that, and wasn't due back until her mother's birthday weekend at the farm with her sisters. Andy couldn't wait to see her again, and he was busy himself, working on his book. He had never felt as at ease with any woman. He called her a couple of times while she was on the road, and she made him laugh with stories about the road show, which sounded arduous to him, but she said it was going well.

"I'm a lot better at business than I am at dating," Charlotte said late one night, on the phone from Chicago. "I usually blow it on the first date, or screw it up totally on the second. I say all the wrong things, or hate their pets, or their children hate me."

"I don't have pets or kids," Andy pointed out to her, "so that's a plus. Actually, I think you've done pretty well so far."

"We've only had two dates," she reminded him, "so I'm still within my norms. And I haven't cooked for you yet. That usually takes care of it, if I haven't said anything sufficiently offensive about the guy's mother."

"I don't have a mother either, so we're good. I do like to eat though, but I can cook, so you get a pass on that. We might actually make it to date three or four before you screw it up completely. I take it phone calls don't count."

"Not really. I can usually get through a phone call," she said cheerfully, undaunted by her poor dating record, about which she made jokes and clearly had no remorse.

"How do you account for your poor dating record?" he asked.

"I think I hated men for about a decade after my miserable marriage and shitful divorce. I'm the only woman I know who paid spousal support, which he spent on all his nineteen-year-old girlfriends. But what really bothered me was that he was such a lousy father and never showed up for his kids. He was always too busy doing something else. It taught them to deal with disappointment at an early age, but it was painful to watch. I hated him after that, and took it out on any guy brave enough to ask me on a date. I punished them severely for everything he did wrong. And then the poor guy died and it seemed a little too rude to speak ill of the dead, and my children's father, so I argued with my mother all the time instead, on any subject. The poor woman was a saint. It's a wonder she didn't cut me out of her will. I would have deserved it. I was just angry, at everything, and for some reason, when I turned forty, I ran out of steam, and I was having so much fun with my business, I stopped being pissed at everything else." She had interesting insights into herself, which he respected and enjoyed.

"It's weird. I've been mellower in my forties too." He was forty-seven, but didn't look it or act it. He had an upbeat innocence and boyish quality that she loved.

"I used to complain all the time, but I even started to bore myself," she said, and he laughed. "Maybe you came along at the right time. I might even make it to five dates with you." And then she grew serious for a minute. "It really ripped my heart out when Mom was killed. I finally got how precious life is, and how unpredictable and how short it can be. I thought she'd be around forever and I could make up to her later for what a pain in the ass I was for so many years. And now she's gone and I can't make it up to her." Andy could hear that she was crying when she said it.

"She told me how brilliant you are, and how smart in business, and what a good mother. She never said you were a pain in the ass," he said gently, "she said you were 'spirited.'"

"That translates to 'pain in the ass.' Look it up in the dictionary. It's an official description. She always forgave me. I try to be like her with my kids. But she was better at it. They adored her. Losing her has been hard on them too. She was their only living grandparent. Now all they have is me, and I'm not nearly in the same leagues of parenting as she was. Maybe I'll get there someday."

"It sounds like you're doing a good job to me."

"They're still alive and aren't serial killers and haven't been to jail, so I guess we're holding our own." He loved talking to her and hearing what she had to say. He couldn't wait for her to come back from her trip, but he didn't say it. He didn't want to sound like a jerk, or desperate. But house-sitting for his father's house was solitary and lonely. He had thought it would be good for his writing, but he was discovering it was bad for his spirits. Charlotte had livened things up immensely, and he wanted to go to another hockey game with her, and he could think of a dozen other things he wanted to do with her. He couldn't wait for her to come back to the farm with her sisters.

When Anson finally showed up at the apartment, he acted like nothing had happened, nothing unpleasant had been said. It was a little awkward at first, but he couldn't wait to go to bed with Veronica, which was what had brought him back after a week of silence and the ice treatment. He showed up on a busy afternoon for him, between meetings, and had to go to Washington that night for a committee meeting at the Pentagon the next day with the Joint Chiefs of Staff of the Navy and the Army, and he was so hungry for Veronica that he couldn't stand it a moment longer. He walked into the apartment with no warning, walked over to where she was standing, and kissed her so hard, he took her breath away. He never apologized when he had been hard on her. He just showed up when he was ready to see her, and made love to her like someone who had been starving for however long he'd been gone. He was the master of the silent treatment and she was used to it. She never resisted him or made him accountable for it when he treated her badly, because he treated her well the rest of the time, and she knew there was no point dragging it out. It was best to put it behind them, and go on. This time was no different. He had wounded her deeply when he had said she was just his mistress and they weren't dating. She was standing in the living room, putting some books away. When she didn't see him, she used the time to do things in the apartment. He pressed her against the bookcase, unzipped the skirt she was wearing and let it fall to her feet, and she was standing there in black lace underwear and high heels. He swept her off her feet and carried her to her bedroom, in the apartment that was his, and made love to her with every ounce of his strength and passion for her, and never said a word. He gave a lion's roar when he came, and he lay there looking at her for a long moment. She could tell that he had missed her, but he didn't say it.

"You're beautiful," he said to her in a hoarse voice, admiring her, as her long dark hair fell around her like a veil. They lay talking quietly for a little while, and then he made love to her again. He was capable of feats with her that he couldn't achieve with anyone else, which bound him to her more than he acknowledged, but he took full advantage of the virility she endowed him with. She was an artful lover and knew how to arouse him and satisfy him in ways no one else ever had. It accounted for the longevity of their relationship, and her role as his mistress. She was a geisha and a courtesan, and she did it well.

She walked across her bedroom naked while he admired her, put on a pink satin dressing gown, went to make him a Scotch on the rocks the way he liked it, and came back to hand it to him. He sat next to her, drinking it, and she lay back against the pillows. She made no mention of the fact that she hadn't seen him in over a week and he had been mean to her the last time she did see him. All was forgiven and forgotten, on his side, and on hers she knew there was no point belaboring the point and angering him again. If she wanted him, she had to play by his rules, with no exception. She was going to do what she wanted and needed to do, with the class at Columbia, and she had her inheritance now, and the farm, but as long as she was with Anson, she was his mistress, and in his eyes, he owned her.

He didn't spend the night with her, leaving at midnight, but the complex machinery of their relationship was back in place, on track, where he wanted it to be. It was the life she had signed on for with him, and accepted for ten years, but she was bigger than his narrow definition of her now. He sensed it and it frightened him, but she wasn't afraid of what he could do to her if she didn't follow his rules. Whether she had meant to or not, her mother had done what she hadn't been able to do in her lifetime. With the revelation of all of her own secrets, Felicia had liberated her children, and Veronica wasn't a prisoner anymore. In her heart, she was free.

The tension between Isabelle and Ian was almost unbearable once he had admitted the affair to her. And for Isabelle, the sadness was overwhelming. She felt as though she was riding a wave every day, and praying it didn't drown her. It was as though talking to her about the affair had freed Ian to do whatever he wanted. He stayed late at the office, or said he did, and came home late at night. He disappeared early in the morning, to spend time with Leila before they went to work. On two occasions he stayed out all night, and only came home to change in the morning. Isabelle felt as though she was seeing the world around her from under water. She didn't even want to talk to her sisters about it. She had never felt so alone in her life. All she could do was hang on and hope the pain didn't kill her. There were times when she thought it might. She had loved Ian so much from the moment she met him, and now he was throwing it all away. It had never occurred to her that it could happen to them, but it had. She felt as though she were watching her life from outside her own body, like a bystander, or a stranger or an alien, with nothing to hang onto. She was trying to focus on the children, and sometimes she thought she was losing her mind, but what she was losing, or had already lost, was Ian. He didn't want to hurt Isabelle, but it was inevitable, and he was in a freefall into Leila's arms, and couldn't stop himself.

It was Ian who finally put a stop to it. He came home early one morning, looking ragged. Isabelle was in the kitchen drinking coffee, before the kids got up. She was smoking a cigarette, which she hadn't done since college, and she looked as though she had been dragged down the street behind a bus. She had dark circles under her eyes, was deathly pale, and had lost weight. She looked like a cadaver.

He sat down across from her at the kitchen table, horrified by how wounded she looked, knowing he had done it to her.

"I can't do this anymore, to either of us, any of us. Leila is upset too." Isabelle didn't answer him. "I thought I could stay here and figure it out. You were right. I can't. It's killing us." He felt as though she was watching him, even when he wasn't there. She was like a ghost following him around. She didn't argue with him. She didn't have the strength.

They pulled themselves together to have breakfast with the children, who seemed quieter than usual too. The whole family was in a turmoil. Making pancakes Isabelle burned the first batch, and the children hardly touched the second, though it was their favorite breakfast. Isabelle got them dressed before the babysitter came to take them to school. Ian packed a suitcase after they left while Isabelle sat in the living room, smoking. She couldn't watch him do it. Every inch of her ached, as though she'd been beaten. Ian dropped his suitcase at the front door, and he came to find her in the living room and didn't approach her. He spoke to her from the doorway. He was afraid to go near her. She looked like she would break.

"I'm sorry I've made such a mess of this. I promise I'll try to fix it. I can't do it here," he said sadly.

"Are you moving in with her?" she asked in a dead voice. "You won't be able to figure it out there either." They had all gotten caught up in his insanity.

"I don't know what I'm doing. You can reach me on my cell, if you need me." But she didn't need him, not the man who belonged to Leila now. She needed her husband back, the one she had loved for twelve years and no longer knew or recognized. Ian was crazy, and Isabelle looked it. "I'll call you." He picked up his suitcase and walked out the door, closing it softly behind him. She heard the elevator come and go, and went back to their bedroom and went to bed. She didn't even have any tears left. She had been awake all night, crying, for days.

She got up when she heard the children come home from school, and she went through the motions of motherhood. Baths, food, tucked them into bed. Charlie wanted to know where his father was and Isabelle told him that he had to go on a trip for work and he'd be home soon. Tyler was listening intently. She didn't know what to tell them, and they hadn't agreed on a story to tell the kids yet. She wondered how you explained divorce to a five-year-old, but they weren't divorced yet.

She didn't answer any calls all day. Veronica and Quinne had called her, but she didn't want to talk to them, or to anyone.

Losing her mother and her husband in the space of two months was almost too much to bear. But there was nothing she could do. She was on an express train to hell that wouldn't stop.

She had ordered pizza for dinner for the kids that night and they loved it. It felt like a party to them, but they knew something was wrong. They asked again when Daddy was coming home, and she tried to look bright and cheerful when she said she didn't know. But the children knew something was wrong. Even Penny was out of sorts and had been wetting her bed at night.

Isabelle got into her own bed after she tucked them in, and she lay there, feeling like a mummy. She finally fell asleep at six A.M., an hour before she had to get the children up. She staggered to her feet when her alarm went off. Disoriented, she got up and woke them. Another day started without Ian.

It was like childbirth, where you wonder how much worse it can get, and then it gets even worse than you imagined. But she knew she had to get through it. She had to stay alive for her kids.

Her life was a blur now, all the days looked the same. It was another day without Ian. She couldn't imagine his coming back now. He was gone, probably forever. She didn't know where he was staying and it didn't matter. He was no longer hers. He belonged to a girl called Leila. Isabelle could guess that he was prob-

Felicia's Favorites

ably staying with her. It was easy, and Ian was making all the easy choices now, and none of the hard ones to save their marriage.

Isabelle had been looking forward to spending her mother's birthday weekend with her sisters, but now she was dreading it. She didn't know what to tell them. Veronica knew, but Isabelle had asked her not to tell the others. At some level, she was ashamed that Ian had left her. She didn't see it as his crime as much as her failure to keep her husband's interest, make him happy, and make him love her. She was feeling terrible about herself, and about him. She would have canceled out of the birthday, but she didn't want to disappoint her sisters. It had been a sweet idea to celebrate their mother's birthday together, but she didn't feel up to making the effort, or even combing her hair.

When the day came, she reminded the children at breakfast that she would be away when they came home from school.

"Will you be like Daddy and not come back?" Tyler asked her, looking her in the eye, and she shook her head and hugged him. She wanted to reassure him about Ian and couldn't find the words. And she didn't want to lie to him. Ian had called them a few times and told them he'd be home soon.

"Of course not. I'll come home on Sunday, and you can call me whenever you want. I'm going to be with all of your aunts." She had already told them weeks earlier, but they might have forgotten. "We're going to talk about our mom. It's her birthday tomorrow."

"Can't you talk to them on the phone and stay here?" Tyler asked in a plaintive tone, and she shook her head. She would have preferred staying home with them too.

"No, it's too hard with so many people. You have a lot of aunts." She smiled at them.

"Do it by Zoom, Mommy." They'd gone to school remotely during the pandemic, and even Penny was computer savvy at five.

"We can't hug each other by Zoom," she said. They went to brush their teeth after breakfast, and she hugged them tight before they left. She wished she could take them with her. It was painful being away from them now. She had lost Ian, and she was terrified to lose them too, not that Ian would take them. But she needed to be close to her children, and instead she was going to spend two days with her sisters. She didn't know what to say to them, and she cried thinking about it. It was going to be a long sad weekend at the farm for her.

Chapter 8

Veronica was packed and ready to leave the apartment on Friday morning. She had seen Anson for two hours the night before. He was flying to Washington, D.C., by private jet later that night. He had two charity events to attend, and meetings with his Armed Forces Committee on Monday morning, so she knew she wouldn't see him all weekend, and she decided not to tell him about the weekend at the farm until Monday. She didn't want to spoil it by arguing with him, or having him forbid her to go. She'd been looking forward to spending the weekend with her sisters ever since they'd planned it. She had read two of her mother's books that week. She was picking Olivia up on the way. Olivia had gotten a substitute to handle her Friday classes. She could have driven her own specially altered car with hand controls, but it would be nicer riding with Veronica and chatting on the way, and more relaxing for her. She'd been busy since they last saw each other.

Isabelle had texted Veronica that she was going to drive herself, after Veronica offered to drive her. Charlotte and Quinne were both coming after work. Charlotte had important meetings, and would arrive by dinnertime. Quinne had preproduction meetings for the new series based on their mother's book. The three who were arriving early were going to start dinner before Charlotte and Quinne got there. Charlotte had promised to bring the wine for the weekend, and Quinne had ordered a cake, the mocha cake their mother loved, from the local bakery near the farm. It sounded a little strange to admit that they were celebrating their mother's birthday without her, but it was a good excuse to be together. When Charlotte told Andy, he thought it was sweet and not weird at all. It was a way to honor and remember Felicia. Charlotte was going to ask the others if she could include Andy on Saturday night, but she hadn't mentioned it yet. Veronica knew they'd had dinner together several times, but the others didn't know they were dating, and Charlotte was a little embarrassed to tell them, but they'd had a great time every time they went out. He had even met Julia, and Charlotte was surprised that she'd been amazingly civil to him. Everybody liked Andy, and so did she, more than she wanted to admit. It was all happening very quickly, and so far seemed very promising.

"So how are things with you?" Veronica asked Olivia as they drove to Connecticut. Olivia sighed and glanced out the window for a few seconds before she answered.

"On the surface, great, I guess. What could be wrong? We just inherited a pile of money and a beautiful farm, our futures are secure forever, which they weren't two months ago, but it seems weird and makes me feel uneasy that suddenly we're rich women. I feel guilty whenever I think about it."

"Guilty, why?" Veronica didn't feel guilty, but she was still surprised. The shock hadn't worn off yet.

"We didn't earn it. It just landed on us like manna from heaven."

"That's what Mom wanted," Veronica said gently. "She wanted to make things easy for us. Why don't you just try to enjoy it?"

"I think I'll feel better when I get the foundation set up, and I can start putting the money to good use. Scott is drawing up the papers for me. That way, donors will get a tax deduction for what they give me to help others in need." She looked happier as she said it. "Have you seen him again?" Olivia asked, curious, and Veronica shook her head. Olivia meant Scott.

"We had a drink together a few weeks ago. I don't think Anson would like it. I haven't seen him since. He advised me about the classes I'm taking."

"How does Anson feel about that?" Olivia had a feeling he wouldn't be pleased.

"He doesn't like it," Veronica said. "But it's important to do it. I want to know what I'm doing when we look over Mom's contracts in future. With the body of work she left, it's serious business, and at eighty-two, Robert won't be around forever to advise us." What she said made perfect sense. Anson had dressed her in head-to-toe Dior and Chanel, but above all she was an intelligent woman, and would have made a very decent lawyer if she'd stuck with it.

The drive to Connecticut seemed shorter than previously. They had a lot to talk about, and Ellen had a platter of her perfect sandwiches waiting for them when they arrived.

After they ate and dropped their bags in their rooms, they went to the grocery store together. Veronica treated Olivia like a human shopping cart, dropping their more fragile purchases on Olivia's lap, while they argued harmlessly about brands, and how many chickens to cook for dinner. They agreed on two, and the teenage boy at the checkout stand carried their purchases to the car for them when he saw Olivia in the chair, juggling the bags on her lap. Ellen put it all away for them when they got home. And they picked up the birthday cake Quinne had ordered at the local bakery. The sisters were well organized, some of them more than others, a trait they had inherited from their mother. Veronica and Olivia were relaxing in front of the fire in the living room when Isabelle arrived. She looked rough. Veronica knew why and Olivia didn't. She was shocked by how thin and pale Isabelle looked. Only Veronica knew that Ian had moved out.

"Have you been sick?" Olivia asked her, and Isabelle shook her head.

"No, just busy with the kids." Veronica knew it wasn't true, and Olivia didn't challenge her, but Isabelle looked noticeably worn out and was very quiet. She went to her room shortly after she arrived, to unpack her things and settle in.

"She looks terrible," Olivia whispered to Veronica, after their younger sister left the room. "Things must be worse with Ian."

"Kids that age are very wearing, that's why I don't have any," Veronica said smugly, and Olivia laughed. "I guess we both got lucky on that," she said with a grin, but she was worried about her sister.

The afternoon drifted by. Veronica went for a walk with Olivia

Felicia's Favorites

rolling beside her. They'd gone to find Isabelle in her room before they went out and she was sound asleep on her bed.

"Poor thing," Olivia whispered, as they closed the door softly and left for their walk.

By the time they got back it was dark outside, and Quinne arrived, happy to see them. Isabelle was awake by then, and had come downstairs looking better. She had called the sitter and the children were fine. And Quinne was excited to see them.

Olivia put the chickens in the oven and Isabelle set a pretty table for them. Charlotte arrived while they were all talking and laughing in the kitchen. She smiled when she saw them.

"Mom would love this, wouldn't she?" They all agreed as she opened the wine she'd brought and handed each of them a glass. "I've been looking forward to this for weeks," she said, and they wandered into the library and made themselves comfortable on the chairs and an ottoman, and the couch facing the fire. They were quiet for a minute, thinking about their mother, paying silent tribute to her, and Charlotte spoke with a sigh. "If Mom were here, I'd be arguing with her. I was such an idiot with her. I hated admitting it when she was right. And she always was, dammit, or most of the time." She wondered what Felicia would think of her budding friendship with Andy, and had a feeling she would like it. It was nice knowing that. She had had to reach the age of forty-two, and her mother had to die, in order for Charlotte to understand that what motivated Felicia more than anything was wanting them to be happy, and she had devoted her life to that.

They had all noticed that Charlotte seemed more relaxed and happier than she had been in a long time. She didn't have any wars to report. She wasn't furious with anyone, wasn't angry at an employee or a friend, and said that Julia had been adorable ever since their trip to Paris. They had turned a corner in their relationship and Julia was a pleasure to be with at the moment. And Charlotte had been on good terms with Sean when he went back to college.

Olivia and Veronica finished preparing the dinner, and Veronica told them about her classes at Columbia. She looked excited and happy when she talked about them, and Charlotte looked at her questioningly.

"How does Anson feel about that?" she asked her, and Veronica paused before she answered.

"He's not happy about it." She didn't want to lie to her sisters.

"Maybe he feels threatened by it," Quinne suggested.

"I think so." Veronica sighed.

"Have you told him why you're taking the classes?" Olivia asked her. "Because of Mom's books, and the contracts we'll have to approve. You're already a lawyer. You can translate them to us so we understand them."

"I haven't gone into detail," Veronica admitted. "I haven't told him about the Morgan Reed books. He still thinks she just edited them, not that she wrote them. I said that I wanted to understand her contracts better, but he has no idea the magnitude of her career. It's a lot to tell him all at once."

"Have you told him about the farm?" Charlotte asked then, and Veronica sighed again.

"Yes, and no. I said that we had inherited a farm, after I spent New Year's here, but he has no idea that it's an estate like this one. He thinks it's some dumpy little farmhouse she left us."

Felicia's Favorites

"It sounds like you've left a lot out," Charlotte said quietly.

"I know. He's used to having me available all the time, with nothing else to do. Now, I'm back at school, even if it's only two mornings a week. But I have homework and papers to write, or I will, and he's hearing about contracts, and a farm. I think he's feeling neglected, or afraid he will be if I get too busy."

"And how many hours does he spend with you every week?" Charlotte said with a critical edge to her voice that sounded like her old persona, not her mellower, more recent one.

"It depends how busy he is," Veronica said in a subdued voice. "That's always been our deal. He sees me when he can. But he was the busy one with a big life, I wasn't. Knowing that we've inherited all this, and Mom's body of work and the responsibilities that will go with it, is going to be a lot for him to stomach."

"It will relieve him of financial responsibility for you," Charlotte said, "if you tell him about it."

"He's never complained about that," Veronica responded.

"Maybe not, but it's a trade-off. If he pays all your bills, he may think he owns you, or has a right to all of your time and attention. And if you can pay for your own now, that changes the dynamic between you. He may feel he's losing his hold on you." Charlotte pursued the thought and had hit the nail on the head. "It sounds like it's all about control," she concluded, and Veronica knew she wasn't wrong.

"That's why I haven't told him all of it. I'm trying to let him know gently, not all at once."

"I'm glad I'm not in your shoes," Charlotte said honestly, "having to massage a man's ego, to make him feel important at your expense. The bigger he is, or thinks he is, the smaller you have to be. If you're honest with him about your new circumstances, he'll feel diminished and is liable to get pissed at you." Charlotte understood perfectly where the reefs were under the surface of the water, and what Veronica was dealing with in her relationship with Anson. Charlotte wondered how much Anson would put up with, and how much control over Veronica he was willing to lose. Charlotte suspected not much, and wondered if that was what Veronica was worried about, and if she was afraid to lose him. Charlotte had never thought it was a healthy relationship for her sister, just as their mother hadn't. Veronica had to have no needs or demands at all in order to make the relationship acceptable to Anson, except the needs he sanctioned, like expensive clothes, which he didn't mind. But it was obvious that he didn't want her to have a life of her own. At thirty-six, she wanted more of a life than just waiting for him to show up when it suited him. It sounded like a bad deal to Charlotte, and even to some of the others. They were less judgmental and critical than Charlotte, who was very protective of Veronica, as their mother had been. Veronica's relationship with Anson was the one subject Charlotte and their mother had agreed on.

Quinne told them about the preproduction meetings for the series based on their mother's book. There were some very big names on the short list for the cast. She said it was very exciting working for a big budget production. She had spoken to Scott about it several times, and Robert. Veronica didn't volunteer that she had met with Scott too, and they'd gone out for drinks. She didn't want the others to know.

"Now that our lives have changed radically, I really want to start my own production company," Quinne told them, as they cleared the table from the main course. The chickens Olivia had roasted were delicious. "Scott is going to help me set it up," Quinne said. It was a huge step for her.

They had gotten to dessert and a local apple pie with vanilla ice cream when Isabelle finally spoke up. She had said very little all evening, and the conversation had been lively about Veronica, and then Quinne's plans to start a production company of her own, with a small part of her inheritance. She could afford to now, and the prospect was exciting. She hoped she could get more of their mother's books onto the screen.

"Ian moved out," Isabelle said in a soft voice, and everyone stopped talking and looked at her. It explained how tired and disheveled she looked. She wasn't at her usual chic best, and they had all noticed it. She looked unhealthy and unkempt, and seemed disoriented, which wasn't like her.

"Where did he move to?" Olivia asked her gently, as Veronica held her hand, and tears swam in Isabelle's eyes as she fought to keep her voice steady.

"I don't know. Probably in with the girl he's involved with. He hasn't told me, but that's the obvious choice. I can reach him on his cellphone. He says he loves both of us, and she's like a drug to him. He wants our marriage, just not now."

"And what did you say?" Charlotte asked pointedly. She hated Ian for the pain she could see Isabelle was going through because of him.

"That he can't have both of us and has to decide, so he moved out. The kids don't know. They think he's on a business trip. But they can't believe that forever."

"What a fool he is," Charlotte said angrily, "and a bastard to you." She had been there herself and knew how painful it was. "Would you take him back now?"

"Yes, if he gives her up. It doesn't seem like he's going to," Isabelle said, as the tears spilled out of her eyes and rolled down her cheeks. "It's a mess at the moment. I didn't expect him to refuse to give her up." She wiped her eyes with her napkin and took a breath. "I just have to deal with it as it comes. I've been having a hard time since he left. It's difficult dealing with the kids and keeping up a happy front."

"I'm sorry," Quinne and Olivia said in unison, and Veronica was still holding her hand. Charlotte was furious at Ian, just thinking about it. She'd been through the same thing with Adam over and over again. But Isabelle wasn't bitter, she looked beaten to a pulp, and they all hated to see it.

"I almost didn't come this weekend, I was such a mess, but I didn't want to miss being with you guys, so I came," she said, smiling at her sisters through her tears. By the end of dinner, they were all talking animatedly to Isabelle, offering their advice, and their support. She looked better by then, more alive and less ravaged, and grateful for their kindness and attention.

To lighten the mood, before they got up from dinner, Quinne asked who had done their homework and they all looked blank.

"I assigned you each twenty-one of Mom's books to read. Isabelle only had to read ten, and Veronica promised to read thirty to make up for it. So? What did you read since we last saw each other?"

Charlotte groaned at the question. "I've been so busy at the office, and I've been working on Julia's exams with her. She had finals. I'm sorry, I didn't read anything."

"Neither did I," Isabelle confessed.

"You're excused," Quinne said immediately with a warm glance in her direction. "You're exempt at the moment."

"I read one," Veronica said, "and I brought two with me."

"Two. And I want to have a baby," Olivia said, and they all stared at her, shocked by the statement.

"You want to adopt?" Quinne asked her. All attention was on her now.

"I don't know. Maybe. I've been thinking about it a lot lately, ever since Mom died. I suddenly realized that I don't want to be alone for the rest of my life, and be old and have no kids. We were Mom's greatest joy, maybe other than Spencer. But we're all here, still loving her, and keeping her memory alive. Think how sad it would be if she had no kids." They were all quiet, thinking about it, and realized that she was right. "After the accident, they said I could still have children, but I never asked about it. I didn't want any, and there's been no man in my life."

"Is there now?" Charlotte asked her, surprised. They seemed to be a family of deep secrets these days. Anything was possible. Olivia lived alone, and might have had a man in her life they didn't know about.

"No," she answered the question. "I don't know that I need one.

I could adopt, or have a sperm donor if I'm physically capable of having a child, or an egg donor and a surrogate. I don't know what's possible. But I'm thirty-seven, and Mom's dying woke me up. I want a baby. And I think I could manage it on my own, with a sitter or a nanny." She sounded serious about it, and they were all stunned. It was a major announcement, and it touched them all deeply.

"Have you seen a doctor?" Isabelle asked, and Olivia shook her head.

"I haven't checked it out. I wanted to tell you first," she said to the group.

"You're braver than I am," Quinne said. "When I listen to what some of you have been through, and think about what Mom must have gone through raising us alone, it would scare the hell out of me to have a child. I've spent the last ten years trying to decide if I should get a dog, and I haven't gotten there yet," she said, and they all laughed. Quinne had been afraid of responsibility and commitment for all of her adult life.

"I think it's an amazing idea," Charlotte said to Olivia, impressed.

"So do I," Isabelle added. "Even with everything falling apart with Ian, my kids are the best thing in my life, and all of you. I think you would be a great mother," she said to Olivia.

"I agree with Quinne," Veronica commented. "Kids scare me to death. But if you think you can manage it, I'm behind you a hundred percent. I'll do whatever I can to help. I don't want to be a mom, but I love being an aunt!"

Felicia's Favorites

They were still talking about it after dinner, the idea of Olivia wanting a baby. It had taken all of them by surprise, and Quinne sat down quietly next to Olivia while the others were talking, and cautiously brought up a subject, not wanting to upset Olivia.

"Have you had any contact with François Vernier?" she asked in a voice no one else could hear, sitting very close to Olivia's chair. He was the choreographer Olivia had been engaged to and madly in love with when she had the accident. She had broken off the engagement so as not to be a burden to him, although he had still wanted to marry her.

"Not in a very long time," Olivia answered quietly. "Five or six years." It had been twelve since the accident. "I know he married about five years ago. He wrote to tell me."

"Maybe you should talk to him," Quinne said thoughtfully.

"And ask him to father a baby? He's married, Quinne. It's been over between us for a long, long time. I hope he's happily married. He married a famous ballerina. He choreographed several ballets for her. That's where he belongs."

"If he married her five years ago, he waited seven years for you. Maybe they're not even together anymore."

"I hope they are. It's over for us."

"You should get in touch with him," Quinne said with a determined look, and went to get another glass of wine. She was alone with her sisters that night. Cooper was coming out the next day to be at the birthday dinner, but Quinne had wanted to spend one night with just her sisters, and she was glad she had. They all had important private things to talk about.

Charlotte slipped away to make a call while the others were talking after dinner. Andy answered on the second ring, as soon as he saw her name and number come up on his phone.

"Hello, Charlotte, how is the sisters' weekend going?" He was happy to hear from her, and he liked knowing she was nearby.

"It's been interesting, everyone seems to have something serious going on at the moment. Do you want to go for a walk?" she suggested, and he was surprised.

"Now? Sure. I'll meet you up there in a few minutes."

"I don't mind walking down to you. I need some air. Listening to them all talking really made me miss my mother. She should be here giving them advice. I don't know that I have any of the right answers for them. I made so many of my own mistakes."

"That just makes you wiser and more human. Don't be so hard on yourself," Andy said gently.

"I'll walk down to meet you," Charlotte said, happy to hear his voice. He was an empathetic person.

"I don't want you walking alone in the dark. I'll ride my bike up to meet you."

"Do you want to come in for a drink?" It was cold outside.

"I don't want to intrude on your sisters. It sounds like you're having important girl time."

"Will you come to dinner tomorrow night? My sister Quinne's boyfriend is coming, he'll be happy to have some male company," and they were all comfortable with Andy. He felt like family now.

"If you're sure it's not an imposition, I'd love it. See you in a minute. I'll meet you outside your front door." She kept an eye out for him at a front window, grabbed her jacket, and slipped out the door when she saw him arrive on his bike. They walked down the drive, with her hand tucked into his arm, while Andy held a flashlight for them.

"My sister who's paraplegic told us tonight she wants to have a baby, if it's possible."

"Does she have a boyfriend?"

"No. She was engaged when it happened, and broke it off so as not to be a weight on him. He wanted to marry her anyway, but she was adamant. He's married now, he's a choreographer. She's never had another man in her life since the accident. She's very independent and lives alone. I think she probably could manage a child, with some help at home. She teaches ballet and designs costumes and scenery for a small ballet company and she's involved in a bunch of charities."

"She sounds like an enterprising woman." Andy smiled at Charlotte in the dark. "You all are. You're a very impressive group. Strong, independent women. And beautiful."

"We're not all independent. One of my sisters sounds like she's being held captive by a control freak. She gave up her law career for him. She and my mother had terrible fights about it. But she claims she's happy and she loves him. Their relationship sounds like a prison sentence to me." But most relationships looked that way to her now. Andy was the first man she'd met in ages who genuinely appealed to her. She felt safe with him and could be herself. He felt the same way about her.

Charlotte went back to the house half an hour later, and he rode home on his bike. He had left his bicycle under a tree while he walked with her. It was nice to be with him after the confessions of the night, about Anson and Ian and troubled relationships. Seeing Isabelle's grief broke her heart to watch.

"Where did you go?" Quinne asked her when she saw her come in. Charlotte's cheeks were bright red from the cold, and she was smiling.

"I went for a walk with a friend," Charlotte said with a peaceful expression.

"I think I can guess who that is." Andy was the only man they knew there.

"He's coming to dinner tomorrow night if that's okay with all of you."

"Coop will be relieved," Quinne answered her. "He was a little nervous about joining our hen party and being the only man here."

"As well he should be," Charlotte said, and laughed. "Although Andy seems to have a calming effect on me." She had been happy and mellower ever since she'd met him.

"I've noticed," Quinne said, and they went back to the others. No one else had noticed Charlotte's absence. They thought she had gone to her room for something.

It was two in the morning by the time they all went upstairs to bed, and Olivia slept in the ground-floor guest room. They all liked the rooms they had chosen to stay in since they first saw the house. It was as though Felicia had set up the house knowing they would be there one day. The rooms were all decorated in soft pastels and soothing colors. The farmhouse was a place to find peace, and they all commented the next morning on how well they had slept. Isabelle looked like a new person when she came downstairs and ate a hearty breakfast. And afterward they all went on a long walk together around the lake. It was their mother's actual birthday, which had a certain magic to it.

They spent a relaxed, easy day. Coop arrived from the city after lunch, and Andy came to dinner. The two men got along well, and it was obvious that Andy was seriously smitten with Charlotte. He sat next to her at dinner, and they were deep in conversation all night.

"I think you've gotten yourself a really good guy this time," Quinne commented to her the next day before they left. Charlotte smiled mysteriously when she said it.

"I have to admit, he seems pretty special. He's sensible and kind and smart, and we have fun together. It's still early days. He can still turn out to be a serial killer or an asshole, but so far everything checks out right."

"Give him a chance, Char. There are good men out there, you just haven't met the right one yet," Quinne said. And she hadn't tried in a long time. Charlotte was deeply engaged in her business and had insisted it was enough for her. But all of a sudden it wasn't. When she was with Andy, everything felt right. She wondered if her mother had felt that way about his father. It was deeply satisfying being with a good man who shared the same values and common interests. It was so easy, like floating or flying.

Before they left the farmhouse on Sunday, Isabelle, Olivia, and Veronica agreed to meet at their mother's apartment in the city the next day. They had to start cleaning it out. They were going to send all her books and antiques to the farmhouse, where the sisters could divide it up. And they would send photographs to Quinne and Charlotte from the apartment by text to help make decisions. The apartment was rented, Felicia hadn't owned it, and they wanted to give it up. They knew it would make them sad to take it apart, but it had to be done. Felicia had been gone for almost three months, and they hadn't had the heart to do it. They agreed to meet the next day.

They hugged each other before they left. The weekend had been a warm, comforting way to spend their mother's birthday, and it had helped all five of them to be together. It was the first birthday without her, and it had been a gentle way to get through it.

Veronica drove Olivia back to the city, and she talked about the baby again.

"Do you think you'll really do it?" Veronica asked her. Olivia's announcement on Friday night had surprised them all.

"I'd like to talk to a doctor and see what's possible. If I can't carry it myself, I think I might like to adopt, or use a surrogate, I just don't know yet, but it's been gnawing at me for about a year, and when Mom died, I really knew it's what I want."

"Do you ever hear from François?" Veronica asked her hesitantly, and Olivia smiled.

"Quinne asked me the same thing the other night. No, I don't, and the poor guy is married. I can't call him and ask if he'd like to father a child, and would his wife mind. And even if he weren't married, I wouldn't. We agreed to close that door forever. It was only fair to him."

"As I recall, he didn't agree about that. He tried to come back for a long time, and you wouldn't let him." Olivia looked out the window, remembering. Losing him had been the worst part of the accident. Or leaving him. He had tried for years to get her back, and

Felicia's Favorites

Olivia never relented. She refused to saddle him with her limitations and be a burden to him. He needed to be with a dancer, and now he was. It was right.

"No, I wouldn't let him come back when he tried," Olivia said softly, thinking back to that time. They were painful memories she didn't want to relive now. She had made a decision to move ahead without looking back, and she had stuck to it for the past twelve years. "It was the right decision. I'm sure he's happy now," she said, and turned on the radio so they didn't have to talk. François was a closed book in her mind, a beautiful love story that had ended.

Veronica dropped her off at her building when they got back to the city, and the doorman took her bag.

"I'll see you at Mom's apartment tomorrow," she said, and Olivia smiled and waved as Veronica drove away.

She drove to her own apartment, not far from Olivia's, and gave the doorman her car to take to the garage. She was in no rush to get home since she knew that Anson had meetings in Washington, D.C., in the morning, and wouldn't be home until Monday night.

She let herself into the apartment, and saw that the lights were on in the living room, which seemed strange. She wondered if the housekeeper had come in over the weekend and had forgotten to turn them off, and then she saw him, sitting stone-faced on the couch. He looked almost like a statue. He didn't say a word and she jumped when she saw him.

"Anson! What are you doing here? I thought you weren't coming home till tomorrow."

"And I thought you'd be here. My meeting tomorrow got canceled. I've been here for four hours, waiting for you." She saw that he had a full glass of Scotch in his hand, and she wondered how many he'd had in four hours, but he had a high tolerance for alcohol. His gaze on her was glacial.

"I'm sorry. Why didn't you call me and tell me?"

"That's not part of the deal, is it? Or it never was before. I don't have to advise you of my whereabouts or my plans. You're supposed to be here whenever I come, waiting for me."

"I told you I was seeing my sisters this weekend. It was my mother's birthday and we wanted to spend it together."

"At the 'farm' you inherited or whatever shack she left you. You seem to be spending a lot of time with your sisters these days," he said icily, "if that's true." Anson looked at Veronica suspiciously and didn't believe her.

"It's been a hard adjustment." She walked over to him and tried to kiss his cheek and he wouldn't let her, turning his head away. "I'm sorry, I really am. It would have been a terrible weekend here alone."

"You wouldn't have been alone if you'd been here today." He stood up then, and reached for his coat.

"Don't leave. I'm really sorry. It won't happen again."

"No, it won't. You're playing with fire, Veronica, and you know it. Are you cheating on me?" He got right to the point.

"Of course not. My mother died and I've been seeing a lot of my sisters. We've all had a hard time with her death."

"So you've signed up at law school, you're never here, and now you own some ramshackle farm with your sisters, and you're not here when I want you. What part of that is supposed to work for me?"

"I don't know what to say. I'm very sorry I wasn't here today." She looked crushed as she watched him leave. She had failed him.

"That doesn't explain the classes at Columbia or weekends out of town. Your life can change in an instant if I want it to. You might want to keep that in mind," Anson said, putting on his coat and walking to the door. He turned to look at her once and she realized that she was shaking. He had threatened her. She didn't want to lose him, and he was a hard man if he wanted to be, or thought he had been betrayed. She had no idea when she'd see him again. She never knew, and she could sense that he was going to make her pay dearly for the hours she had kept him waiting. She felt sick after he left, wondering what he would do to punish her. And she had no doubt that he would. His silences and absences were punishment enough without threats. Veronica suddenly felt as though she had grown wings that were too large for the small space that he had allotted her. She had crossed a line for him, and she had the sick feeling that there was no turning back to the way things had been before. She had grown bigger since her mother's death, and Anson was not going to tolerate it.

Chapter 9

Robert Farr called Quinne on Monday morning. She had been confirmed as one of the executive producers of the show, and they were offering Cooper an audition for the part they had for him. It was big news for Quinne and Coop, and they were ecstatic at the news. Quinne called the others to tell them, and they were happy for her.

She reached all of her sisters except Olivia, who was at a doctor's appointment and couldn't pick up.

She was having a sonogram that morning, and a pelvic exam by her gynecologist afterward, and the doctor told her that as far as she could see structurally, there was no reason why she couldn't conceive and have a healthy pregnancy. They had taken blood to check her hormone levels. She was thirty-seven, so her age could be an issue.

"If we have any doubts, we can run tests using dye to check your fallopian tubes, but your periods are regular and you have a very straightforward gynecological history. Do you have a sperm donor in mind? If your numbers are good, we can still use your eggs. Or if we need to, we can use a donor egg. Yours should be fine, if your hormone levels are in normal range."

"I don't have a sperm donor yet," Olivia said, trying not to get too excited, but it was all good news so far. And her thought of having a baby suddenly seemed real.

"The trauma from the accident affected your spinal cord, but not your reproductive organs." The doctor wrote down the name of the sperm bank she recommended and preferred to work with, and handed Olivia the paper with the name. "You should be able to carry a baby to term without a problem. I assume you'll have help with the baby."

"Of course."

"We won't need to do IVF, in vitro fertilization, if your hormone levels are in normal range. In that case, we would do IUI, intra-uterine insemination, which is much simpler. We can use IUI fertilization, it's an easy process, and if your hormone levels are good, there won't be hormones involved. It's a simple procedure. Let us know when you want to get started. You should have a baby in your arms within a year." She smiled at Olivia, who left a few minutes later, feeling excited and hopeful. She took a cab to her mother's apartment, where Veronica and Isabelle were waiting for her. They had already gotten started taking their mother's clothes out of the closet, and Olivia's heart ached when she saw familiar things she recognized. She saw the dress her mother had been wearing the last time she saw her alive, which brought tears to her eyes.

"Sorry I'm late. I had an appointment."

"No worries," Isabelle said. She looked better after the weekend than she had when she arrived at the farm, and she'd had a nice evening with the children the night before.

"Was everything okay when you got home?" Olivia asked Veronica, as they continued to take clothes out of the closet and lay them on the bed.

"Anson had been waiting for me for four hours. He wasn't pleased. He came back early from D.C. I told him I was with you all weekend, and he asked me if I've been cheating on him. I think he's suspicious about the farm and why we keep going there."

"Why don't you take him to see it?" Isabelle suggested, and it was hard for Veronica to explain why she didn't think it was a good idea. It was much bigger and more substantial than he expected, and Veronica still hadn't told him about the inheritance and all that their mother had left them. Veronica had the feeling that he would be threatened by the fortune she had been left as her share. In some ways, it changed the balance of power between them. He had sensed it, but he didn't know for sure. Seeing the property in Connecticut put Veronica in a whole different league in his eyes. He wanted her dependent on him and what he gave her, not independently wealthy. She didn't want to explain it to her sisters. There was nothing equal about her relationship with Anson. All the power was in his hands, not evenly divided between them. This relationship had never been equal.

It was a painful process packing their mother's things into boxes. Her papers were all in good order. She had neat stacks of manuscripts in file cabinets in her well-organized office. It was a small apartment in perfect order, and many of her papers were at the farm, where she had a large storeroom full of file cabinets. What she had at the apartment were mostly old manuscripts and documents, and albums of her daughters' childhood, and a mountain of books. There were framed photographs of the family on every surface, and Olivia wrapped them carefully to send to the farm. Felicia's more valuable paintings were at the farm, but there were some others that were sentimental for the sisters. The kitchen equipment was old and they decided to donate it. The decisions were easy, but the emotions were raw. They were glad they were doing it together, and it was strange now to see the apartment where they had visited Felicia. It looked tiny compared to the farm. The apartment was such a small piece of her life, but all they had known as her home while she was alive.

They finished in a day, and had divided everything between donations and cartons marked for the farm, and some specific boxes marked for each of them, with their childhood photo albums. They texted photographs to Quinne and Charlotte of things they weren't sure about, some lamps, a number of Baccarat vases since Felicia had always had fresh flowers around the apartment. It went faster than expected with three of them working. They kept some of her dresses and coats, but donated most of her clothes. They were finished by four o'clock. It was an entire life divided into some boxes, and they were quiet when they left. It was a sad task, but it had to be done, and they notified the building that the apartment would be vacant by the end of the week. They left together, and took separate cabs to their homes.

Veronica had kept her cellphone in her pocket all day in case Anson called her, but he didn't. She guessed she wouldn't hear from him for a while, after not being there the day before, which he considered a capital offense. Her cellphone rang as she walked into her apartment. But it wasn't Anson, it was Scott Freeman. She was surprised to hear from him.

"How are the classes going?" he asked her.

"Great. I'm getting decent grades so far."

"I'm not surprised. I've got the signature copies of the streaming contract from Robert. Would you like to go over them with me? It might be a good exercise for you. They've added some interesting clauses. Or I can just send them to you, if you don't have time." But it sounded like fun to look at the contract with him, and Veronica responded spontaneously.

"I'd like that."

"Do you want to come to the office tomorrow? We could have lunch, and check the contract then."

"Sure." She said she'd meet Scott at his office, and as soon as she hung up, she realized that if Anson called her or showed up, he wouldn't like her going over contracts with Scott, but she wanted to learn what complex contracts like that looked like. She felt torn, and she didn't want to risk angering Anson again. She thought about canceling the appointment, but she didn't want to, and the next morning she told herself that it wasn't a big deal, and Anson was busy at the office and unlikely to show up for lunch because he was still punishing her. She wore slacks and a red sweater and a matching red coat, and boots, and appeared at Scott's office on time. He was wearing a suit and tie, and had her sit next to him at his desk to go over the key points in the contract that he wanted to show her. He leaned close to her while they worked, and it was fun going over the contracts with him. He showed her what to look out for and where they could get tricky. They worked for an hour, and then he stood up and she walked around his desk. He had noticed her perfume again when he sat next to her, and he had to force himself to concentrate on the documents. He could feel an electric current pass between them. Something happened every time he was near her, and he was pretending not to notice, but as she tucked her hand into his arm and they walked to the restaurant nearby, he was excited to be with her.

He talked about his family at lunch and made her laugh. He was from L.A. and had gone to UCLA, and to law school at NYU, and stayed in New York after that. He was twelve years older than she was and didn't look it. He was boyish and athletic, and they discovered that they were both avid skiers and loved to play tennis. He had to keep reminding himself that it wasn't a date, she was a client and had a serious boyfriend, but somehow it didn't matter, he was so attracted to her that he had to keep telling himself that the best that could ever happen would be that they could be friends. He talked about her mother and how much he had liked and admired her, and how proud she was that Veronica was a lawyer and had graduated magna cum laude.

"And then I threw it all away," she interrupted him. "It took her a long time to forgive me. She was furious."

"Why did you give it up?" He was curious and wanted to know everything about her.

"I had to. The man I was in love with wanted me to. It was either him or the law firm. I was twenty-six years old and madly in love with him. I thought it was the right decision. My mother didn't. She was right, I guess. But things look different at thirty-six than they do at twenty-six. I'm trying to make up for it now, putting my toe in the water with my mother's contracts. I love being back at Columbia, it's fun going to school and challenging my brain again."

"It's a very good legal brain," he complimented her. "You should hang onto it." Scott wanted to see more of her, but there was no way he could. The contract he had shown her was a very thin excuse. He had the feeling that her boyfriend or lover or whatever he was had a death grip on her, and she followed the rules he set for her, out of either respect or fear. Giving up her career for him had been a major sacrifice and he could easily understand why Felicia had been upset. He would have been too.

Veronica was wonderful to be with but he could sense the walls she had around her, and Scott wasn't sure if they had been built by love or a desire to control her, or maybe both.

The lunch ended too quickly and with it his excuse to see her. She called an Uber at the end of lunch and left a few minutes later, and he felt bereft after she was gone. He had never been as intrigued by any woman as he was by her.

Anson hadn't called her while she was with him, and there was no sign of him at the apartment, and she was relieved. She had been worried about it at lunch, but Scott was so much fun and so easy to talk to that she had stopped worrying about Anson, and just enjoyed Scott. She would have liked to see more of him, and even be friends, but she knew that there was no way she could. He was another sacrifice she had to make for Anson. She wasn't going to jeopardize her relationship with Anson and the life he provided her for a man she barely knew, no matter how attractive he was. There was something fascinating and exciting about Scott. She loved his enthusiasm and his energy. Anson was much more serious, more intense, and demanded her full attention. Scott was so much more lighthearted about everything. He made it fun to be with him. She wondered if it was because he was younger than Anson, or if it was just his personality. There was a dark side to Anson, while Scott was all light and kindness.

She had homework to do after that, and spent the rest of the day studying, into the evening. Anson didn't show up, and she got her assignment done for school.

She dreamt of both men that night. They were fighting over her, and fought a duel with pistols. She heard a shot ring out in her dream, and she couldn't tell who had won, and she woke up before she found out. It was an interesting symbolism, and she lay awake for a long time afterward thinking about Scott, and knowing she shouldn't. It was the first time in ten years that she had been attracted to another man, and she wasn't going to give into it. She felt that same electric current every time she saw him, but that was all it was, a current, a spark, and nothing more. There was nothing she could do about it. Sooner or later she would have to see him again. He had mentioned that he was helping Quinne set up her production house, and he had been their mother's attorney and Veronica would have to go over new contracts with him. She felt as though she was being pulled toward him by forces beyond her control that she didn't understand.

Felicia's Favorites

* * *

Andy and Charlotte's relationship was deepening steadily, and they were both enjoying it. He came to the city to see her and take her to dinner. They went to another hockey game. And she took him to an opening at a gallery she'd been invited to. He had met Julia several times, and they got along, which was unusual for Julia since she usually hated her mother's dates, but Julia was his biggest fan, and put in a good word for him whenever she could. Charlotte didn't need any encouragement, she genuinely liked him. And Julia reported his appearances to Sean, who was intrigued too. Charlotte hadn't had a serious boyfriend as long as they could remember, so Andy seemed significant.

Charlotte's sisters were wondering about it too, but didn't want to ask, and spoil anything. She seemed much more lighthearted these days. She wasn't taking things as seriously, and never said anything bad about Andy, a first for her in the last decade. Charlotte and Andy had dinner with Quinne and Cooper one night, and Olivia asked Quinne about it afterward.

"Do you think she's in love with him?" Olivia asked her, intrigued.

"For normal people, I'd say yes, but you never know with Charlotte. She's avoided serious relationships for a long time. But they seem to enjoy each other." Charlotte was busy with work and her daughter. She had a full life, and she had stopped mentioning Andy to her sisters. She didn't want to encourage them or feed the rumor mill. She wasn't sure herself what was happening, where the relationship was going, or what she wanted. Andy sensed that about her, and didn't want to rush her, or spoil anything, so they found fun things to do when he came to the city, going to the movies and to the theater to a play they both loved, and they went ice skating. They couldn't seem to stay away from each other. He stayed in the city for a weekend when it snowed and they had a snowball fight. They were like two kids together, fun and lighthearted, and he let her read the manuscript of the book he had just finished, and she loved it. And she was reading her mother's books on the list Quinne had given her. They were beautifully written, challenging and intricate, and she could never guess the endings. She was in awe of her mother's skill and couldn't tell her now.

"She was a brilliant writer," Andy confirmed when Charlotte mentioned her books to him.

"I never read them because I thought she only edited them. I wish she had told us about the books when she was alive," Charlotte said wistfully over dinner.

"I don't think she ever told anyone except my father," he said seriously. "They had something very special together, and it just seemed to get better with time."

"We never really knew her," Charlotte said. It was her greatest regret. "We know more about her now than we did when she was alive." She could hear her mother's voice in the cadence of the books, and she loved that. It was like hearing her mother read the books to her, as when she read to them as children.

Charlotte hadn't been back to the farm since her mother's birthday, and neither had the others. They were busy with their own lives. Isabelle was trying to take care of her children, still pretending that Ian was away. They hadn't seen each other since he moved out, and didn't want to get together. They communicated by text, which Charlotte thought was pathetic when Isabelle told her. She assumed that he hadn't given up the girl yet, or he'd be pursuing Isabelle. He was buying time, and Isabelle was adjusting and looking better. She had a healthy glow to her cheeks again, and her eyes were bright and alive when Charlotte saw her.

Veronica was engaged with school and none of them had seen her since they emptied their mother's apartment after the birthday weekend. They all had lives and problems to deal with and were trying to adjust to the windfall they'd inherited. Quinne was working on the series, attending preproduction meetings, and trying to start her production company. Olivia was teaching her classes, and the others wondered if she had made any decision about a baby, but she hadn't said anything about it again and they didn't want to ask. The weather had been harsh, so none of them had gone to the farm. They knew it was there if they wanted to go, but none of them had time.

Charlotte was the first one to go back, when Andy invited her to spend Valentine's weekend at the farm, since Julia was planning to spend the weekend with friends. Charlotte had avoided getting any deeper into the relationship with Andy. They'd been having a great time, but she was leery of a bigger commitment, and didn't want to make a mistake and fall head over heels in love with someone who'd be leaving in a few months anyway. When his father came back from London, Andy was going back to Aspen. She'd had all the flings she wanted in one lifetime. But he was hard to avoid because she enjoyed him so much. She had tried to slow things down, and being with him on the Valentine weekend was the opposite of what she was trying to do. But it was so tempting that she finally decided to accept, and told herself she could handle it. She'd be staying in her own house, and he in his, and as long as they stayed sane and relatively sober, she thought they could stay out of bed, and just have a nice time together, as they had for the past two months. They hadn't known each other for long, but they had learned a lot about each other, and themselves, in the time they had spent doing fun things in New York. She relaxed and was happy with him, and he was wonderfully creative about dreaming up events for them to go to, places to see, and just having a good time together. Charlotte was more relaxed with him than she had been with anyone in a dozen years. She knew she was tempting fate by going to the farm on a weekend dedicated to romance, but they were both sensible adults and she thought she could manage it without misleading him and deluding herself that they had suddenly each met the love of their life at forty-two and forty-seven. She was trying to be reasonable and sane for both their sakes. Neither of them wanted to get hurt, and she was sure they wouldn't. She was looking forward to reading what Andy had been writing that week. She was thoroughly enjoying the rough drafts and manuscripts he let her read. She felt honored to be included in the process of his creative life, and they spent an equal amount of time talking about her business. Everything they did was fun, and she was trying not to be swept away by the illusion that it was a fairy tale or a dream come true.

She explained her theory about the weekend to Quinne before she went, and her sister laughed at her. "Oh, you are in big trouble here. You're trying to reason with your heart and convince him, me, and yourself that you're not falling in love with him. You're human, Charlotte, just like the rest of us. Flesh and blood and a beating heart. You love him and you're scared. That's normal, but thinking that you can go up there, be alone for two days, and not wind up in bed with him, and in love with him, which I think you already are, you're crazy if you think you can pull that off. Why don't you just let life happen, and let go of the controls for two days and see what happens. You deserve to be happy, Char, and so does he. Let him be your hero, if he wants to be, or your Prince Charming. He's a great guy and I think he loves you, and you finally found the one guy who I think won't hurt you or disappoint you. So go up there and have a good time, and if you fall in love with him, you'll be a happy woman."

"Don't be such a romantic," Charlotte scolded her, and sounded like the curmudgeon she used to be before she met him.

"Stop holding on so tight," Quinne told her.

"I'm not," Charlotte insisted.

"If you were holding on any tighter, your fingers would break," Quinne scolded her back. "Have a happy Valentine's Day, Charlotte. I'm giving you permission to be happy," she said, and they hung up a minute later, as Charlotte thought about what Quinne had said. Her words haunted her on the drive up to the farm. She got to the house and unlocked the front door with her key. It was five o'clock and Ellen had already gone home for the evening. Charlotte flipped on the lights when she walked in, and saw a huge vase of red roses in the front hall, another one when she walked into the living room, another one on the coffee table, and yet one more vase of roses in the library, and a big basket of red roses in the kitchen with a note. When she opened it, it said "Happy Valentine's Day, love, A." She smiled as she read it, he had outdone himself. It looked like a florist shop, and there was a path of rose petals all the way down the hall to her bedroom, where another vase of red roses was waiting for her, and another note from him. He had made it fun for her, like everything else he did. He was thoughtful and funny and kind. Ellen had been in on the rose secret. She loved the roses and he had pulled one out and handed it to her. It was turning into the most fun Valentine's Day Charlotte had ever had. She called to thank him for all the roses, smiling when he answered. He showed up a few minutes later with an enormous bouquet of red roses he handed her. It was excess delivered with charm and creativity and everything he felt for her, and had never felt before in his life. He put his arms around her and held her close to him, and as he did he chased all her fears and demons away. All her resolutions were forgotten, her reservations, her vow to herself not to fall in love with him or even sleep with him. He kissed her, and they were in bed five minutes later, making love just as Quinne had predicted would happen. Reason took a back seat to desire, and their lovemaking had all the passion of two people who had run from love for years. Now they were vulnerable and sincere, and Charlotte knew she loved him and would never find another man like him. He was the last of the good guys, and the first good man in her life, and she hoped he wouldn't break her heart, but there were no guarantees that it would turn out the way they wanted. They both took the chance, which was all it took to make love happen and sweep them both away to a magical place where only they existed. All she had to do was open the door and let love in. It had finally arrived in the person of Andy York, the best man she'd ever met, and in an odd way he was a final gift from her mother. They would never have met if he weren't the son of the man Felicia had loved. They fell asleep and woke up and made love again.

They spent the night together at her farmhouse, and it felt totally natural to be with him. They had dinner at midnight and went back to bed, talking and laughing and sharing secrets. They were the two happiest people in the world. Neither of them had ever felt that way before.

In her apartment in New York, Olivia had been staring at her computer for an hour and didn't know what to do. She finally wrote a brief email to François Vernier, asking him how he was. It was her way of putting a message into the universe. She had no idea if he'd even answer. She had told him she wanted no further contact with him and had meant it at the time. And maybe whether or not he responded didn't matter. She had finally taken the first step back into life. It had taken her twelve years to do it, but she had finally found the courage to take a chance, to reach out to someone she had loved greatly, and destiny had intervened cruelly. She couldn't be with him after the accident. It wouldn't have been fair to him. He deserved a whole woman who could dance his ballets and be an active woman beside him, not one in a wheelchair for the rest of his life. She couldn't be that person and condemn him to a life with someone like her. And now she was reaching out to him to say hello. She had been thinking about it for weeks after her sisters asked about him. He was a ghost from the past now, and so was she.

Ghosts didn't answer emails, and he probably wouldn't either. She imagined him happy with his wife, and possibly children by now, after five years of marriage. She didn't want to intrude in his life. She just wanted to peek through a window for a minute, and see him in his world. They had been perfectly synchronized, minutely in time with each other, like a ballet of their own. He had been a flawless dancer, technically and emotionally, and she had been the perfect match for him, floating in the air, totally in harmony with him.

The email to François was just a brief greeting, a flutter of wings from the past. It served no purpose except to communicate with him for an instant, their wings barely touching as they brushed past each other, wanting to know the answer to an unspoken question, if she still loved him, and if he loved her.

Chapter 10

"So what do we do now?" Andy asked Charlotte on Sunday morning. It had been an idyllic weekend, with most of it spent walking, sitting by the fire, and in bed.

"Should we pretend this never happened?" Charlotte asked him. Andy looked crestfallen when she said it. That was not the answer he wanted. He wanted to go on doing this forever. "You're leaving in a few months, aren't you?" she asked him. "When your father comes back. So it will end then anyway. You'll go back to Aspen, and I'll be here, in New York, starting a new business."

"Why can't we make both work? I'm flexible and can come to New York, maybe you can spend some time with me in Aspen, and I'm not married to Aspen, I can work here too. We've found something amazing, Charlotte. Are you really willing to give that up, hide from it, or avoid it because of geography?"

"It's not just about geography," she said seriously. "I've been hurt before, so have you undoubtedly. We didn't get to the age we are without making mistakes, picking the wrong people, and winding up with wounds and bruises. Are you willing to take a chance on that again? Is it worth it? Geography is the least of it. I have a ball with you. You make me happy. And then what? One or both of us get wounded and it's over."

"If something goes wrong and we're both decent people, which we are, we fix it. We don't just walk away because we might get bumped one day. That's why we're alone, both of us. I've been terrified for years of making another dumb mistake. I'm not afraid of you. Look at our parents, they were older than we are when they found each other, and it worked. It probably wasn't easy. Your mother was living some kind of crazy secret life, hiding how famous she was under a pseudonym, and my father is not an easy guy. He's a good man, smart and kind, but he has his complications too. And they were crazy about each other, and happy. I can tell you for certain, my father will never love another woman after your mother. She was perfect for him, and he knew it. I saw them together, you didn't, and they were happy. I want what they had. I want you, and I'm willing to work for it, and if I have to live in New York instead of Aspen, so what. I love you, Charlotte. Life has just given us an incredible gift, and I'm not willing to ignore it or shove it under the bed or put it in the trash. I'm not afraid of you, and you don't need to be afraid of me. I'm willing to fight for what we have, and I'm not going to sleep with you for a weekend, and walk off into the sunset to find someone else. I'm here for you. I love you, and maybe we'll be lucky and find the kind of magic our parents did. Don't you want that too?" he said, looking at her intently. What he said took her breath away. She didn't know a single man in her entire history who had said anything like it to her. "By the way," he added, "my father is coming to New York next week. He wants to meet you and your sisters." She smiled when he said it.

"I want to meet him too, we all do. Is he moving back?" She looked somewhat worried. Maybe Andy was leaving sooner than she thought.

"No, he has a meeting with Robert and his publisher. I think he wants to see me, and make sure I'm taking decent care of his house. And as I said, he wants to meet all of you. I offered to stay at a hotel but he wants me at the house with him. So what do you say, Char? Are we going to be brave?" He made it sound so appealing, and so easy to do, it made her want to say yes, but she wasn't sure. She didn't want to get hurt again if things went wrong. "A monthly renewable contract? A daily one?" he said with a grin, and she leaned over and kissed him.

"I love you too, so shut up. We don't need a contract." She looked at him long and hard. "I'm in," she said softly. "You have the family vote, by the way. And Cooper, and everyone who knows you. I'm the difficult one here," she said.

"No, you're not. You've got some scars. We all do. And you've dealt with a lot. And losing your mother in an act of violence recently."

"And everything she left us," Charlotte added. "I'm still not used to it. I still worry about money, and then I remember that I have more than I'll need in my lifetime, even with a new business. I love this house now, especially since we've spent time here together."

"I need to get a new place in Aspen, if we're going to spend time there together. My house is barely big enough for me. I'll look around there one of these days. We're fine here for now." They were better than fine. They were happy. Andy was right. What they had was too good to throw away.

"Thank you," she said softly, and didn't want to leave him to go back to the city. But Julia was coming home that night from her friend's house. "I love you, Andy." He pulled her close with his arm around her.

"I love you too. Do you want to stay here tonight?"

"I have Mom duty. I should go back." She almost asked him to come with her, but she didn't want him staying at her apartment with Julia, yet. It was still too soon for that.

"I'll come to the city this week. See what works for you." She was suddenly sorry that they had given up her mother's apartment. He could have stayed there, and the rent was cheap. She didn't know anything about his finances, but his books were successful, and their sales had improved with each book. His father was one of the most successful writers in the country. He and Felicia had been an even match, in many things, just as Charlotte and Andy were. They were what Charlotte had always wanted, equal partners. It was a whole new style of relationship for her, and he said it was for him too.

They made love again before she left. Now that she had said she was "in," they both felt closer than ever. They had taken an important step. They were together because they were choosing to be. It was no longer a fortuitous accident. They meant it. Charlotte liked the feel of it.

Andy kissed her tenderly before she left, and she drove back to

Felicia's Favorites

the city, smiling most of the time. She had been terrified of making a commitment to Andy and their relationship, and now it felt completely right. She wondered if her mother had ever felt like that in the beginning. She would have liked to have her advice. Charlotte thought of all the times she had argued with Felicia about her opinions, and she realized now what a fool she had been. Her sisters had known better when they said that Felicia was almost always right. And Charlotte thought she would have approved of Andy. It gave her a good feeling, she was on the right side of things now, the smart side, the loving side, the side she shared with Andy. He was exactly what she had needed for so long. They didn't make the rules for each other, and neither of them wanted the upper hand. There was no boss. They were just two good people figuring things out as they went along, and so far it was working well. If they hit a rough patch or stumbled, they would figure it out and help each other, just as Andy said.

Veronica had a quiet weekend in the apartment. She had a lot of reading to do for school. She didn't want Anson to catch her doing it. She had a desk drawer half open where she could throw the book she was reading, if he walked in. The others she had with her were in the backpack she wore to school. There was so much he didn't know now. It worried her at times. He knew nothing of her inheritance. She still hadn't told him how famous her mother had been, and the additional income her writing generated now that they had sold one book for a series, and there would be more in the future if the current one was a success. Anson thought the farm was some kind of ramshackle old barn and maybe a cabin. He had no idea how beautiful and substantial her new Connecticut home was, that she shared with her sisters. Anson was handsome and charming, and he had supported her well for ten years. But she continued to suspect that he wouldn't like it if she had a fortune of her own and could support herself. She wanted to be with him now, but she didn't "need" him to pay her bills, only for emotional support. But his kindness to her was sporadic. Sometimes he was wonderful to her, and at other times he was cruel. She hadn't seen it as clearly in the beginning, but she did now. The demands and restrictions he put on her were controlling and abusive and demeaning to her.

She had almost finished her reading assignment when she heard his key in the lock. It was late Sunday afternoon, and normally, he didn't show up on weekends, unless he went to a party he hated and left and came to the apartment. Whether or not he spent the night depended on whether or not his wife was in town. Occasionally, he showed up on a Sunday night, but very rarely. But these days, she was being very careful not to ruffle his feathers. She had the impression that he was watching her closely and didn't trust her. There had been no friendly texts, warm messages, or surprise, loving phone calls. He showed up or he didn't, with no warning. And he didn't stay long. They had only made love a few times, and it was perfunctory and mechanical. He seemed to have lost interest in her. It was a slow deterioration over the last two months, ever since she had signed up for the class at Columbia, and had spent a weekend at the farm with her sisters. He had questioned her several times about whether she had met with Scott Freeman.

Felicia's Favorites

Anson didn't trust him either. He was treating Veronica like an enemy agent, or a woman he no longer had faith in. She didn't know how to stop the freefall their relationship seemed to be in, making it impossible to tell him anything about what she had discovered about her mother and the inheritance she had left.

Veronica slipped her textbook into the drawer and locked it when she heard his key in the door. She was wearing jeans and a Columbia sweatshirt since she didn't expect him.

"You look like a college student," he said with a smile when he walked in, and seemed in a better mood than she had seen him lately. She smiled too and walked over to put her arms around him to kiss him.

"Are you hungry, do you want something to eat?" He hadn't stayed for a meal with her for a month. He was always rushed and busy. They sat down in the living room after he helped himself to a drink.

"I'm having dinner with Anne and the kids at a restaurant. I had a spare hour so I thought I'd come by and see how you are. What's been happening to you lately?" he asked her. "You seem different, and I think you're keeping things from me." She hadn't expected him to confront her and she didn't know what to say. She didn't feel ready to make confessions that might upset him.

"Not really," she said in a gentle voice. "It's been a rough time since my mother, and we've had some things to sort out for her estate."

"What about this farmhouse she left you? What's with that?"

There was no avoiding his direct questions, so she answered him. "It turns out that she had done some writing none of us knew about, under a pseudonym, and she had saved some money, and left it to us. She'd bought a farmhouse in Connecticut. It's very old and a nice place. We didn't know about that either."

"And you want to spend time there?" he asked her, and she hesitated.

"Not necessarily. I want to be here for you."

"But you haven't been here much lately, have you, between school and the mysterious farmhouse. It sounds like your mother was a very secretive woman. You must have gotten that from her," he said, watching her closely, to see her reactions to what he said.

"Not really secretive. She was modest and very discreet. Humble, really. She didn't want any recognition for her writing." Veronica was grateful that he didn't ask the pseudonym Felicia wrote under. He didn't care.

"You've been different since the farmhouse came into your life."

"Maybe different since she died. It's been hard for all of us."

"I'm sorry about that. You seem more independent lately, as though you don't need me as much."

"Of course I need you. What I got from my mother has nothing to do with us. It doesn't change anything," she said soothingly, and moved a little closer to him on the couch, but he didn't respond, which scared her. It was Anson who was different and seemed very cold. She wondered why he had come to see her. He didn't kiss her, or seem interested in making love to her. Previously, he had wanted to have sex with her as soon as he saw her, now he didn't.

"How big is the inheritance?" he asked her bluntly, and Veronica didn't want to answer him. She was afraid it would change things between them.

Felicia's Favorites

"I don't know. They haven't figured it out yet," she said vaguely.

"Why don't you want to tell me, Veronica? Are you afraid I won't want to spend as much on you anymore?"

"Of course not. That's not why I'm here."

"Really? Isn't it? The lifestyle I give you is part of our arrangement. You had no income when you came to me, nothing, and I was happy to take care of everything. If your mother left you some money, I'm happy for you. It means you don't really need me anymore, do you, Veronica? You want to go back to law school, and spend weekends with your sisters. You inherited a home from your mother. That's all very nice for you. I don't want to just be your sugar daddy, and I do want you here, available for me all the time, and lately you haven't been. I think you're ready to move on, don't you?" He said it in a silky voice and she stared at him, shocked. He wanted her at his beck and call night and day, whenever he wanted. For sex, for an hour, for however long he wanted, at any time of his choosing. Veronica had never seen it that way, but he treated her like a hooker, a high-end call girl.

"I'm sorry I wasn't here, Anson, when you wanted me. It only happened one time."

"You were late another time," he corrected, "and you haven't told me how much you inherited." Seeing the steely look in his eyes, she wasn't going to tell him.

"I don't think that's an appropriate question. I don't know how much it is."

"I think you do. And I don't think it's appropriate for you to expect me to support your lifestyle when you have money of your own."

"I'm sorry, I should have offered to pay for rent or something, it's all been very new. I'm not used to it yet."

"And clothes and jewelry. I know every penny I've spent on you for the past ten years. It's a lot of money. I think you were worth every bit of it. So I don't want what I spent back from you, Veronica. You don't want to lead this life anymore. It's written all over you, so it's time for you to go, before it turns nasty and I start charging you for being here." He stood up with an icy look in his eyes as he looked down at her, sitting frozen on the couch, shocked by what he had said. "You're not suited to this life anymore, Veronica. It's over. You can keep the clothes, but leave the jewelry. The artwork and decorating stays. Be out by six P.M. tomorrow. My lawyer will pick the keys up from you at five. And that's it, I guess." She stared at him as ten years of her life evaporated in a puff of smoke. He had spelled it all out, and the way he did it suggested that he had made the same speech before. She had lasted longer than most of the women in his life, except his wife. He had told her that before. "You signed a confidentiality in the beginning, so you know the rules on that."

"Yes, I do," Veronica said, as she stood to face him. "I'm an attorney," she reminded him, "so I made a copy of what I signed. Most of it isn't legal, but I'll respect it anyway. I wasn't planning to take the art or furniture. And *my* lawyer will bring the keys to you, you don't have to send yours to me. Thank you for everything you did for me, Anson. I've loved you, and I'm sorry if you feel I've fallen short recently." She didn't complain about the cold, merciless way he was ending it with her, or try to change his mind. No one had ever treated her as coldly, and she was shaking, but it didn't show. It was over. He had become her jailer, and she was glad she hadn't told him the amount of her inheritance. It was none of his business now. Her mind was racing as she thought of what she had to pack. She only had a few suitcases, and she'd have to get more, and be out by six the next day. She realized now that she was just a commodity to him. He didn't love her and never had, and if he did, he wouldn't let it show now. He felt betrayed by her because she had a strong bond to her sisters, wanted to expand her education, and had a brain. He just wanted a willing body and pretty face available to him when it suited him, and she had been just that to him for ten years. He strode to the door then, put his coat on, and looked at her, as she stood tall and straight facing him.

"You were a good girl, Veronica," he said in a demeaning tone. "One of the best I've had," and he walked out, leaving ten years of her life in ashes behind him.

"Goodbye, Senator," she said, as the door closed behind him.

Her whole body shook after he left and she sat down on the couch. She was angry and sad, scared and humiliated. He had treated her like a hooker in the end, any tender moment they had shared forgotten. In the end, it meant nothing to him, or maybe it had. But he could sense that she was no longer willing to be his slave as she once had been. Her mother had been right yet again, and now Veronica understood why she had been so upset and so worried, and so outraged to think of Veronica in that life. She had given up her career at the law firm for him, in exchange for a few suitcases full of clothes. It was insulting that he wanted her to leave all the jewelry he had given her as birthday and Christmas gifts. In fact, they weren't gifts, he considered them loans, and had known that he would take them back in the end. All she wanted to do now was get out of the apartment as fast as she could. She had loved him once, but she didn't love the way he had treated her in the end. He was treating her like a whore, not the decent, loving woman she had been to him. He wanted to be her jailer and control everything she did. At the slightest sign of independence in any form, he was throwing her out of her home.

As soon as she stopped shaking, she called Isabelle and asked if she could borrow some suitcases. Isabelle traveled and Veronica knew she had valises.

"I'm sorry, I don't have any. Ian came and took a lot of his stuff, he took my suitcases and he hasn't given them back yet. He says he's living out of them. Are you going on a trip? Anywhere fun?" Veronica realized when Isabelle asked the question that she had nowhere to go, and had no idea where to stay. She didn't have time to find an apartment the next day. She'd be packing, and it might take all day to do it.

Veronica's voice still sounded shaky when she answered. "Anson just told me to move out of the apartment. He's been upset since we found out about the inheritance."

"Did you tell him how much it is?" Isabelle sounded shocked.

"No, I didn't. It would only have made things worse. He felt that if I inherited anything from Mom, he shouldn't have to support me anymore, but I've been his beck-and-call girl for ten years."

"Did he give you some warning?"

"He just came to tell me. I have to be out by six P.M. tomorrow, and leave any jewelry he gave me. I get the clothes."

"What a rude bastard," Isabelle said, furious on her behalf.

"He was as cold as ice. He stayed for about an hour, told me to get out, and left. Mom was right."

"She always was," Isabelle confirmed. "I'm sorry, Veronica."

"He was angry that I went back to school. I was supposed to be in the apartment at all times, waiting for him."

"Where are you going to stay?" Isabelle was worried about her. But in her own current state of turmoil, having Veronica move in with them would have been another unsettling element for her children. And Veronica could afford to stay anywhere until she found something more permanent. They were both at a time of enormous change.

"I don't know. I have to figure that out. I have to pack. I'll let you know." But she had plenty of money for a hotel now. She called Quinne, who said she had no real suitcases since she always took carry-on. Charlotte was in meetings, so Veronica texted her, and Charlotte said she needed the ones she had and couldn't spare them, which left Olivia, who said she only owned two, and Veronica needed way more than that. She estimated six or seven. In the end, on Monday morning she took an Uber to a luggage shop she knew and bought eight suitcases for her wardrobe, her books, and the contents of her desk. And then she took another Uber back to the apartment.

Before that, on Sunday night, she had lain in bed all night, thinking of how cold Anson had been when he left her. No goodbye, no kiss, no gentle touch, just his ordering her to get out like a cheap trick. She was up at six, emptying closets, and she took a cab to the luggage store at ten. She was back in less than an hour and packed for the rest of the day. Before she left to buy her luggage, she called Scott Freeman.

"Well, this is a nice surprise," he said happily.

"Thank you. I need a favor. I'm moving today. Could you possibly go to my landlord's office at six to return the keys? It's not too far from your office. He wanted to send his lawyer to get them, and I said I'd send mine." Her voice sounded shaky and serious. She hadn't mentioned moving before.

"I'm glad to be of service. Is this short notice, or have you been planning it yourself?"

"It's short notice," Veronica said, trying to sound calmer than she felt. "He told me yesterday."

"You can refuse to move if he didn't give you proper written notice. You can even refuse to pay your rent. It will take him a year to evict."

"I'd rather not get evicted. It's not my apartment, and I don't pay rent. I just want to go quietly." Suddenly he realized what had happened. She was breaking up with the boyfriend who kept her on such a short leash, and was considerably older than she was. Or at least she was moving out. Scott considered it good news, and was delighted to help.

"I'm sorry. What time do you want me to pick up the keys?"

"Around five-ish. Thank you so much," and before that she had to figure out a place to stay, and get everything she owned into suitcases.

As soon as she came back from the luggage store with eight big suitcases, she put things in them as quickly as she could. She tried to calm herself and not panic. She wondered if Anson would call her to apologize for being so cold the day before and tell her he would miss her, but he never did. When she picked up her cellphone to look up hotels, it was dead, and she realized that he had cut it off since he paid for it. She used her computer and the landline in the apartment.

She booked a room at the Mark, as she had to stay in the city so she could go to her class. Isabelle dropped by with a sandwich for her at lunchtime, and they sat and talked for a while. She was halfway through her packing and took a break. She was happy to see her sister.

"He didn't give you any kind of warning?" Isabelle was still shocked, but in some ways not surprised. Men like Anson Phillips were ruthless, and he had always made it clear that she was his mistress, even though he had been generous and treated her well.

"Maybe he was right," Veronica said quietly. "I didn't want to sit here waiting for him all the time. After Mom died, I suddenly realized I was wasting my time and my brain, which is why I went back to school. I didn't say anything, but I wanted some freedom."

"Are you okay?" Isabelle looked her in the eye and Veronica nodded with wide eyes.

"I think I am, or I will be. I wasn't expecting it, and he was so cold." She went back to packing then and Isabelle left. By four o'clock she was finished, and everything she owned was packed into the eight bags. They were standing in the hallway, and she was wearing jeans and another Columbia sweatshirt, and heavy boots. There was snow on the ground outside.

She walked around the apartment before Scott arrived, thinking of all that had happened in ten years there. She had been so proud of it at first and felt so grown-up. He had made her feel so important, and took her shopping to buy clothes he liked to see her wear, like a doll. Veronica hadn't seen it that way then, but her mother had when they argued about it. She knew that her mother would have been pleased that she was moving out, even if it wasn't her decision. At twenty-six, she had felt so proud and happy there. At thirty-six, she felt humiliated and ashamed. She had wasted ten years of her life with a married man who didn't love her and had used her, and she had consented to it. She couldn't blame Anson for her part in it, and blamed herself.

Scott arrived promptly at five o'clock, and she was ready to leave. She had ordered a van with a driver to take her bags the short distance to the hotel. She had to look for an apartment, and thanks to her mother she could afford one. She felt as though Anson had shot her out of a cannon into a new life she wasn't prepared for, but she would have to learn. And after her refresher class, she could get a job in a law firm and work her way up from the bottom. She was ten years late getting started.

"Are you okay?" Scott asked her. She didn't look heartbroken or distraught. She looked nervous, and her hair was piled on her head in a clip. She looked younger than when he had seen her looking chic and polished in Chanel. All her Chanel was packed, and she had a lot of it.

"Yeah, I think I am," she said. "Thank you for helping me." She had put the keys in an envelope. She had three sets and she knew Anson had his. She left all the small kitchen appliances. She would have to buy everything new when she found an apartment, but maybe it would be fun. And she had packed all the jewelry in their original boxes in a briefcase she had. It was all there, every piece of it, as he had instructed. She handed Scott the briefcase and asked him to return it with the keys. She wasn't sad to give up the jewelry. It felt like an affront now, and it made her feel cheap.

Scott rode down in the elevator with her, after she took a last look around the apartment. She took two photographs of herself with Anson, and left the rest in their silver frames. She had emptied the desk and all the closets and drawers. The van was waiting for her downstairs, and the doorman filled it with her bags.

"Can I call you?" Scott asked her, and she shook her head.

"No, you can't." He looked disappointed, and she smiled. "I think he canceled my cellphone, it was his. I have to get a new one tomorrow." He was relieved to see her leaving, but he was shocked too, by the brutality of Anson's behavior.

"It sounds like he didn't miss a trick."

"I'm staying at the Mark. You can call me there. I'll text you my number when I get a new phone." He wondered if she would go out with him, but he was afraid to ask. Maybe she needed more time to recover. Ten years was a long time. But she felt strangely invigorated and excited. She hadn't expected to feel that way, but she felt as though she was getting out of jail, and in some ways she was.

Scott left on his mission in an Uber with the envelope of keys and the briefcase, and Veronica headed for the Mark with all her worldly possessions. She had booked a suite, and the lobby looked chic and fashionable and was full of well-dressed people. The bellman set up all her bags in her room. There were some she knew she wouldn't use now, with summer clothes. She ordered a glass of wine, and sat down on the couch to catch her breath. She realized that Anson had thought he had left her penniless. He had canceled the credit cards he had paid for, with no idea that she had a fortune of her own now.

Scott was back forty-five minutes after he had left her, and handed her a small package when she let him in, saying it was from him, not her "landlord." She offered him a glass of wine and he was happy to accept. She opened the package while they waited for his wine, and she smiled and was touched when she saw it. He had bought her a phone, and got a referral from her old number. Anson's cruelty was matched by Scott's kindness to her.

"I can set it up for you," he said, taking it from her and handing it back a few minutes later.

"Your new phone number is on a piece of paper in the box," he told her with a smile, and they sat down in the living room of the suite. She was dying to ask Scott about Anson but was embarrassed to do so, and he could guess what was on her mind. "I didn't see him. I left the keys and briefcase with his assistant. She was very nice." Veronica had spoken to her hundreds of times during the five years the woman had been there, but she wouldn't be speaking to her again. It was strange that the man who had been the mainstay of her life for ten years had vanished completely from her world overnight. She didn't miss him yet, she hadn't had time, and all she could think of was the cold way he had spoken to her the day before. She was shocked to realize that she had no feelings for him, that she just wanted to get on with her life now, start living again. She wasn't sure where to begin, but she had class the next day, which would ground her. She saw that Scott had something to say, and he hesitated.

"Would it be inappropriate to invite you to dinner tonight?" he asked her, and she smiled. She felt the same current pass between them that she had felt before, but it didn't frighten her now that it would upset Anson.

"It would be fine," she said, feeling freer than she had in years.

"There's a nice Italian restaurant near here, or Sant Ambroeus around the corner." It sounded great to her, and she could imagine her mother smiling, now that she was out of Anson's control at last.

They sat and talked for an hour, and walked to the restaurant. She didn't change, she just combed her hair, and she tucked her hand into his arm as they crossed the street. It was only a few blocks to the restaurant, which was crowded and lively, and she looked up at Scott and felt as though her life was starting over. She was liberated and free and young again, as they sat down at a table. She was giddy with excitement, and so was Scott. He hadn't expected this to happen, nor had she. Veronica sensed that she was exactly where she was meant to be. Anson had done her the biggest favor of her life by setting her free, and she smiled as she looked around. It was one of those moments when everything was perfect and she'd been given the chance to start her life again. And she knew her mother would have been thrilled for her.

Chapter 11

After class the next day, Veronica started the search for an apartment. She saw three and hated them. They were in dreary modern buildings with no charm. It took her a week to find one she loved. The apartment was small but all she needed, a floor-through in a townhouse that had been divided into apartments in the East Seventies. It had a bedroom, a study, a big living room, a dining room, and a kitchen. There were high ceilings and tall French windows with antique curtains provided by the owner, a retired opera singer who lived on the three upper floors. And there was an elevator so Olivia could come to see her. Isabelle dropped by after Veronica signed the lease, and loved it. Veronica noticed that Isabelle looked tired and pale. She and Ian were still living separately, and they had finally told the children that they were living apart for a while and trying to work things out. They had cried, but they were spending two nights a week with Ian. He had rented a furnished apartment while he continued to figure things out. He was still seeing Leila, and telling Isabelle he didn't want to lose her or their marriage, which sounded less and less real to her. He said that he hoped to have worked things out by the summer, and wanted to rent a house in the Hamptons with her, and he said he could come out on weekends. She could guess that he would be with Leila in the city during the week. Isabelle had turned down his offer to rent a house in the Hamptons with him, and had talked to Scott about a divorce. It broke her heart to think about it, but she was losing hope that Ian would ever be able to let Leila go. There was something about her that seemed to be more addictive than any drug. He was seeing a therapist to figure out what he wanted. He still wasn't sure.

Scott had helped Quinne set up her production house too, and she was up and running. He was eager to see more of Veronica once she settled into her apartment. She had all her sisters to dinner at her new home. Cooper came, fresh from the set. He was working on Felicia's series. Andy was there with Charlotte, and Veronica had invited Scott.

"The Weston ladies are keeping me busy," he said to Andy, and he laughed.

"They keep us all busy," Andy commented.

Olivia admitted to Isabelle that she had written to François Vernier, and he hadn't responded.

"I'm sorry, Ollie," Isabelle said. They were sitting in a corner talking. Everyone in the group got along. Isabelle had helped Veronica furnish her new apartment quickly. It was comfortable and inviting. They had combed the vintage shops and antique stores, and Olivia had tagged along. The result was exactly what Veronica

Felicia's Favorites

had wanted. It was her first apartment on her own. She'd had roommates when she worked at the law firm ten years before.

"It's okay," Olivia said about François. Isabelle remembered how madly in love they had been. "It means he's happy now. I'm glad for him." Olivia was philosophical about François. She wasn't even sure why she had written to him. They were ancient history.

And Andy's father was due to arrive on Friday. All five of the sisters were going to the farm on Sunday to meet him for lunch. Charlotte and Andy were spending weekends at the Weston farm in Connecticut whenever Julia went to friends on the weekends. Andy stayed at his father's house during the week, except when he came into the city to see Charlotte.

They had a fun dinner at Veronica's new apartment, and Scott stayed after the others left. She seemed to be blossoming in her new life. She and Scott were enjoying getting to know each other better. He didn't want to rush things. She was fresh out of a ten-year relationship that had left its mark on her. She realized now how oppressive it had been, and how Anson had controlled her. It had seemed normal to her after a while. And she saw clearly now how unhealthy it had been. She was enjoying school and Scott, her sisters and her freedom.

"Do you think Isabelle and Ian will get divorced?" she asked him, as they sat in her living room with a last glass of wine.

"Professionally, I can't say anything. Personally, I think he's pushed it to the outer limits. She's been very patient." Isabelle wasn't dating anyone, but the affair with Leila had gone on for almost a year now, and Ian still hadn't given her up. Isabelle had lost hope for their marriage.

* * *

The same group assembled at the farm on Sunday, without Scott, who was a newcomer to the group as Veronica's date. Quinne and Cooper drove out. Olivia and Veronica came from the city together. Andy and Charlotte had spent the weekend, and she had met Spencer before the others, on Saturday, and was deeply moved by him. He had cried and hugged her when he met her. And Isabelle brought her children on Sunday, so he could meet them. He looked a lot like Andy, although bigger, broader, and older. He was a serious person, but had a good sense of humor. He teased them all about things their mother had said about them, and he was sweet to Isabelle's children, who loved playing outside. Andy and Coop played ball with Tyler and Charlie, and Penny stayed close to her mother. It felt like a real family gathering. The only one missing was Julia, who had plans in the city with friends. Spencer told Charlotte and Andy that they had made Felicia's fondest wish come true, that one day they would meet and fall in love.

He'd come to New York to negotiate a new contract with his publisher and promote his latest book. Robert Farr had taken Spencer to the set of the series they had started to shoot and he was duly impressed seeing Quinne in action. They talked about it at lunch on Sunday. He was aware of all their jobs and activities and from the stories he told, they could tell how much their mother and he had talked about them.

"She loved this place so much. I'm so glad you've kept it. She always hoped you'd spend time here. She wanted to introduce us, but she wasn't ready to reveal all her secrets yet, and she thought she had time." He had tears in his eyes when he said it. Andy had

Felicia's Favorites

asked him the day before if he was ready to move back. He and Charlotte had been trying to plan what they would do when he did, and hadn't decided yet. Their plans were somewhat dependent on Spencer's. He had surprised Andy when he said that he didn't think he could ever live there again. He had been thinking about it a lot. He and Felicia had been so happy there that he still couldn't bear the thought of living there without her. He had enjoyed meeting her children immensely, and they were as wonderful as she had said, and made him feel welcome. But he felt too lonely being there without Felicia, and Andy could see that he was. He felt so sorry for him. He wondered if he would ever recover. He was only seventy-two years old and youthful for his age, but Andy could see that losing Felicia had aged him.

"What'll you do, Dad?" Andy asked, worried about him.

"I don't know. London suits me, and I've rented a cottage in Hampshire, it's the dower house on one of the great old estates. Felicia would have loved it." He still measured everything by her, and Andy thought he was making the right decision. It would be too hard to live in the Connecticut house without her. His memories of her there were too vivid. "I'd like you to move in, not just house-sit," Spencer said to Andy. "I'll put my things in storage if you like, if you don't want them. Why don't you live here with Charlotte and make it your home?"

"I'd like that, Dad, and it's a generous offer. Charlotte's daughter has another year of school in the city, so she has to live in New York until Julia leaves for college. I go back and forth from here and her daughter seems fine with it. She's a lovely girl."

"They feel like my family now too," Spencer said at lunch on

Sunday, and the sisters all agreed. They hadn't grown up with a father figure, and Spencer was warm and generous and loving to them. He had heard fifteen years of stories from Felicia and already felt as though he knew them well. The only ones missing in their midst that day were Charlotte's children and Felicia herself. Spencer gave an emotional toast, and they all cried, but they were warm tears of love and joy and happy memories. It was a day she would have loved. They took a walk after lunch, and Spencer told them stories about their mother and what a wonderful woman she was.

The sisters left Connecticut reluctantly on Sunday afternoon after their day with Spencer. He was appearing on *Good Morning America* the next day to promote his new book, and they all promised to watch. Andy was going with him to keep him company, with his publicist. It was easy to forget what a big star Spencer was. He was so unassuming and easy to be with that one forgot how famous he was. He and Felicia had that in common, and many other things. Spencer had been struck by how much Felicia's daughters looked like her, although each in a different way. And their personalities were so exactly as she had described them. Spencer felt as though he had known them for fifteen years through Felicia. He was planning to spend another week in New York, and then go back to London.

* * *

When Olivia got home from the country, Veronica dropped her off. She had a date with Scott for dinner that night, since he had missed the lunch, and she was looking forward to it. She hadn't heard a word from Anson since he had evicted her from the apartment. His absence wasn't painful, and she didn't miss him, which surprised her. It just felt strange. She was startled by how easy the separation had been. She had been more ready to leave the relationship than she realized. His constant control had been stifling in the end. And the brutal, cold way he had ended it had killed any feelings she had for him.

She wondered if she had already been replaced by another innocent malleable young woman he could form in the image he wanted and keep trapped in the apartment, waiting for him to appear. There had been no fallout from it, no unpleasantness, just silence. She felt as though she could breathe again and do what she wanted. And being with Scott was so easy. She realized now how difficult and demanding and above all controlling Anson had been. She didn't miss it, and embraced her freedom.

Veronica and Scott had Thai food that night and she told him all about Spencer and what a nice man he was.

After she'd had dinner in her kitchen that night, Olivia rolled up to her computer table to check her emails. She hadn't looked that morning or when she got home. On Sundays she liked to take a break from her obligations, students, classes, and charitable causes. She had a full schedule all week and got a flood of emails on some days. She glanced through them and didn't see anything important at first, and then she saw it, the response from François. It had been weeks since she'd written to him and he hadn't answered, which she thought was a gentle way of letting her know that he was long since over her and didn't want to hear from her. She didn't blame him, and was relieved for his sake to know that he had moved on. It had been agonizing leaving each other after the accident, and he had done everything he could to convince her to remain in the relationship, which she flatly refused to do, for his sake. She wanted him to have the happy full life he deserved, not be chained to a paraplegic for the rest of his days. But letting go had been a tragedy for both of them. It had been years before he gave up.

When she saw the email among a long list of others, she just sat there and stared at it. She didn't want to open it. It was probably a short, polite response. She had only written saying that she wished him well, and hoped that things were going well for him. He was much more famous than he had been twelve years before. His success had been meteoric and he was an immensely talented choreographer, working all around the world.

It took her a long time to have the courage to click it open, and finally she couldn't wait any longer. Her hands were shaking when she opened it, and she took a breath as she read it. His last email to her had been five years before, to tell her he was marrying a very famous Russian prima ballerina. He had choreographed a magnificent *Swan Lake* for her, which Olivia had watched on the internet and cried because it was so powerful. He was a brilliant artist. She could hear his voice as she read his email.

Felicia's Favorites

My Dearest Olivia,

What a splendid and unexpected surprise to hear from you. Apologies, I was in Russia when your email arrived, working night and day on a very nice Giselle, and had terrible computer problems. Back in Paris now. How are you? Well, I hope, still teaching your classes. Lucky students to have a teacher like you. I hope that you and your lovely family are all well. I am coming to New York to do three shows for the American Ballet Theatre. Always fun to be in New York. It would be very special to see you. Staying at the Plaza.

He gave her a range of four days.

Kiss your wonderful mother and sisters for me.

Always,

François

It was warm and friendly and congenial, and polite. He sounded happy and as full of life as always. His Russian wife was obviously good for him, and Olivia stared at the dates he was coming, and wondered if she had the courage to see him. By now, the last drop of emotion between them must have dried up and it wouldn't be dangerous, but she didn't want him to think she was chasing him. He was married now, and she was still in a wheelchair and always would be. He had trained as a dancer himself, with the Bolshoi and the Paris Opera Company, and had fallen in love with choreography. She had been eighteen with a promising career ahead of her when they met and he was twenty. They were in love for seven years, and had finally gotten engaged when she had the accident that ended her career and life as she knew it, and she ended the relationship. He had refused to let go for so long, and now he sounded exuberant and happy and engaged in his life. She wondered if he and his wife had had children in his five years of marriage. She would love to see him, and wondered if it was wise. It seemed foolish now, but also rude not to answer him, especially since she had initiated the correspondence. She didn't even know why she had, except that her sisters had suggested it.

She stared at the blank screen for a long time, and then typed a brief message.

So happy to hear from you. You sound great. I'm sure the Giselle in Russia was wonderful, and your ABT performances will be too. Tea when you're here, if you like? Whatever fits your schedule, mine is flexible. Dry martinis on demand. See you soon.

She sent it before she could change her mind, teasing him about the dry martinis he had discovered in New York and loved. He'd gotten terribly drunk and her mother put him to bed until he sobered up. Felicia had loved him. They all did. Olivia was twenty-five when she had the accident, and François twenty-seven. Now they were grown-ups. He was married and very famous, and her life had more or less stopped twelve years before, but she kept busy and involved in ballet and charitable causes. It would be fun to see him, but perhaps emotional too, and he obviously didn't know that her mother had died. She could tell him when she saw him. She didn't want to put it in an email. She rolled away from her computer, thinking about him. It felt silly to have written to him, and exciting too. Everything about François was exciting— his talent, his looks, his passion for ballet, his exuberance, his love of life. He used to make her feel like she could fly when they danced together. And then it was over so soon. Felicia had thought they were too young to marry, and had convinced them to wait a year. If they'd been married, Olivia would have stayed with him, but destiny had decided otherwise. Probably for the best, she told herself. She didn't bother to answer her other emails. His was the only interesting one.

The dates he had mentioned for his New York trip were a week away and she had time to decide if she would see him. It was so tempting. He was a married man now. Maybe his wife was coming to New York with him, although he didn't mention her.

She went to bed early and dreamed of dancing, as she often did, leaping across the stage, and then François was lifting her up until she felt as though she could soar to the sky. In her dreams, she could still dance.

Isabelle was in a deep sleep that night when she dreamed that she heard a child crying. Then she woke up. It was Tyler. She jumped out of bed and went to him immediately. He said his stomach hurt. She tried to soothe him and stroked his silky hair, but nothing helped. She could hear that he was in acute pain. She waited a few more minutes and called the pediatrician. When the emergency service answered she gave them her name and explained the problem, and a few minutes later, the doctor came on the line. He was the youngest member of the practice, whom she had only met once.

"It sounds like we should take a look." He told her to go to the emergency room at New York–Presbyterian and he'd meet her there. She tried to comfort Tyler but he was inconsolable and said the pain was the worst he'd had in his whole life. She put on jeans and a sweater, slipped her feet into sneakers, and came back to bundle Tyler in a blanket. Charlie and Penny were sleeping soundly, and she went to tell the nanny where she was going.

She carried him to the Uber waiting outside. It was two A.M. on a Sunday night and there was very little traffic. The hospital wasn't far.

It was at times like this that she really missed Ian. They'd had a few ER runs since he had left. Nights like that were always better shared. It was so much more reassuring to have someone with you. But she didn't want to wake Ian if it was nothing.

The young pediatrician was waiting for her, and together they laid Tyler down on an exam room table. He pressed lightly on Tyler's abdomen and he screamed, and the right side was distinctly worse. The doctor looked at Isabelle with a serious expression.

"You were right to call me. We've got a hot appendix. I'm going to order a sonogram to be sure, but I'll call the pediatric surgeon now, so they can prep the OR. I think we got it in time. Has he been uncomfortable for a few days?" he asked, and she shook her head.

"No, he was fine today, he ran around in the country. He woke up out of a sound sleep screaming."

Felicia's Favorites

As she talked to the doctor, he was already moving Tyler on the rolling table to the sonogram lab, where they confirmed his diagnosis. He called the surgeon to let him know, and they took Tyler back to the ER.

"He'll be fine," he said, and explained the situation to Tyler in terms he could understand, and Tyler screamed even louder and clutched his mother's hand.

"I don't want him to cut me open."

"We're going to take it out through a little hole, and you're going to feel so much better, Tyler, when we get rid of that silly old appendix that's making you hurt."

The surgeon arrived twenty minutes later, and explained the procedure to Isabelle.

"We'll have him back to you in an hour, good as new," he said. They gave Tyler a shot to relax him, and everything happened quickly after that. They let Isabelle go to the doors of the OR and then they whisked Tyler away. He had already stopped crying and was getting drowsy, and she stood there alone for a few minutes. There was no lonelier place on earth than a hospital with a sick child when you had no partner.

She went to the waiting area, to wait for Tyler, and she called Ian. He sounded groggy when he answered. It was three A.M. by then.

"I'm sorry to wake you," she said. "Tyler has appendicitis, and they're taking it out now. They just took him to the OR. He was in a lot of pain," she reported.

"Did it burst?"

"Not yet, but they were worried it might."

"Poor guy. I'll be there in fifteen minutes. Thanks for calling me," he said, sounding friendly and warm. She was trying to see him as little as possible. It just upset her, knowing he was still with Leila, and their life had been in turmoil for months because of him.

Isabelle was sitting quietly in the waiting room, thinking about her son, and waiting for news of him. It wasn't a complicated procedure but it was still surgery. She was staring straight ahead when she saw Ian walking toward her. It startled her for a minute to see him. He was so handsome, tall and sexy in jeans, a black sweater and an old distressed leather bomber jacket, and black loafers without socks. His hair was slightly tousled, as though he hadn't thoroughly brushed it before he left the house in a hurry. She looked up at him with a smile, and as she gazed up at him, a woman stepped out from behind him, her hair, fresh from bed, uncombed in a loose casual knot, wearing tight jeans and a bustier top under a weathered man's oversized black leather motorcycle jacket, with high-heeled black boots. She looked incredibly sexy, somewhat cheap, and could only be Leila since she was glued to Ian, and had been hidden from view standing behind him. When she stepped aside, Isabelle got the full view. The two women had never met before and Isabelle felt like someone had just hit her in the solar plexus and knocked the wind out of her. Leila was an impressive sight at three-thirty in the morning, in high heels and a bustier, and she looked far younger than her twenty-three years in a kind of Lolita way. Isabelle found herself staring at how big Leila's breasts were. She could readily see what Ian saw in her, she looked like the star of a porn movie, and Isabelle was annoyed at Ian and couldn't believe he'd brought her. She didn't belong there.

This was about their son. But Leila seemed to feel totally at ease being there.

She plopped down in the chair next to Isabelle, who was trying to ignore her so she didn't say the wrong thing, or snap at Ian.

"Hi, I'm Leila," she said, as friendly as a large Labrador or golden retriever with tail wagging. Bringing his girlfriend, who had coincidentally broken up their marriage, to the hospital to meet his wife, during their son's emergency surgery, was ample proof of Ian's poor judgment in the circumstances. He seemed totally unaware of how awkward the moment was for Isabelle.

"Leila wanted to come," he explained, and sat down on Isabelle's other side so she was sandwiched in between them, and she nodded at Leila. "She really loves the kids," Ian added.

"Hi," was the best Isabelle could muster, while they sat there silently, waiting for news of Tyler. Isabelle was sorry she'd called him, but she had to. It never occurred to her that Ian would bring Leila, for their first meeting. Leila took a candy bar out of her purse and offered Isabelle some, which she declined. Finally, what felt like hours later, the surgeon appeared in scrubs to report that Tyler had done well, and that the appendix had been about to burst so it was a good thing they'd come. He was doing fine, and was in the recovery room and would be for another hour, and then they'd take him to a room.

"He's going to be pretty sleepy for a few hours. If you and your daughter want to go home and get some sleep, you can come back in the morning." Isabelle, too stunned to speak, nodded and thanked him. The fact that the surgeon had mistaken Leila for her daughter made Isabelle want to hit someone, preferably Ian.

Isabelle wanted to stay in case Tyler woke up, but the surgeon made it sound unlikely, and she wanted to get a few more hours of sleep so she could be alert for him in the morning. Leila stood up then and was ready to go. She wanted to go outside and smoke, and Ian told her he'd be out in a minute. He waited until she had gone before speaking to Isabelle.

"I'm sorry, I wouldn't have brought her, but she really wanted to come. She loves our kids," he said again.

"That's because she is one. How could you bring her here? Our son is in surgery and you bring your hot girlfriend to the hospital to meet me? Where is your brain?" She knew where it was but didn't want to mention it in public. "That was possibly one of the most socially awkward moments in my life. Next time one of our kids needs surgery, please come alone. I take it you're still living with her," she said through pursed lips, well aware that she looked a mess. She had thrown on her clothes and hadn't bothered to comb her hair at all. She felt like Leila's great-grandmother.

"We're kind of going between her place and mine," he explained, a detail that Isabelle didn't really want to know. But he clearly wasn't over her, and Isabelle could see why, and the fact that she "loved their kids" was evidence that Leila was obviously spending time with their children during visitation, but was too discreet to say so. Isabelle wasn't in love with that idea either. Her conclusion was that Ian was an idiot.

She left them outside the emergency entrance to the hospital and hailed a cab to go home. They got into another one right behind her, and Isabelle sat in the cab thinking about Leila. She couldn't believe that Ian had brought her to the hospital, with Isabelle there, and seemed to think it was normal to do so. He was oblivious to Isabelle's feelings.

The whole night seemed surreal when she woke up the next morning. She called the hospital to check on Tyler, and the nurse said he was still sleeping but had had a good night, and she called Olivia just to have someone to talk to and told her about her first meeting with Leila, and Olivia laughed.

"You've got to hand it to Ian. For a bright guy, he puts his foot in it every time. It sounds like quite a scene. There's nothing like a narcissist to be oblivious to everyone's feelings but his own."

"And they're more or less living together," Isabelle added.

"I'm sorry. You have to admit it's funny though. It sounds like a scene in a movie," Olivia said.

Isabelle smiled at the memory. It was funny in retrospect, a little less so while it was happening. Leila was so unbearably sexy and looked so damn young. It wasn't surprising that Ian was flattered by her attention and didn't want to give her up.

"I'll call you later to check on Tyler." Olivia didn't tell her that she'd exchanged emails with François. It was still too close to the bone for her, and he was a married man now with a beautiful wife. She still didn't know if she'd see him. It might be too hard.

Isabelle took a shower and dressed to go back to the hospital. At least this time Leila wouldn't be there, she hoped. But nothing surprised her anymore.

Chapter 12

The following week, Veronica was studying for a quiz when her phone rang and she picked it up without looking. She was shocked when she heard Anson's voice. She wasn't expecting him to call, he hadn't called her since he evicted her.

"How are you?" he asked her in a satin smooth voice. "I miss you. I think about you every time I go to the apartment. I hate to be there now, it makes me too lonely for you. Are you doing okay?" he asked her. It was a little late to be calling her to find out. She couldn't help wondering why he went to the apartment. For random sex? Or did he already have a new girlfriend living there? Anson moved fast. "I worry about you," he said in a gruff voice, and she didn't believe him. If he worried about her, he wouldn't have thrown her out on one day's notice, and he would have called a lot sooner. He sounded lonely, which was probably the only reason for the call. Maybe he hadn't found a replacement yet after all. But with the benefits he offered, apartment, wardrobe, and jewelry to wear if not keep, it wouldn't be a hard spot to fill. "Are you still in school?"

"Yes, I am," she said simply. She wanted to ask how he was, and if he missed her, but she didn't want to engage. He had thrown her out, and it was better that way now. "How's the campaign going?" It seemed like a safe subject. She wanted to end things civilly, even if he hadn't.

"It's heating up. I miss you, Veronica," he said again, in case she hadn't heard him the first time. "Would you have dinner with me sometime . . . like tonight?" he asked, and she was surprised. He had been so cold with her, so heartless when he told her to leave, cutting his last ties with her like a knife, and invited her to dinner now. She didn't want to see him again. She had been his mistress for ten years, a role she no longer wanted in his life, and they weren't friends, he had seen to that. It was over for her. Just talking to him gave her a chill.

"No," she said simply, "I can't."

"Are you seeing someone?" He sounded angry for a minute.

"No. Just friends." That's all Scott was for the moment. She hadn't wanted to rush into anything right away, no matter how attractive he was, but the relationship was headed in that direction.

"So you're an heiress now, and don't need me." He sounded wounded as he said it. The narcissist as victim, a classic switch.

"I loved you, Anson, and not for what you gave me. For you. All those perks were nice but that wasn't why I was there or why I stayed. I stayed for you," she said, so gently that it unnerved him and cut through him like a knife.

"I was upset. You were different after your mother died, and I thought you didn't need me anymore once you inherited from her. And you went back to school." He viewed it as a betrayal, and acted accordingly. It was a major new insight into his character, and who he was. He was cruel beneath the surface. He had banished her from her home, and taken back everything he had given her. This punishment of her was merciless.

"I needed to feed my mind, and it was a hard time for me. But that didn't make me love you less." He had done that on his own, especially in the end.

"I thought you were cheating on me."

"I didn't and I never would," she said seriously, and he believed her. He had always believed her to be an honest woman, until the end, when he could sense she had secrets.

"I made a mistake. I acted hastily. Come back to me," he said, pleading with her. Anson never humbled himself to anyone and Veronica was stunned.

"I can't," she said quietly. "You threw me out of the only home I had. I don't want to depend on anyone anymore, or be a mistress."

"I need you. Where are you staying?"

"I found an apartment, I'm okay." It was actually prettier than his, much smaller but more distinguished, and more elegant the way she'd decorated it. She loved it, and it was hers. And no one could throw her out at a moment's notice ever again.

"Can I see you?" he asked, and Veronica squeezed her eyes shut. This was harder than she expected, but her life was a one-way street now, away from him. There was no going back. He was too possessive and controlling and cruel in the end. She knew he would squeeze the life out of her if she went back, and she might never have the guts or the opportunity to leave again. He had done her a favor by evicting her.

"I can't, Anson, I'm sorry."

"You can, but you won't. You're punishing me, and that's not fair." It was more than fair but she didn't say it. There was no point. "I told you I'm sorry. What more do you want?" Anger edged into his voice when she didn't give in to him.

"I don't want anything. I told you, I don't want to be a mistress anymore."

"If I divorce Anne, it will destroy my political career. You know that." But Veronica didn't want to marry him either. She just wanted out. She already was out, thanks to him, and she wanted to stay there, away from him. He was toxic. She understood that fully now.

"I'm not asking you to get a divorce. I never did. I knew the rules, and I followed them."

"You stopped needing me."

"I need to rely on myself now. You did me a favor. I needed to grow up, and you forced me to. I'm trying to be a grown-up now. I couldn't be dependent on you forever. It's not right." She could breathe now. She was free to live and move and do what she wanted, not waiting for him to show up and being alone for the holidays for the rest of her life. And he had said he missed her, not that he loved her. Anson didn't love anyone, she knew now.

"Just see me. We can talk about it. I liked you the way you were." She had been honorable, and he knew it. Too late.

"There's nothing to talk about," she said softly. She was gone and he knew it. There were tears of anger and frustration in his eyes. The world was full of younger and even prettier girls, although she was a beauty. He wanted her. He had seen what was out there, and they wanted him only for the money. Veronica didn't.

"Call me if you change your mind," he said, and hung up. It was too humiliating listening to her refuse him. He couldn't bear it.

She knew she wouldn't go back to him. She would never give up her freedom again. And thanks to her mother, she didn't need to. Even without her inheritance, she wouldn't have gone back. She would never get back the ten years she had spent as Anson's bird in a golden cage and his slave. She knew that whatever she did now would be better for her. He would be fine. He'd have another girl in his love nest in no time. A girl he could control, as he had her. She was shocked that he had called her, and flattered, but he hadn't changed her mind.

She took the quiz she'd been studying for and got an A. She wrote a paper for the class, which the teacher loved, and Scott took her to dinner on Friday night. He'd had a long week and he was tired, but happy to see her. They went to their favorite little Italian hole in the wall after that. They walked back to her place for another glass of wine afterward. She had told Scott at dinner that Anson had called her and he wasn't surprised. Anson was no fool. He'd had a diamond in his hands and he knew it, and he had thrown her away. Scott guessed that he had probably thought he could get her back if he wanted to. But he'd been wrong. She wasn't for sale. Veronica realized now that she didn't love Anson.

He was a bad habit she had broken. Scott admired her for it, and for other things. He knew she was free now. He hadn't been sure until then.

While they were talking, he leaned over and kissed her, gently at first, as his lips brushed hers, and then it became a searing, passionate kiss, heightened by all the times he had seen her and wanted her and knew he couldn't have her. He had spent many nights thinking about her after he saw her, wishing that he had a chance with her, but she had been in Anson's control then, and she no longer was. She could really give herself freely now, and as they kissed, she melted into his arms and he wanted to love and protect her, and be part of her life. They stopped kissing for a minute and he looked at her.

"I wanted you for so long, Veronica." She nodded and smiled shyly.

"Me too. I thought that would never be possible," she said, looking at him, soaking up the feelings between them.

"I thought he would hold onto you forever. I never thought this could happen." He kissed her again and neither of them could stop, and they didn't want to. They answered to no one but themselves. They were two free people who had fallen in love. They stood up together and went to her bedroom, and he slowly undressed her, and admired her in all her beauty, unable to believe that he was here with her, and as she pressed him to her, and lay on her bed with him, she gave him her heart, but knew that she belonged to herself, and what she gave him came from the depths of her soul.

Felicia's Favorites

* * *

As the dates for François Vernier's trip to New York approached, Olivia wondered if he would call her, and if she would be brave enough to see him. Having contacted him, she had cold feet. Seeing him made no sense. He was married now, and she was still in a wheelchair. They had broken up twelve years before, after the accident, and she had ended it for valid reasons, for his sake. Nothing had changed. It would just be a form of torture to see what they could no longer have. She made an appointment at the sperm bank to get her mind on other things that were important to her. She still wanted a baby. She was going to try IUI, and if it didn't work, adoption. She didn't want to try IVF on her own, the hormone shots sounded too debilitating and the process too complicated. She preferred the more natural route of IUI or adoption. The other options didn't appeal to her. She would have preferred to have a baby with a man she loved, but that route was no longer open to her. At thirty-seven, she wanted to move ahead now. Her doctor had told her it was best not to wait if she was sure she wanted to have a child, and she was. She knew it would give deeper meaning to her life, and thanks to her mother she could provide a wonderful life to a child. Olivia glowed just thinking about it.

She had just made the appointment at the sperm bank, and sat thinking about it, daydreaming, when the phone rang and she answered, and François's voice filled the space around her like magic from the past. She was too startled to speak for a minute.

"Olivia?" he said, with the same deep voice full of excitement and energy.

"You're here!" she said. She could feel her heart pounding, with the same thrill his voice always gave her, and she had to remind herself that he was married. She hadn't heard his voice since seven or eight years before, when he called her again to try to convince her to come back to him and she wouldn't. "How are you?" she asked him.

"Wonderful! I love New York. And I'm happy to talk to you. I arrived two days ago, and it's been madness since I arrived. I didn't want to call you until I knew when I could see you. We're in rehearsals all day." His life was huge now compared to hers. "When can I see you?" He sounded eager and happy. He had a buoyant personality along with his immense talent. They had had a terrific time working together, and then they fell in love. They had both been at the top of their game then, with the strength and power of youth.

"You've got the busy schedule, tell me what works for you," she said.

"Is today at six too soon? I won't finish until then, and we have an eight P.M. rehearsal tonight. We're working everyone hard. They have some exceptional dancers. It's a wonderful company." He always liked dancing with the American Ballet Theatre, and Olivia didn't ask if his wife was there too. She probably was.

"That's great for me. I'll have finished my classes by then too." He wasn't surprised that she was teaching. He knew she would find meaningful work to do.

"What do you prefer," she asked, "the Plaza or the Russian Tea Room?" The Russian Tea Room had always been one of their favorite spots. It was old-fashioned and romantic and traditional, while the bar at the Plaza was dynamic and modern and crowded, with fashionable, powerful people meeting and making deals.

"I know it sounds silly, but I love the Russian Tea Room, if you still like it. It reminds me of Russia in another century. And caviar and vodka doesn't sound bad," François said with a laugh. He was an immense success now, and had probably made a great deal of money, undoubtedly highly paid for his productions and his rare performances. He was a huge star, still dancing at thirty-nine for special appearances. He wouldn't for much longer and would only choreograph after that.

"The Russian Tea Room sounds perfect. I haven't been there in . . . since . . . a dozen years." Not since before the accident, with him, and she had never had the heart to go back after they broke up. The memories were too poignant. But going back with him sounded right, to dispel the old ghosts. They were no longer the same people. They had moved on.

"See you tonight then, six o'clock at the Tea Room," he said, and they hung up a minute later. Even on the phone, he sounded like a strong summer breeze that had blown through the room.

She dressed and hurried off to work then, and had to struggle all day to focus on her classes. She finished at five, brushed her hair, and put on makeup in the bathroom of the gym where she held classes. She had brought a big soft white cashmere sweater and a white coat she had bought recently, shopping with Isabelle at Bergdorf, and black velvet ballerina flats that looked better than running shoes. She'd worn black slacks, and her hair hung down her back. Excited to see François, she hailed a cab and slid into the back seat as the driver put her chair in the trunk. She was a pro at managing for herself now, and she arrived at the Russian Tea Room at five to six, got settled in the chair, and wheeled herself into the restaurant. François walked in seconds after she had settled down on the banquette in a booth. She looked like any other diner sitting there, with the illusion of normalcy. He spotted her and came straight across the restaurant to her. He had seen the wheelchair being rolled away, which didn't surprise him, and she looked no different than he remembered from a decade earlier when he'd last seen her. She was beaming up at him and he slid into the booth next to her, in a black turtleneck and black jeans, and black boots, and whatever he wore, he looked like a dancer. His sapphire-colored eyes were vibrant as he held her hands in his.

"Let me look at you," he said, drinking her in. "I still see your face when I do jumps, and I can hear you whisper to me 'Higher!!'" He had dark hair and he looked young and strong. "You look perfect, Olivia. More beautiful than ever." He kept her hands in his as they talked, and she felt his energy coursing through her. "Tell me everything about you. What do you do every day? Tell me about your classes. I want to know everything," he said, and she smiled. She had almost forgotten the sheer power of being with him, and how he infused that into his choreography and his dancers, who could achieve things they never had before under his tutelage. He had made her a better dancer too.

"I teach at a tiny dance company, but I love it. I design some of the costumes and scenery. I do charity work, and give free dance classes to underprivileged kids. Whatever I can to keep my hand in." She admired a career like his so much. That had once been her destiny too, but it no longer was.

Felicia's Favorites

"You're happy?" he asked her, as though he needed to know.

"Yes. I have a good life," she reassured him. And he could see that she did, she looked healthy and well.

"And your family? You know I am in love with your mother." Her face clouded as he said it, and she squeezed his hands. It was as though, with their hands joined, they became one person and gave each other strength.

"My mother died five months ago," she said gently, and he looked shocked. Felicia was so youthful and alive when he last saw her, but it had been a while.

"Was she sick?" he asked with tears glistening in his eyes.

"No, she was shot by a deranged person while she was running a marathon. Nine people were killed and she was the first. It was hard for all of us. We're starting to get used to it, and she left us a lot of surprises." She smiled at him, and he wiped a tear from his cheek. She told him about the books and the farmhouse, and about Spencer York, and he smiled broadly.

"That is so perfect. She was brilliant! Of course she would be a best-selling writer, and in secret. I love it! You must be very proud of her."

"We are." Olivia loved that François embraced the positive side of their news instead of clinging to the tragedy. That was how Olivia was trying to live it too. It was a much better place to be. François had been an orphan, with no siblings, raised by an aunt who was a ballerina, so he loved her big family. "And the farm is really beautiful. She lived there and we didn't know it, and we just met the man she loved and he is wonderful. He's already like a father to us, and we've only met him once. He adored my mother.

He still does. And Charlotte and his son are in love." She smiled at him.

"And the others, your sisters? Is Charlotte still so fierce? I was always afraid of her."

"She was fierce, until she met Andy. Now she is much mellower. She's happy. Quinne just started a film production company. And she's working on a big series based on one of my mother's books. The man she lives with is an actor. Veronica just broke up with the man she was with for ten years."

"Ah, the senator, yes? You told me about him one of the last times we spoke. He sounded elusive, and he was married, as I recall."

"Yes, and he stayed married. And sadly, Isabelle and Ian are having some problems, they're trying to work them out. Charlotte has two children, teenagers, and Isabelle has three little ones. So that's us. What about you? Do you have children?" François looked startled by the question.

"No, I have dancers. That is much more complicated than children!" They laughed and Olivia knew it was true. There were some divas even in the small ballet company she worked with. They talked about dancers they knew and had lost sight of, and the cities he worked in, Paris, London, Berlin, Moscow, and New York. He said he was always on the move and he liked that. Listening to him, Olivia knew she had done the right thing when she freed him. François had a big life and enjoyed it to the fullest. He couldn't have done that if he was taking care of her. The early years after the accident had been rough. Her mother had done everything for

Felicia's Favorites

her until she learned to do it herself, and now she preferred it. "And you," he said softly, "in that chair . . . you have no pain? Do you suffer?" It haunted him when he thought of her.

"Not at all. I'm fine. I have no pain. I can do everything, except walk. I live alone and I manage well." And then, she felt so comfortable with him that she shared her most private wish with him. He had been the love of her life, and she had never been as at ease with anyone else. "I'm thinking about having a child. More than thinking. I'm planning to."

"You have a good man in your life?" François frowned. He had such an expressive face, every emotion was there.

"No. No man. I'm going to do it alone. I've been thinking about it for a year or two, and when my mother died so tragically, I realized that you have to take life by the horns and not waste a minute. I thought she hadn't really lived, but she did. She had work she loved, a home she loved, and a wonderful man, and they adored each other. So I decided not to let anything stop me, and I'm going to have a child." She looked determined. François knew that look.

"Are you able to have one yourself?" he asked her, unembarrassed.

"Supposedly, and if it doesn't work I'll adopt." It was obvious she'd given it a great deal of thought.

"And the father? A friend? A man in your life?" he asked her again.

"There's no man," she said simply. "I'm alone and it's fine. I can have a sperm donor, a stranger. You pick them on paper, kind of like computer dating. You never meet and you don't know each other's identities. I'm a little iffy about that, but people who meet in bars take bigger chances."

"But if they meet a bad man in a bar, they don't see him again. If you have a child with a bad man who lied, you will have his child forever."

"I know. And if it doesn't feel right, I'll adopt. I would be happy with that too."

"It's a very big decision. You have not been idle, my darling Olivia." She had always liked her name with his accent, which was pronounced, but he spoke fluent English, German, French, and Russian. "You're a very brave woman. Sometimes too much," he said. Then he spoke softly. "I still think of you all the time. You never left my heart. You will always be there." Olivia couldn't imagine that his wife liked knowing that, but she was touched, and he hadn't left hers either. It was just a fact of their lives that they couldn't be together, but they still loved each other. She knew that now, seeing him. It was no longer a knife in her heart, it was a soft, ever-present feeling of a special part of her, locked away, that belonged to him. It wasn't painful but it was real. She was used to it, like her chair. She lived with it, without letting her injury stop her or deprive her of anything.

At ten to eight, François looked at his watch with deep regret. "I have rehearsal in ten minutes. I hate to leave you, but I'm going to be late." There was always more to say. There always had been. They talked as much as they danced, and laughed a lot. "When can I see you again? Do you have time?"

"I do, and I'll make time." It was like being with her best friend, only better. "But I don't want to cause an awkward situation for you," she said. It had troubled her before she saw him.

"How? What kind of awkward situation?" He looked surprised.

"How does your wife feel about our seeing each other? I don't want to screw anything up for you," she said, and he looked blank for a moment and then laughed.

"You mean Natasha. I was an experiment for her. She wanted to see if she liked men as much as women. She didn't. And she needed a French passport. It took two years to get it. We've been divorced for three years." Olivia looked relieved at the news. She had felt guilty about it. "I'm glad you said that. So now that's out of the way. And you have no boyfriend?" he asked her to be certain.

"No."

"Good. Then we can eat caviar together again," he said, and she laughed. "Or hamburgers. I want an American hamburger again before I leave. And a corn dog." She remembered that he had a passion for American junk food. "I'm in rehearsal tomorrow until eleven at night. Is that too late for you? Can we have a hamburger tomorrow night at eleven? Do you remember that place we went to once? JG Something?"

"JG Melon," she said, it had been the chic, trendy place for great hamburgers for decades.

"That's it. There was a trucker's diner too, but that was a little rough."

"Yes." She laughed at him. "Let's do JG Melon after your rehearsal. I'll reserve if you want."

"Perfect." Olivia slipped into the chair while they were talking and François didn't attempt to push, remembering that she did it herself. They stood on the street for a minute before he left her for rehearsal a few blocks away. "It was wonderful seeing you, Olivia," although he was sorry about her mother. "I'll tell Natasha you asked for her," he said, laughing, teasing her.

"Oh, shut up." Everything was the same as it always had been between them, as if no time had passed.

"See you tomorrow," he said, and hurried into the crowd on Fifty-Seventh Street, and she stood there smiling. He was still the same crazy wonderful best friend and best man she had ever known. It was nice to know he wasn't married. She refused to pursue the thought any further. It was a simple statement of fact with no innuendos or illusions. He was divorced.

François was in New York for seven days. The rehearsals went smoothly, and the performances were extraordinary. He got Olivia tickets backstage for all three. They managed to see each other for some amount of time at odd hours every day. He had a day off on the last day, and they were all over New York, doing errands he hadn't had time to do. He loved New York, and they ate at a diner on Second Avenue on the last night. He had a triple cheeseburger with everything on it, although he was very thin and usually careful about his weight, and they shared a banana split.

"Thank God you're leaving. I'd get fat if you stayed." Olivia went to the gym every day to exercise her upper body, but she couldn't exercise the lower part. She had no muscle strength and no sensation in her legs from her spinal injury. Her legs were very thin from lack of use.

They went back to her apartment afterward to talk. François was leaving the next morning. They hadn't crossed any lines, and he had been careful not to cross her boundaries. He knew what they were. They were two best friends, celebrating each day, enjoying each other, and living life to the fullest in the moment. He brought out the best in her, and he said she did the same for him.

"I want to make you a proposition," he said, careful not to use the word "proposal" so he didn't scare her. They were having a wonderful time together and he didn't want to spoil it. "I want you to have my baby, not some total stranger as a sperm donor who might be a serial killer, or hate ballet. Our genes are perfect for each other and we might be the parents of the greatest dancer that ever lived. Consider it a genetic experiment, for the benefit of future dance companies. I would like to be your sperm donor, on one condition."

She looked thoughtful as she listened, cautious but intrigued. "What's the condition?"

"You marry me to do it. I don't want the brilliant dancer we give birth to to have unmarried parents. It won't look good in his or her biography in the dance program," he said seriously and she giggled. "I'm serious," he said. "So we get married, you have your baby. We can live together or not. Or I can live in Paris and on airplanes, and you live here in this incredibly tiny apartment."

"I'll get a bigger one if I have a baby," Olivia said.

"That's good to know. And if you hate me, or decide that I have an intolerable personality, you can divorce me whenever you want.

Natasha can tell you I'm very easy to divorce. So that's my proposition." She loved the idea of having his child, but she looked suspicious.

"And if we live together? What would that be like?"

"You make the rules. I travel all over the world for work. It would be like now, best friends who love each other. I would be honored to be the father of your child," he said gently, and she was touched. François had found a way to package it in such a way that she didn't feel like she was ruining his life being married to an invalid, which she wasn't. Having his baby would be her dream come true.

"How would we do that?" she asked him.

"You have to ask your doctor. I don't know what the mechanics are in our situation," he said honestly.

"No, not that part." She laughed at him again. "I mean you'd want to get married first, before the baby. Like when?"

"Oh, that. I suppose you're in a hurry to get the baby started," he said. "We can get married in any break in my travel schedule. I've got some openings in May, June, July, August . . . would you want a big wedding?"

"No, small. Maybe just the family and a few friends at my mother's farmhouse, our farmhouse now. I think you'd like it. It's very pretty." Olivia couldn't believe she was planning a wedding with François, but with the baby as their excuse, it all made sense and she wanted to do it.

"Next month? May? A month from now. Is that enough time for you to plan? And after the wedding we go straight to the doctor's office, let him do his job, and with your permission, we could go

Felicia's Favorites

on a honeymoon to Disneyland or Marine World, or Venice, or somewhere you think is appropriate. Nine months later, our prodigy is born. I love the idea," he said to her, his eyes brimming with nineteen years of love for her since the day he met her.

"I like your proposition," she said, smiling gratefully at him. "Thank you, François. I accept."

"I should really send Natasha a text, thanking her for divorcing me. She's living with a prima from the Bolshoi and they're very happy."

"And you get me," Olivia said. "You really don't mind about all this?" She waved at her legs, which were why she had broken their engagement before.

"You would be the best possible mother I can imagine for my children, and the best wife for me. I think we've suffered enough in the last twelve years, now let's seize the gifts we've been given and enjoy our life together." It was what her mother had done with Spencer and Olivia realized now that they were right. She had never stopped loving François for a single day, nor had he her. And now it was time to celebrate. The baby was an added bonus.

"You don't mind adopting if the IUI doesn't work?"

"If that's what you want. I will let you run the baby factory, I'm a mere choreographer, and a dancer."

"Do you want to spend the night?" she asked him.

"I do but you may hate me for it. I have to leave for the airport at six A.M. and pick my bags up at the hotel on the way. I'm packed. I should leave you around five, is that okay?" François asked her, and she nodded, and he moved toward her on the couch, put his arms around her and kissed her, as he had wanted to since the day he arrived in New York and didn't want to scare her off. Her email had been providential. And now they were getting married and planning a baby.

"I've never proposed and planned a family before I even kissed a woman," he said. "We're a little bit crazy, but I love that about us," he said, and she looked serious.

"What if the insemination doesn't work?"

"Then we'll keep trying until it does. Perseverance is a good thing." He had been trying to marry her for fifteen or sixteen years, and they were finally going to do it. He could hardly wait.

They got undressed and into her bed, and she lay in his arms, smiling at him.

"Thank you for not giving up on me," she whispered.

"Thank you for loving me and giving me a chance," he whispered back. They were going to commute between Paris and New York depending on his performance schedule. François said his apartment was big enough for them and several children. And Olivia was thinking that she needed a bigger apartment. There was so much to plan and think about and hope for. So much to look forward to and be grateful for, as she fell asleep in his arms. He got up at four, and showered and dressed without waking her, and then he sat down on the bed next to her and gently kissed her. She stirred and opened one eye and smiled at him.

"See you in a few weeks," she said, and rolled over on her back and he kissed her again.

"I'll call you when I land. I think Olivia Vernier is a very nice name, don't you?" he asked, and her smile widened, and he was smiling too. They had been here before at this giddy place, dreaming of a future together, and now they were here again. He didn't want anything to spoil it this time. "Give your sisters my love. I'll see them all next time, at the wedding." He beamed. Neither of them had expected this.

He left a few minutes later, and she got up and rolled around her apartment. She had to call caterers and a florist in Connecticut. She wanted to call her sisters, and take time off from her classes. And she had to tell her doctor and plan for the IUI. There was so much to think about. She felt like she was flying when she called Quinne first. She was the one who had pushed Olivia to write to François.

It was seven-thirty in the morning and Quinne was about to leave for work. Coop was on the set, already in hair and makeup by then.

As soon as Quinne answered, Olivia blurted out the news. "I'm getting married!"

"Oh my God, to whom?" Olivia wasn't usually given to impulsive acts.

"My sperm donor." Quinne was genuinely shocked. Olivia had gone off the deep end if she was marrying a stranger.

"When?"

"In four weeks."

"Do you know anything about him? This doesn't sound reasonable."

"He's a choreographer and a dancer, he's French, thirty-nine years old . . ." Olivia was laughing by then. "François and I are getting married," she said. "Thank you for making me write to him. We're very happy. It was his idea when I told him I was going to have a baby with a sperm donor. He's divorced." Quinne was laughing by then too. "I want to get married at the farm."

"You can get married at the top of the Empire State Building or the Eiffel Tower, and I'll be there," Quinne said. Olivia had been through so much and now she was getting her happy ending. It seemed very fair.

"I need a dress, an apartment, a caterer, a florist."

"We'll help you," Quinne promised, ecstatic for her. "Where are you going to live?"

"On Air France mostly. We'll figure it out as we go. Quinnie, thank you," Olivia said with deep feeling. The next person she would have wanted to tell was her mother. But somehow, in her heart of hearts, she was sure her mother knew, and was celebrating for her. Maybe she even had a hand in it, wherever she was.

Chapter 13

Once the news was out and Olivia had spoken to each of her sisters, they all moved into action. Olivia and François had chosen Memorial Day weekend in May as their wedding date. Olivia had called the local florist and told them what she wanted. Ellen, the housekeeper, knew a good caterer. Andy knew a great photographer. François told Olivia to do whatever she wanted. So they were having the family, and Robert Farr, and Scott Freeman, who was deeply involved in a relationship with Veronica, and they were happy.

All four sisters went with Olivia to Bergdorf's bridal department with her to pick a dress. It had to work with her chair and not get tangled up in it, but they all thought it should have a train and a cathedral veil. Olivia didn't want something enormous but she wanted a traditional wedding dress. It took them three hours to choose all of it, with the right Manolo Blahnik shoes, with special-order cameo blue soles for good luck, for "something blue."

Even for a small wedding, there were so many small component parts that it took all five of them to divide up the tasks and tend to everything. The sisters had decided to wear simple white piqué dresses and carry bouquets of field flowers. Olivia's dress was white organdy, which floated around her, and a lace veil. Julia and Penny were going to walk down the aisle together as flower girls in white eyelet broderie anglaise dresses, carrying daisies. The boys, Sean, Tyler, and Charlie, would wear white jeans and white button-down shirts and blazers, with white buck shoes. And since Olivia's dress was a formal wedding gown, François had decided to wear a formal gray morning coat with striped trousers and gray top hat. So the bride and groom would be formal, and the wedding party less so. Quinne had booked a fabulous hairdresser from the set, and she was bringing two assistants for the sisters.

They were going to have dinner outdoors, on the large patio, and they were putting in a dance floor and hiring a band for dancing. It was a small wedding but every detail had been tended to. Charlotte had agreed to oversee everything since she was the most organized and had more assistants at her office, and Quinne was on set for long hours every day for the series and couldn't take calls when there.

Before any of it got put in place, Olivia had booked the IUI insemination for the morning after the wedding. They were doing it naturally without hormones, because Olivia didn't need them. Her hormones and reproductive organs were fine, the only problem was her spinal cord injury, which wouldn't interfere with the pregnancy, or getting pregnant. She was going to have the baby in New York, by Caesarean section, a week before her due date, because

Felicia's Favorites

labor would be too complicated and C-section was safer for her and the baby, if the IUI succeeded. And if it didn't, they would try again.

François called her morning and night during the weeks before the wedding. He couldn't believe his good fortune to finally marry the love of his life, his soulmate. They had long conversations when he had time. The wedding worked perfectly with his schedule. His last scheduled performance was ten days before the wedding, and he left the next day to be in New York with Olivia. She had found a bigger apartment on Central Park West with four bedrooms, close to Lincoln Center for when François worked in New York, and they were planning to move in September. If she got pregnant, the baby wouldn't be due until February.

François was handling the honeymoon, which was a secret so far. He was mysterious about it, and teased her by saying they were going camping. Olivia had called Spencer in London and asked him to walk her down the aisle, and they both cried when she asked him. He said he was delighted, since it would be his only opportunity with no daughters of his own. When François returned and met Andy, they got on so well, that he asked him to be the best man. And all of Olivia's sisters were her bridesmaids.

In all, the wedding party consisted of fifteen people, including the five grandchildren, and in addition they had invited Robert Farr. Scott Freeman was Veronica's date. It was a lot of fuss for a wedding of fewer than twenty people, but it was a jubilant celebration, and Olivia had always wanted an intimate wedding. All she needed there was François.

Isabelle had ordered a beautiful flower arch of white roses, tiny white orchids, and lily of the valley for the ceremony, and Olivia's bouquet was lily of the valley and tiny orchids. She had gone to the nearest Episcopal church and the minister had agreed to do the ceremony at the house, in the garden where they were holding the wedding.

François looked happy and relaxed when he arrived ten days before the wedding. He loved reacquainting with Olivia's sisters, whom he had known well before, and he enjoyed Andy, Coop, Scott, and Spencer when he arrived from London. They organized a bachelors' dinner for him at the Racquet Club, where Scott was a member, and Olivia's sisters threw a party for her at her favorite restaurant in the Village. It was all she wanted as her bachelorette night.

Ian had been left out of the family gatherings, because he and Isabelle were still on very tenuous terms, but she had decided to invite him to the wedding, since they were still married and he was her husband and the children's father.

The ceremony was to be at seven o'clock, dinner at eight-thirty, before which the little children would be put to bed, and then everyone else could dance as late as they wanted to. Everything about the wedding was easy and relaxed, joyful and about family, which was what they were all about, and at every event, François and Olivia were beaming and happy.

The day of the wedding, everything went according to plan. The hairdressers and makeup artists were right on time. The photographer recorded Olivia getting dressed with her sisters' help. He left the wheelchair out of the pictures as much as possible. The dinner tables had been set with exquisite flower arrangements, and when Olivia was dressed, she looked like a princess. The train came from her shoulders and trailed fifteen feet behind her, draped over the back of the wheelchair, so you couldn't see it, and Penny held it for her aunt.

Every single detail was flawless. The women looked beautiful and the men handsome. And Olivia could feel her mother near her as she rolled slowly down the path next to Spencer, in gray morning coat and top hat, toward the flower arch where the minister and François were waiting, and the scent of lily of the valley hung in the air. François was in the same formal coat as Spencer, without the hat. Tyler was holding François's top hat for him.

Spencer walked solemnly beside Olivia, and gently touched her shoulder, lifting the veil from her face when they reached François, and then Spencer stepped back and François got a full view of his bride, holding her bouquet, looking adoringly up at him with wide eyes full of love, trust, and hope. François stood beside her during the ceremony, after Spencer took his seat, wishing that Felicia was beside him. And when the minister asked, "Who gives this woman in marriage?" Spencer and Olivia's four sisters spoke up in strong clear voices and said, "We do."

When Olivia and François exchanged their vows and Tyler and Charlie handed them the rings, the minister gave his blessing, presented them as husband and wife, and told François that he may kiss the bride. François bent down and kissed her, and scooped her out of her chair and held her in his arms, and walked down the aisle with her, with the photographer following them closely, and the bridal couple beaming. It was the most romantic thing any of them had ever seen, and he gently deposited her on a chair where she could talk to everyone and enjoy the reception. He was holding her hand and he never left her side. He had been dreaming of this day since he met her. The wedding had been as beautiful as any ballet they had ever danced together.

Charlotte noticed as the group circulated and talked to each other that Ian looked uncomfortable, stayed slightly apart, and followed Isabelle with his eyes. Charlotte had the feeling Isabelle was avoiding him. She sat next to him at the ceremony but moved away from him after that.

Everyone had fun at the first dance. Olivia had picked all the music, and then they sat down to dinner and Isabelle's children were led off to bed by the nanny. They had eaten dinner before the ceremony. All five sisters had thought of everything between them.

Isabelle left the table between courses to sit at a distance in one of the garden chairs, and smoke a cigarette. She enjoyed watching her sisters, and everyone having fun and celebrating François and Olivia. The music added even more romance to the balmy evening. She was watching them when Ian came up to her and sat down on a bench near her chair. He looked strained.

"I guess everyone hates me by now," he said to Isabelle, who looked uncomfortable as soon as he sat down. It was hard having him there, but she had thought it was the right thing to do. He was still part of the family for now.

"No one hates you," she said quietly. "They're sorry for us. How are you?" she asked him. She hadn't spoken to him since Tyler's appendectomy.

"Confused, sad. I've screwed everything up." He was in a dark mood, despite the joyous occasion. "Leila and I are trying to break up. The relationship isn't working for her either," he paused and then looked at his wife. She looked beautiful in white, and almost like a bride herself. She had been a spectacular bride when they married in New York. "I want to come back, Isabelle. I've learned my lesson. You and the children mean everything to me." Now that Leila wanted out. Their affair had gone on for a year and destroyed Ian and Isabelle's marriage, and shown Ian to be weak, dishonorable, and foolish.

"I'm not exciting enough for you," she said. "I don't have a career or a talent, I'm just a wife and a mom. It's what I love. It wasn't enough for you, or Leila wouldn't have happened. I think you're looking for sparkle and glamour, and everything I'm not. I've finally realized that Leila, or someone like her, is more your style. But now isn't the time to discuss it."

"I want to come home. Leila wants to take over the apartment, and I don't want to get some other sterile furnished apartment," he said, as Isabelle looked at him, seeing him clearly now. He was devilishly handsome and pathetic, but his looks weren't enough to justify his selfishness.

"That's not a reason to come home, because you're homeless and like my decorating. You've stayed with Leila a year, trying to figure it out. If we were right for each other, you would have come home a long time ago. You've squeezed that lemon until you've had every drop of juice out of it, and now you want to come back, until you find someone else more exciting and do it again. I've learned a lot in these months. I deserved a lot better than what you gave me for almost a year now while you had fun with Leila. Your parents told you in the beginning that I wasn't good enough. And you believed them. You can't come back, Ian. I'm done. I want a divorce. Or more exactly, I don't want one and I never did. I loved you, truly. But now I need a divorce, so I can have a life, by myself, or maybe with someone who appreciates me. You don't. I guess you never did." She said it all in a flat, even tone, and when she had said it, she got up and walked away. He didn't argue with her, or tell her she was wrong. He watched her go, then quietly slipped away, found his car in front of the house, and drove away.

One of the caterers saw him leave and discreetly removed his place at the table. Isabelle saw it, and she was sad, but what she had said was true. Whatever he did with Leila now, it was over for her. He had kept her waiting and broken her heart for too long. She was better off without him and she knew it. He wasn't good enough for her, didn't treat her well, and hadn't respected her.

The wedding guests kept the party going until after two in the morning. They danced and had fun, and finally let the band go at two. Even Charlotte's kids had had fun, and she and Andy sat quietly at the end of the evening, enjoying the warm atmosphere. Spencer had gone back to his house at one. His heart was full of memories of Felicia but he'd had a good time. He had danced with all the sisters and enjoyed talking to them. It was a beautiful evening, and before anyone left, Olivia had turned her back to them in her chair and tossed the bouquet over her shoulder behind her. It whizzed past Quinne, who moved aside and dodged it, and

Felicia's Favorites

Charlotte took a step back—she'd already been married once—and it hit Veronica squarely on the chest and she caught it as everyone clapped, and she and Scott looked at each other and laughed. He kissed her while she was still holding the bouquet.

"You're next," Quinne said with a grin, as she walked past them to Cooper at the bar. She still didn't feel ready for marriage. Veronica wasn't sure she did either, but she and Scott had been happy together so far, and he spent many nights at her apartment.

Charlotte had asked Isabelle how things were with Ian. She had seen that he left before dinner, after he and Isabelle talked.

"I told him I'm done. He and Leila are thinking of breaking up, so he wants to come home. I can't. I want a divorce."

"Are you sure?" Charlotte asked her.

"Very. He's been with her for a year. If it took him this long to figure it out, and only because it's not working for them, I don't want him back. I want out. I deserve better than that," she said, and Charlotte nodded. Isabelle seemed sure now.

"Yes, you do. I'm just sorry for you and the kids."

"They're fine, and I will be too. I'm feeling better. Game over," she said, and Charlotte hugged her and went to find Andy for a last dance.

By three A.M., the house was silent and everyone was asleep.

They all had brunch in the dining room the next morning at eleven, and at noon, François and Olivia drove away to start their new life together.

They stayed at her apartment in the city that night, and at eight o'clock the next morning, they went to Olivia's doctor for their appointment. They were both excited and hopeful, and François reminded her that if it didn't work, they would keep trying for as long as Olivia wanted.

They did an internal sonogram to confirm that she was ovulating. She had been testing and taking her temperature all week, and the test had been accurate.

François was going to go into a private exam room to provide the sperm sample. The room was small and depressing, with dog-eared girly and porn magazines. There was even a video if he wanted it. Olivia asked him to stay with her, and laughing and nervous and feeling self-conscious but very much in love, she assisted with the sperm sample. A nurse took it from them, and the doctor returned to inject it directly into Olivia's uterus. The procedure wasn't normally painful, but she felt nothing at all. They suggested she lie down for half an hour afterward, and they left the office two hours after they had arrived, possibly with a baby on the way. They wouldn't know for two weeks. They'd still be on their honeymoon then, and Olivia had bought two pregnancy tests to check.

She still didn't know where they were going on their honeymoon. François had kept it a secret. He had told her to bring casual summer clothes and a few silk shirts and gauzy dresses for the evening.

They picked up their bags at her apartment after the medical appointment, and a limo he had ordered arrived on time and took them to the airport.

François put a hand over her eyes when they got to the gate so

Felicia's Favorites

Olivia couldn't see their destination, and a steward announced on the flight that they were going to Saint Martin.

"We're going to Saint Martin?" She looked excited, and they accepted champagne. It had been a busy morning. Olivia dozed on the flight, after the excitement of the wedding two days before and the doctor visit that morning. Two handsome young men in white naval uniforms were waiting for them when they landed and whisked them to the port, where François led her to an enormous white yacht. He carried her onboard, a deckhand set up her wheelchair, François gently lowered her into it, and she rolled herself around the deck to check out the boat. It was the most beautiful yacht she'd ever seen.

"Are we on it for the night?" she asked him, and he kissed her. The yacht was called *The True Love*.

"*The True Love* is ours for three weeks. We can go wherever you want, eat what you want, do what you want. If you get bored with me, there is even a movie theater. The minute I saw the name on the brochure I knew we had to have it for our honeymoon." Olivia was staring at François in amazement, and he sat down next to her and put his arm around her as the crew fired up the engines, removed the ropes that moored them to the dock, and took off for the Caribbean seas, where they were going to spend their honeymoon.

The first test that Olivia took two weeks later showed negative, and François thought she had done it too soon. She was disappointed by the negative result but they were having a fabulous honeymoon. And on the last two days of the trip, five days later, she tested again, and got a positive result this time. Two clearly pink lines that said she was pregnant, and at dinner that night she told François. They had just spent the most incredible three weeks of their lives on the most elegant yacht, and now Olivia's dream was coming true, she and François were having a baby. There were moments in life when everything came together and was perfect, and this was one of them. He kissed her and for a moment he didn't know what to say. He had mourned her for twelve years after the accident and thought he had lost her forever. And now they had a whole life together to look forward to.

They watched the sun set over the water that night, and they both knew that this was a day and a time in their lives that they would never forget. Their True Love had set sail on their wedding day, and long before that. François kissed her, and they smiled at each other.

"Thank you for the perfect honeymoon," she whispered to him. It was more than that, it was a perfect life together.

Chapter 14

Olivia and François went back and forth between Paris and New York after the summer they spent at the farmhouse in Connecticut. The others came and went, Charlotte and her children, between other trips, a rafting trip in Colorado, and a ranch in Wyoming. Andy went with them. Isabelle moved to the farm for the summer with her children and the nanny, after she filed for divorce from Ian in June. She heard rumors that Leila had left him too, and moved to L.A.

Quinne and Coop were working through the summer on both her own production house and the series, but enjoyed a day off here and there, and a hiatus on the set for four weeks.

Veronica and Scott came out on weekends. Spencer came from London for two weeks to spend time with Andy. Andy had taken over the house, at his father's insistence. Olivia and François spent time at the farmhouse when they could in the fall and were excited about Olivia's pregnancy, which was going well.

It had been a fruitful and challenging year, the hardest year of their lives after losing their mother, and the best year in other ways. New babies, new work, new marriages, new loves, disappointments like Isabelle's divorce after suffering through Ian's affair, and true love and a happy ending at last for Olivia and François. There were good people and good times, and some incredible obstacles and griefs to overcome.

They all spent the day together in Connecticut on the anniversary of Felicia's death, realizing that a year before, brokenhearted, it was only then that her children had discovered who she was. They all wished they had known her better, and discovered the truth sooner. With the pain of losing her had come blessings for them all, thanks to her. And Spencer, her great love, was part of their lives now. He had lost the woman he loved, and gained her entire family surrounding him now and loving him too.

They scattered her ashes on the anniversary. It had taken them a year—they couldn't face it before that. The sisters had ordered a beautiful white marble heart, which they put under a tree in the garden to honor Felicia, with her name and the dates, and an inscription: "Extraordinary mother, grandmother, partner, writer, friend. So beloved, so greatly missed, the brightest star in our sky, forever loved." Spencer cried when he read it and was touched by the addition of "partner" for him. They said the Lord's Prayer, sang *Amazing Grace,* and each of Felicia's daughters scattered a portion of her ashes, and Spencer too. They all cried but they knew she would want to be there, and be part of the flowers and the trees and the peace and love she had found there, and now for eternity, to be remembered by those who had loved her.

Felicia's Favorites

The day ended with a big meal that they all prepared and enjoyed at the farm. It was painful remembering the day a year before. And yet a year later, there was hope, a baby on the way, a series, new loves. On the anniversary of Felicia's death, Olivia was six months pregnant, a symbol of life and hope and the future for them all.

They spent Christmas and New Year's together at the farm. It had become the center of their world, the place where they came to find peace and solace, where they laughed together, ate together, shared their victories and their dreams, and folded their wings in order to take flight again with renewed strength.

Isabelle's divorce from Ian was final in January. Leila had moved to L.A. Ian had a new girlfriend by then.

And in February, they all went to the premiere of the series, and saw the first episode aired. There was a big party that night. The ratings went through the roof, and the reviews were fabulous. Quinne had begun writing some of the screenplays herself. Robert Farr was proud of all of them, and knew Felicia would have been too.

They went to the party after the premiere, sponsored by the streamers who had created it from Felicia's book, and Charlotte asked Olivia if she was okay when they got there. Her face was flushed and she said she had a headache and her shoulders were sore but she was fine. She was two weeks away from her due date and she and François were excited and anxious. He watched her like a mother hen. Charlotte thought she didn't look right at the party, and said something to Isabelle. Olivia had worn a gold dress to the event, François had flown in from Paris that day, and wasn't leaving again, since her C-section was a week away. The baby seemed huge. She let François push her wheelchair at the party, she said her arms were too tired. She was at the end of the pregnancy, and had been busy with their new apartment. They had bought a duplex at the Dakota on Central Park West.

Charlotte and Isabelle didn't want to worry François, but Isabelle finally said something to him when Olivia went to the ladies' room with Charlotte.

"We don't know what, but Char and I think something's up with Olivia. Something's off."

He looked surprised. "She said she feels fine." Neither he nor Olivia had any experience with pregnancy and she'd been healthy the entire time.

"Don't forget, she doesn't feel anything from the waist down," Isabelle reminded him. "She won't know if she starts labor." Olivia's doctor had told her what signs to watch for. As Isabelle spoke, Charlotte appeared pushing Olivia's chair as fast as she could through the crowd.

"Get the car," she said tersely to Isabelle. "Or an ambulance, whichever you find first."

"What's wrong?" François asked her, and looked at his wife. She was suddenly deathly pale.

"I'm bleeding," she said, looking frightened.

"A lot," Charlotte added. François took over the chair and pushed through the crowd at full speed, pressing through. They had a limo outside and Charlotte and Isabelle climbed in, leaving the others at the party. Isabelle and François laid Olivia on the floor of the

Felicia's Favorites

limo on her coat, and François told the driver to get them to New York–Presbyterian Hospital as fast as he could. Olivia was in and out of consciousness as they watched her.

Charlotte ran a hand under her and it came away covered with blood. "She's hemorrhaging," she said, as Olivia passed out again, and François held her hand and looked desperate.

When they got to the hospital, Isabelle ran into the ER and two orderlies came out running with a gurney and blankets and lifted Olivia onto the gurney, with François running alongside as they raced into the ER.

"How pregnant is she?" they asked him.

"Thirty-eight weeks," François answered. They took Olivia straight to maternity to a delivery room. They called her doctor, and an attending obstetrician examined her. They ran an IV into her arm and cut her clothes off, and François stood there, shocked, terrified he would lose her and the baby. They explained that they thought the placenta was delivering first, so she was hemorrhaging, and because of her paraplegia, she had felt none of the pain or the warning signs.

"We're going to do a C-section right away," the obstetrician told them. They had a fetal monitor on the baby and the heartbeat was strong, but Olivia's was thready. She had lost a lot of blood, she was bleeding out. Once in the operating room, the anesthesiologist had a mask on Olivia's face, and they told François to leave. Everyone was moving fast and monitors were beeping.

"They said I could stay for the C-section," he said, terrified.

"This is an emergency, we'll come to tell you how they are," a surgical nurse said, hurrying him to the doors. He found Charlotte and Isabelle outside. They sat down in chairs together, silent, praying, afraid, and tears were rolling down François's cheeks.

"We shouldn't have tried it," he said. "She said there was no risk."

"This could happen to anyone," Charlotte said softly. The only difference was that Olivia didn't feel anything. Someone without her spinal injury would have felt the pain hours earlier.

They sat for what felt like an eternity waiting for news. François was pacing, his dancer's body tense, like a lion ready to strike, but there was nothing to strike at, nothing to do, nowhere to go. And then the obstetrician came out of the delivery room. His scrubs and apron were covered in blood, but he was smiling at them.

"Your wife is fine," he said to François. "And so is your son. Your wife lost a lot of blood. We've given her three units, and she'll need another one. The placenta had detached and was delivering first. If you'd waited half an hour longer, we would have lost them both." A nurse came out then with a small bundle wrapped in blankets, with a little blue knit cap on his head, and a perfect face. He looked like François, and weighed eight pounds, ten ounces. He was beautiful, and François cried when he saw him.

"Can I see my wife?" he asked the doctor.

"We're closing now. You can see her in the recovery room in about half an hour." The nurse took the baby to the nursery then, to check his vital signs again and scores, and clean him up. His aunts watched him go with tears in their eyes, and they hugged François, who sobbed in relief.

Felicia's Favorites

"If you two hadn't noticed that something was wrong, they would both have died." He couldn't have borne losing her again.

"Congratulations," Charlotte said, wiping away her tears, and they took a walk outside to get some air. It had been a terrifying night with a happy ending.

"Maybe Mom was looking out for them," Isabelle said softly, and François looked shaken and nodded agreement.

"I would have given my life for both of them," he said. They went back inside, and François went into the recovery room to see Olivia.

She opened her eyes and smiled wanly when she saw him. They were still giving her blood. "Is he okay?"

"He's fine, and so beautiful. I love you, I'm sorry it was so hard."

"It was scary," she said, and drifted off to sleep while talking to him. François sat next to her and she slept for a long time, and then they took her to a room. Charlotte and Isabelle had gone home by then. The others were waiting for news and they texted everyone saying Olivia and the baby were fine.

They all came to visit the next day. Olivia looked terrible with dark circles under her eyes, and François stood next to her, looking at her and their son in wonder. She was holding the baby, but she was very weak and a nurse took him from her. François was acutely aware of how lucky they had been and how blessed they were. When they were alone again, Olivia looked at him and smiled.

"It was worth it. I would do it again," she said.

"I'm not sure I'd survive it," he said.

"My mom did it five times. C-sections with all of us," she said.

"She was an amazing woman and so are you," he said, and sat next to her. A nurse came in and handed François the baby, and then they carefully put him to Olivia's breast. She lay there, holding their son. She looked like a Madonna as he gazed at her, and as he did, he could see Felicia's face in hers, just for an instant, and their strong resemblance, and then he saw Olivia clearly again, and he knew that Felicia was with them, guiding them, protecting them, loving them. He wondered if she had brought them back together when Olivia wrote to him. He looked down at Olivia then, radiant with their son in her arms, as she nursed him. They named him Felix, and François had never been as grateful in his life. He knew a miracle had occurred. Many of them. Felicia was their guardian angel now.

They christened Felix on their first anniversary in May. Spencer was his godfather, and Isabelle his godmother. Charlotte and Andy got married on the same day, in a simple civil ceremony at the farm, which was all they wanted. All of the family was there as witnesses, to celebrate them and their union. Julia and Sean were best man and maid of honor. And they celebrated Olivia and François's son. There had been many miracles. Olivia and François had reconnected, and Olivia's and Felix's lives had been saved at the delivery. Charlotte and Andy had found each other and were happy. Veronica and Scott were engaged and getting married on Christmas. Veronica had just gotten a job at a law firm. Quinne and Cooper were happy and doing well, with their careers and the production house. Isabelle and her children had found peace after

Felicia's Favorites

a tumultuous year. She was happy again and thriving. And Spencer had the family that Felicia wanted to give him and didn't have the chance. They had him now and he had all of them to warm his heart. They were Felicia's final gift to him. Her family to love him in her absence.

Every one of them had been touched by a miracle, by the woman who had loved them, more than they ever knew when she was alive.

"I guess we were her favorites after all," Olivia said, holding her son on her lap in the wheelchair. He was sound asleep after being baptized. And Andy had just kissed the bride.

All of them were Felicia's favorites, the special people she had loved, and left to care for each other. They were a chosen few. They were Felicia's favorites, every one of them, and she lived within them now forever, to protect, to bless, and to love them, just as she had when she was alive.

About the Author

DANIELLE STEEL has been hailed as one of the world's bestselling authors, with a billion copies of her novels sold. Her many international bestsellers include *The Devil's Daughter, The Color of Hope, The Portrait, For Richer For Poorer, A Mother's Love, A Mind of Her Own, Far From Home,* and other highly acclaimed novels. She is also the author of *His Bright Light,* the story of her son Nick Traina's life and death; *A Gift of Hope,* a memoir of her work with the homeless; *Expect a Miracle,* a book of her favorite quotations for inspiration and comfort; *Pure Joy,* about the dogs she and her family have loved; and the children's books *Pretty Minnie in Paris* and *Pretty Minnie in Hollywood.*

daniellesteel.com
Facebook.com/DanielleSteelOfficial
Instagram: @officialdaniellesteel